Born to Die

Born to Die

Dorian Sykes

www.urbanbooks.net

Urban Books, LLC
300 Farmingdale Road, N.Y.-Route 109
Farmingdale, NY 11735

Born to Die Copyright © 2025 Dorian Sykes

All rights reserved. No part of this book may be reproduced in any form or by any means without prior consent of the Publisher, except brief quotes used in reviews.

To the extent that the image or images on the cover of this book depict a person or persons, such person or persons are merely models, and are not intended to portray any character or characters featured in the book.

ISBN 13: 978-1-64556-723-3
EBOOK ISBN: 978-1-64556-724-0

First Trade Paperback Printing June 2025
Printed in the United States of America

10 9 8 7 6 5 4 3 2 1

This is a work of fiction. Any references or similarities to actual events, real people, living or dead, or to real locales are intended to give the novel a sense of reality. Any similarity in other names, characters, places, and incidents is entirely coincidental.

Distributed by Kensington Publishing Corp.
Submit Orders to:
Customer Service
400 Hahn Road
Westminster, MD 21157-4627
Phone: 1-800-733-3000
Fax: 1-800-659-2436

The authorized representative in the EU for product safety and compliance
Is eucomply OU, Parnu mnt 139b-14, Apt 123
Tallinn, Berlin 11317, hello@eucompliancepartner.coM

Born to Die

Dorian Sykes

CHAPTER ONE

Lil' Keith and Marcus's latest victim was a Nigerian man, well-dressed in a business suit, who looked to be in his mid-fifties. They came up on him late one evening getting out of this white Mercedes-Benz 420 on a deserted street within the Lake Chateau Estates community, an affluent section just on the outskirts of New Orleans. They had been stalking the vic's mini-mansion from the shadows of a large cluster of bushes three houses down, where they lay in silence for hours, determined to wait out their prey. He was late, but Lil' Keith and Marcus were seasoned when it came to the murder game. They'd wait him out all night until sunrise if need be. They'd done it before. Murder was their hustle. Killing came naturally to them; it was one thing they were good at.

As the man pulled into the driveway, Marcus snatched his hoody over his dreads, clutched his chopper, then nudged Lil' Keith to be on point. They watched the man exit his vehicle and walk over to the trunk, where he lifted two black briefcases.

"Let's go around," Marcus said in a whisper. He and Lil' Keith slid out from the bushes in lockstep. The vic cast a worried glance over his shoulder, locking eyes on the two black figures rushing toward him. It seemed like the call of death. After a few more quick glances, the vic neglected the house altogether and made a run for his life, cutting across the street with both heels touching his ass.

"Fuck," growled Marcus. He had a feeling the nigga was going to run on them. They always do when they see that stick in hand.

Lil' Keith and Marcus gave chase. They found the man at the end of a dead-end alleyway, regretting his turn. The vic frantically searched wide-eyed for an out but was doomed by the ten-foot cement wall sealing his fate. Feeling their presence, the man suddenly spun around, his loafers sounding like a match striking against the summer pavement as he backstepped his way into the wall, his final resting place. In a last attempt for respite, he offered up the two briefcases in exchange for his life.

"Take 'em, please. Just don't kill me," he pleaded with tears welling in his eyes. "I'll give you anything. Just please."

Without answering, Marcus and Lil' Keith simultaneously upped their twin Russian AK-47s and took aim at the man's frame. His final pleas were muffled by the rapid gunfire from the two assault rifles. The first burst of rounds knocked a bloody gray patch from the man's dome, sending him crashing against the alley's concrete. Together, they stood over him and emptied both 30-round clips, as ordered.

Through the thick cloud of gun smoke, Marcus looked down at their work. All it takes is to be on the murder scene of an AK-47 just once, and you'll understand why they call 'em choppers. The man's flesh looked as if he'd been mauled by a pack of lions. He was torn open to the bone. But it was nothing to the two head bussas. They'd been stomaching murder scenes since they put their first demo down when there were just fifteen.

Lil' Keith kneeled down and began probing the man's lifeless corpse for all valuables. He snatched the gold Rolex from his wrist and nearly broke the man's pinky finger for the matching gold ring.

Seeing back porch lights flick on up the alley, Marcus urged Lil' Keith to hurry up. "Leave that yeah, round."

"Hold up there, round," said Lil' Keith, still probing. "I know dis nigga holding out on me, ya heard me?" Lil' Keith didn't believe in leaving anything behind. He had the man out there damn near naked with his pants down around his ankles.

The screened porch door of the house they were in back of screeched open, and out stepped an old white woman dressed in her house coat. Marcus met eyes with the woman.

"What in God's name . . ." Her words began to trail off as her eyes took in the gruesome scene.

Marcus upped the .357 Bulldog from his waist and licked six shots off in her direction, causing the woman to scramble back inside. "We out, round," announced Marcus. He snatched up both briefcases and made a run for the getaway car.

Monay sat nervously behind the wheel of the stolen burgundy Impala SS. She heard the hail of gunshots, so what was taking them so long? Her stomach did a backflip as she glanced at the clock mounted on the dashboard. *I'ma give y'all two minutes, and I'm out,* she thought. Just then, she saw Marcus's 6-foot 2-inch solid frame bend the corner, heading toward her at full speed. Her heart fluttered as she scrambled for the locks.

"Where's Keith?" she asked as Marcus jumped inside the passenger seat.

Out of breath, Marcus realized for the first time Lil' Keith hadn't been running by his side as he'd thought.

"Where is he?" demanded Monay, her voice laced with fear.

"He's coming. Just chill."

Marcus knew his partna best, and one thing was for sure: Lil' Keith was going to make it out of that jam, so he wasn't worried.

4 Dorian Sykes

Relief washed over Monay at the sight of Lil' Keith banging on the back door for them to let him in. He was so little and crafty that they didn't even see him when he came from the side of the house they were sitting in front of.

"Go! Go!" yelled Lil' Keith as he skidded into the back seat.

Marcus couldn't do anything except shake his head at his lil' partna. "Round, what chu gone do with the nigga shoes?"

Lil' Keith had taken the man's Gucci loafers from his feet.

"Shid, these ma'fuckas chea brand new, and they're my size. Ya heard me?" said Lil' Keith, pulling back a wide grin, revealing his gold-capped teeth.

"Really, Keith? snapped Monay. She and Keith met eyes through the rearview mirror.

"Bitch, shut the fuck up and drive, ya heard me?"

Monay turned a few corners before she turned the headlights on. A blur of red and blue lights shot past them as they waited to cross the intersection on Loyola Ave. A lone ambulance tailed the flashing lights at a slow speed. They were in no hurry to make it to the scene. They got the call over the radio that the victim was D.O.A.

Monay eased the Impala into the midnight traffic, and for a few minutes, they rode in silence, waiting to get as far away from there as possible and back to the hood where it was safe. Lil' Keith's popping of the locks on the briefcases broke the still silence as they drove.

"I thought we was gonna wait till we got back," said Monay, her sexy hazel eyes dancing through the rearview.

"And I thought I told you to shut the fuck up and drive," Lil' Keith shot back, his eyes never leaving the four kilos of what he was sure to be pure heroin, fresh from Nigeria.

"What we looking like back there, round?" asked Marcus, turning halfway in his seat to try to steal a glance.

"Jackpot, ya heard me?" said Lil' Keith.

Monay sucked her teeth, letting her irritation be known. She and Lil' Keith locked eyes again through the mirror, but this time, she held her tongue from wanting to say something. She knew better than to press her luck when it came to Lil' Keith because Keith was always going to do Keith no matter what she or anybody else said. Plus, she wasn't trying to piss him off because not only would he not hesitate to put his paws on her, but she could now feel it in his demeanor that he was looking for any reason to say fuck breaking bread with her.

Lil' Keith and Marcus had been stalking their victim, Brett, for almost a month but could never catch him because he was always changing cars and going out of town for days at a time. They had tried following him home one night as he was leaving Club Metro up in the Central Business District. They had thought they'd get him done for sure that night because he was leaving an upscale club located in the C.B.D., and they thought he'd fall asleep and not expect anybody to be on his line. But as Lil' Keith and Marcus followed him on the interstate, the nigga all of a sudden punched his Porsche 911 and came up on an exit after hopping four lanes over. Marcus was driving, but he chose to fall back and let the nigga live to see the next day because it would've been too obvious had they come up on the exit behind him.

But little did Brett know, he had just baked his own cake. When he left the club, he had a little something he'd scooped up inside who was riding shotgun, giving him dome as they drove on the interstate. Lil' Keith recognized the young woman off the bat: Monay. She

6 Dorian Sykes

used to go to Fortier High School with him and Marcus back in the day. Marcus couldn't place her, but Lil' Keith was one hundred percent certain it was her.

"I'm tellin' you, round, that's her." Lil' Keith could pick that wide ass out of a line-up if his life depended on it. He used to study her tiny waistline from the back as she would walk the halls of Fortier, shutting shit down with her home girl, Sasha.

"Damn, she still looking good," said Marcus.

Lil' Keith came up with a plan, seeing as though they had discovered this nigga's weakness was pussy—just like most niggas. He was going to slide up under Monay and have her run down Brett's whole layout for them. He'd put the charm on her at first, then that dope dick to get in her head, and then she'd be ready for the business.

Lil' Keith smiled wickedly to himself because his plan was brilliant, he thought. Not only would they smash this nigga who'd been ducking them, but he'd also get to fuck on some pussy that he'd been scheming on since high school. Marcus stole a glance over at his crime partna and saw that grin on his face.

"What the lick read, round?"

"I got this nigga, ya heard me?" said Lil' Keith. He ran down his plan to Marcus on Monay, and that they'd fall back on the nigga for the time being.

Instead of stalking Brett, Lil' Keith was now stalking Monay. He knew the circles that she moved in, and where he'd most likely find her. It wasn't a full two days when he ran into her and Sasha at Cricket Club, a nice spot uptown on St. Charles Avenue. It was one of the spots where the big boys came out and play to get their shine on, so Lil' Keith donned the Girbaud and Soulja Reeboks and slipped into a cream linen outfit with the matching ostrich skin loafers. He slid off into the spot with a fresh fade and his jewelry game on point, Cartier

Born to Die

watch and matching bracelet blinging under the club lights. He and Marcus stood under the entrance door for a moment as they came in. All eyes were on them from around the club.

Lil' Keith spotted Monay and Sasha playing the bar, trying to act unimpressed by their arrival. But it wasn't high school anymore. Lil' Keith put his spiel down on any broad who crossed his path. He glided over to the bar while Marcus got them a V.I.P. booth. Lil' Keith leaned against the bar and gave his order to the bartender for two bottles of Cristal, and then told the bartender to put on his tab whatever the two ladies were drinking, "All night," he said. And without saying a word to either of the women, he took the two bottles of Cristal and headed for the section where Marcus had posted up, leaving both Sasha and Monay speechless. He could feel them watching him from across the room, but let them stew in their wonder.

"They on you, round," said Marcus, taking a sip of the champagne.

"I know."

It wasn't a full five minutes before Monay, flanked by Sasha, were off their bar stools and switching their way over toward the V.I.P. They tried to play it cool by acting like they only came over to say thanks, but really their pussies were jumping to know who these two ballin'-ass niggas were. Lil' Keith invited them to join him and Marcus, to which Monay and Sasha smiled and accepted. Marcus and Lil' Keith entertained them all night until the club let out. When Monay saw what Lil' Keith and Marcus were rolling in, a platinum Lexus 400 sitting on chrome, any thoughts she may have had on playing coy were out the window. When Lil' Keith asked her if they were coming with them, Monay answered "Yeah" for both of them.

8 Dorian Sykes

It was crazy, though, because the whole night at the club, even after they fucked all night and woke up the next morning in bed together, Monay still hadn't remembered Lil' Keith from school. He wasn't about to wake her up, either, because it wasn't like he was looking for love. He had one agenda with Monay, and that was getting the rundown on Brett. He knew one thing was for certain: if she was putting that platinum head game on him like she'd done to Keith last night, she knew all of the nigga's business.

As they crossed back into the city of New Orleans, everyone began to breathe easy and relax.

"Turn that radio on, ya heard me?" Lil' Keith said from the back seat as he patted his pants pockets front to back, looking for the yeah stamped *911*. It was his second favorite pastime to murdering shit. He'd been snorting dope since he came off the porch like it was weed.

"I think I lost the yeah back there," Lil' Keith said, agitated 'cause he'd waited all day to do some, and now he couldn't find his yeah to save his life.

"I got some, baby," Monay said in an ass-kissing tone, happy to be of some help.

But Lil' Keith crushed her when he snapped back, "Bitch, you see me back here searchin' and shit while you up there with some yeah on you?" He snatched the foil package from her extended hand and tore into the package, nose first.

Monay watched him through the rearview, hoping the dog food would calm him down because he was in a dark, evil mood, and she couldn't stand being around him when he was like this.

"You wanna hit this, round?" Lil' Keith asked, holding out the foil for Marcus.

"Yeah, let me get right with chu."

"It ain't that 911, but it's some straights," said Lil' Keith, now starting to feel the high coming on. Monay was still eyeing him. She let her lizard-like tongue slide over the sexy gap she had in her teeth in a teasing way, hoping to change Keith's mood.

Bitch, you just don't know, Lil' Keith thought. He leaned forward and tapped Monay's shoulder, signaling for her to make the next turn.

Monay drew a question mark with her brow but made the turn anyway. She thought they were supposed to be going to the Marriott Hotel, where they had a sell setup for the dog food, and she'd get her cut. But they were now in Hollygrove, her section of the 17th Ward, where she lived and grew up.

From the back seat, Lil' Keith's murderous green eyes searched the blackened sidewalks for any souls, all the while easing his .40 caliber from off his hip. Monay never saw it coming. Lil' Keith grabbed a fistful of her hair and stabbed the .40 into her skull. The interior lit up like the night sky on the Fourth of July from the thunderous flash. Her brains and bone fragments blew all over the dash, but before her head could touch the steering wheel, Marcus had caught the wheel and pushed her out of the car against the curb. Marcus hadn't known Lil' Keith was going to down Monay, but then again, what's already understood need not be said. He was sure his partna had his reasons, which was good enough for him.

As Marcus drove back toward the hood, he saw Lil' Keith back there eye-fucking the work again, so it came as no surprise when Lil' Keith came with the larceny.

"Say, round, this chea is enough for us to make forty keys. I know this chea standing at least a ten, ya heard me?"

"You right, round," Lil' Keith said, dreaming with a smirk on his face. Boy, would it be nice, though, to have their own personal stash of the best dope known to New Orleans.

Marcus, seeing that his partna was in a zone about the work they were holding, decided to put a genuine smile on his partna's face. He told him, "Go 'head and clip us a nice piece, round, ya heard me? Tank won't miss a couple ounces."

CHAPTER TWO

1996

Club 360 had become the newest happening nightclub in the N.O. They named it 360 because of the panoramic view the club provided from its multi-level structure and many terraces. On any given night, there'd be star athletes from the Saints in the spot, ballers from around the city, and out-of-towners, with nothing but the baddest bitches New Orleans had to offer. There'd always be a line wrapped around the club outside from the entrance to the parking lot. Most people would show up knowing that they'd never make it inside because you had to be somebody to get in or be rolling with somebody who had weight in the city. Broads would be in line, hoping a baller on his way in would pick them out of the many faces to join them in V.I.P.

Tank was loving every minute of being part-owner in the new club. He'd always wanted to own his own club, but he never had the type of legal money it took to build a mega club from the ground up and obtain a liquor license. Tank was an official street nigga from out the Third Ward, bred straight out the Magnolia Projects. The streets gave him the name Tank because it was all about a dollar with him. Niggas feared Tank because he was a deadly combination of a street nigga who could think and a mean hustler, and he was known to be treacherous when needed. Murder was always the answer. That was how he kept niggas in line and how he built his ever-growing empire.

Even with the nightclub he muscled his way into, he had forced a loan shark to move on a couple of Arabs who owned a chain of strip clubs, knowing that they wouldn't be able to keep up with the payments because their clubs were going down. When they fell behind on the interest, Tank put his muscle hand down by making them front the club, with him as co-owner. At 28, he was living every dope boy's dream. He was a self-made millionaire. He had a fleet of exotic cars, private estates, and some of the baddest chicks in the N.O. at his beck and call. But still, Tank was like Tony Montana when it came to ambitions. He wanted the world and everything in it. He was going to start with New Orleans and had a hand in the dope game with some of the biggest spots in the city, but he wanted everything to go through him.

The only thing standing in the way of Tank dominating the city's heroin trade had been Brett, since he had Raw dope straight out of Nigeria that the city had fallen in love with. Tank had tried two approaches so Brett would become his connect. He first approached Brett with his million-dollar smile and vision of how, together, they could lock down the city from uptown to downtown. When Brett didn't bite, Tank doubled back with an offer he thought Brett wouldn't be able to refuse. Tank set Brett's Range Rover on fire in broad daylight, right outside the barbershop where Brett was getting his hair cut. When he came out with his guns drawn, Tank told Brett that next time, he would be inside the trunk unless he got with the program and started moving through him. In fear for his life, Brett agreed to start supplying Tank with his raw heroin, but he went underground and kept feeding the streets himself. For Tank, that was as good as a slap to the face, and so Brett had signed his own death warrant.

The blinds upstairs in Tank's office were drawn shut. He was laid back, chilling big-dick style behind his cherry oak wood executive desk, watching the floor activity of the club below on the video monitors mounted against the wet bar. His newest hostess, Unique, was at his feet, giving him head fit for a king. He'd been plotting on the fine young thing since she first started working at the club a couple of weeks ago. She was only eighteen, just how Tank liked 'em—fresh with low mileage. Unique favored Stacy Dash, from her skin tone to her eyes and slick body. Tank was already thinking about sponsoring this young thang and putting her up in a condo before some other baller snatched her up. He wouldn't want another nigga to ever feel the platinum treasures she was putting down on him. If Tank ever had any weakness, it had to be women. Bad bitches, in particular.

Tank didn't know what felt better, the head Unique was giving him or the sight of his two head busters on the video monitor making their way through the club. The two briefcases could only mean one thing: they'd downed Brett. A victorious grin stretched across Tank's clean-shaven face as he closed his eyes and exploded in Unique's mouth. She swallowed every drop and sucked him till he fell limp. She finished with a seductive smile that assured Tank there was more yet to come. He put her on file and walked her to the door.

"Call me," she said teasingly as Tank opened the door.

Lil' Keith and Marcus were on their way in. They both took a moment to enjoy the ass as Unique fox-trotted down the hall into the elevator.

"Who was shorty?" asked Marcus, closing the door.

"My new hostess," Tank said as if it were nothing.

"Ol' nigga sweatin', round, knowin' he just finished playin' in that pussy," said Lil' Keith. "Hostess, my ass," He flopped down on one of the plush sectionals and set the briefcase he'd been carrying onto the marble coffee table, as did Marcus.

Tank couldn't keep the grin off his face as he began rubbing his mitts together in anticipation of what was inside the cases. And more importantly, he wanted to confirm they'd definitely downed Brett.

"Round up outta here, ya heard me?" Marcus said, letting Tank know that they'd handled the situation.

"I never doubted y'all for a second. I knew it was just a matter of time fo' the nigga slipped up. . . . Anyways, spare me the details. What y'all got chea in these cases, ya heard me?" asked Tank.

Marcus popped the latches on both cases and waved his hand over the four kilos while looking up at Tank, waiting for his approval.

Tank walked over and lifted one of the keys from the table. "Yeah, youngins, y'all did real good chea, ya heard me?" Tank looked over the other keys. His brow drew a knowing question mark as he lifted the busted kilo Lil' Keith had dipped in already. "I'm not even gonna ask what happened to this one," said Tank, still grinning like a Cheshire cat.

"I see you ain't finna offer a nigga nothing to drink neither. Niggas just downed some African mu'fucka we been chasin' for damn near a month, and bring you damn near fo' of them thangs, and we can't even get as much as a drink, ya heard me?" Lil' Keith joked, but he was really trying to change the subject off the busted key.

Born to Die

Tank was standing there laughing, "Damn, round, how long you been holding all that in, ya heard me?"

"I mean, damn, round, am I lying?" Lil' Keith laughed.

Tank turned to Marcus, who was on his way around the wet bar. "Would you bring this nigga a drink, ya heard me?"

"Bring me the whole bottle. Some Remy, round," Lil' Keith said from his nook on the sectional.

Marcus brought the drinks back over, handing Lil' Keith a fifth of Remy Martin VSOP and Tank an ice-cold bottle of Cristal.

"I see you know my drink," said Tank, accepting the bottle and popping the cork in a celebratory manner. He raised his bottle toward Marcus and Lil' Keith. "To family," he toasted.

The pair gave a head nod, and they all took a drink. This was the part Tank could've missed Lil' Keith with—all the family shit. Tank was always preaching his spiel about loyalty and them being a family first, and it was them together against the world "'til they caskets dropped." Lil' Keith had been peeped the nigga for what he was, which was a nigga out for self and who didn't care whose back he had to step on long as he made it to the top.

How this nigga gonna love me when he still got his own momma in the projects, but he's got two three mansions? thought Keith as he sipped from the Remy, listening to Tank's latest sermon on how much he loved Lil' Keith and Marcus like they were his very own sons.

Lil' Keith stole a glance over at his partna, who was eating up every word Tank was spieling as if he'd been anointed by God himself. Marcus was Keith's partna for life, but it sickened him sometimes to see how open Tank had his mind.

Tank was a vicious nigga all right. He played on the fact that Marcus and Lil' Keith grew up with no one ever showing them love, so he'd fill that void by always preaching how important family was. Lil' Keith grew up the hard way, but he still knew what love was and what it wasn't. But he'd always been one to lay low, play slow, and see how far a nigga would go. Really, he was wishing Tank would wrap up his T.D. Jakes sermon because he wanted to get back to his car so he could do some blow. That raw he'd clipped earlier was burning a hole in his pocket.

But Tank was in full character of a Mafia Don as he paced the marble floor with his hands interlocked behind his back, delivering his hood doctrine. He looked the part of a street boss, from his clean-shaven head and face to the jewels to the dope boy gut he kept tucked under an always crisp white T.

"Family's gotta look out for family," he stressed, stopping to face Marcus and Keith with those soulless eyes of his. "So, I'm sending y'all down to Miami for a few weeks to clear y'all's head and relax for a while. Y'all been putting in a lot of work lately, and I wanted to reward y'all with this trip. I got the spot down on South Beach for y'all to rest up 'cause when ya get back, we got a few mo' loose ends we need to tie up before this family can take its position on the food chain, ya heard me?"

The only thing Lil' Keith kept hearing was "we" and "family," the same shit Tank came with every time he wanted them to down somebody for him.

"When do we leave for Miami?" asked Marcus.

"In a couple of days," said Tank as he walked around the back of his desk and slid the bottom drawer open. He pulled out two manila envelopes and joined Marcus and Keith over on the sectional.

"I've been waiting to give y'all these," he said, handing them the envelopes. He watched as they opened their envelopes and pulled out their contents. "Y'all first-class tickets, right chea, ya hear me? Got a lil' spending money,

Born to Die 17

twenty Gs, and the keys are to the two 600s y'all seen parked outside when y'all came in."

"Them cars been sittin' out there for weeks, round," said Marcus.

"Like I say, I have been waiting to give y'all this chea."

Tank was sensing that Lil' Keith wasn't as impressed with his gifts as Marcus was, so he did what he'd always done best: he uniqued more. "This chea lil' money ain't nothing but toilet paper." He met eyes with Keith. "I'ma roll out the red carpet fo' y'all soon as y'all get back, ya heard me?" Tank grabbed his bottle of Cristal from the table and stood with a grin stretching his face. "In the meantime," he said, walking over to the blinds and opening them, "I want y'all to ball out with me tonight."

Marcus and Lil' Keith joined Tank by the office window, where they stood looking down at the club below. Biggie Smalls had the spot going AWOL.

Tank put his hand on their shoulders and said, "Let's get down there, 'cause I see some ladies tonight that should be having my baby."

CHAPTER THREE

Two Days Later

Lil' Keith pulled up on the set of his hood, Valence and Magnolia Streets, sitting low and creeping in his brand-new pearl blue S600 Benz tucked on chrome blades. He hadn't parked it since Tank gave him the keys to it. He'd been club-hopping and riding around from uptown to downtown, getting his shine on. He kept the tool on his lap at all times, though, cause even though they were seeing money now, his blood had been beefing with the 17th Ward since he could remember. It was on sight with them niggas wherever. That applied to being out on the set, as well, because niggas from both sides were known to drop their nuts sometimes and come put the play down in a nigga's own hood, so Lil' Keith stayed with his .40 cal with the extended clip that they called "the dick." In the N.O., damn near every nigga had a 30-round clip hanging from their gun, which they called their "yeah." If a nigga ain't have a dick in his shit, he was faking.

Lil' Keith's hood was on the merk side of the set. It was split up by two sides: the money side and the murder side. It especially went down on the merk side. Niggas getting they issues out there. Directly on the corner of V.L. was the Chinese store. That was where niggas from the hood held court and posted up. There was always a line of empty liquor bottles and teddy bears by the phone

20   Dorian Sykes

in memory of homies who got smashed back in the day answering their beeper. That corner and everything it embodied was legendary. That was why when Lil' Keith got out of the car, he had his "yeah" tucked under his baggy white T-shirt.

Black Boy and Samuel, two of Keith's partnas, were posted up outside the store, nursing a pint of Hennessy between them.

"What's up, wodie?" said Lil' Keith, climbing the curb and giving his partnas some dap. "What the lick read, ya heard me?" he asked, putting his back to the storefront and taking in the block and its traffic.

"The Impalas been ridin', ya heard me?" advised Black Boy.

"Yeah, round, that bitch Lewis and his flunky Tate been through here all yesterday and twice this morning," added Samuel.

Lil' Keith wasn't shaken, but probed further. "Who they lookin' for?"

"Them bitches got a picture that they keep lookin' at when they roll through, but nigga as much ain't see who it is," said Samuel. He turned the last of the Hennessy up against his ashy black lips and killed it. "Say, round, you got some squares on you?" he asked, now needing a cigarette for the rundown he just gave Lil' Keith.

In the hood, Samuel and Black Boy were like the word man from the old movie *Original Gangstas*. They always knew what was going on because all they did was post up on the set.

Lil' Keith handed Samuel his pack of Newports, then lit one himself. "Say, round, grab us some bottles," said Keith as he passed Black Boy a Benjamin from his knot of bills. "Grab me a Remy VSOP, ya heard me?"

"I got chu, round," said Black Boy. As he opened the store's door, crackhead Lisa stumbled into him on her way out. She smacked her lips and proceeded to brush

Born to Die

off her battered clothes, as if somehow they'd just been ruined. "Boy, ain't you got no damn sense, runnin' in ta folks?"

Black Boy apologized to Lisa and then went inside the store. "I forgot she was in there," Samuel said in almost a whisper. He knew how Lil Keith hated seeing her on the set.

"Keith!" Lisa yelled. "I know you ain't gonna stand there and not speak to ya momma! Gimme twenty dollars."

Lil' Keith flicked the short of his square against the sidewalk, refusing to acknowledge his mother.

"You hear me, Tyrone? I am still your mother," said Lisa as she got right up in Lil' Keith's face, forcing him to look at her.

"Bitch, you ain't my momma. Ain't never been no momma. Look at chu. You's a hype, ya heard me? Fuck I'ma give you twenty dollars fo'? So you can go smoke it up? Better find a dick to suck, ya heard me?"

Tears were welling in Lisa's eyes as she stood there under Lil' Keith's relentless blast. Samuel felt sorry for Lisa because, after all, she still was his ol' bird, but he knew better than to get into the family business. He stood there, looking up the block, trying to pretend he wasn't witnessing the onslaught. He saw Lewis and Tate bend the corner down the block on Freret Street. They were speeding for some reason. Samuel tried tapping Lil' Keith to put him on point, but he was zoned out, still going in on his mother.

"Round, them Impalas is comin', ya heard me?" said Samuel. But Keith hadn't heard a single word.

Lewis slammed the Impala into park as he and his partner Tate pulled to the corner. They both sprang from the car, Glocks drawn, advancing with a dead aim on Lil' Keith.

22 Dorian Sykes

"Get the fuck on the ground, now!" ordered Lewis as Lil' Keith turned to face them. "Down on the ground," he ordered again. Lewis was a redneck homicide detective who had just as many bodies under his belt as most head bussas in the hood. He was itching to kill Lil' Keith right there on the corner because he was tired of building cases on him and Marcus only to have them beat them in court. "Give me a reason," Lewis said through clenched teeth. "I'm only gonna tell you once more to get down—"

Before he could finish his threat, Lil' Keith had shoved Lisa between him and his partna, making a run for it. Lisa hollered out for Keith to just stop, but he was barreling full speed up the block.

What the police knew from the moment they pulled up was that there was definitely going to be a foot chase with Lil' Keith. Never would he just go down without taking their asses on a tour through the hood. Keith had his .40 cal on him too, and he was trying to get that up off him because the feds had been picking up gun cases lately, especially when niggas got caught with that dick hanging from their shit.

Lil' Keith knew the hood like the back of his hand, so he thought that shaking them would be a piece of cake, but when he looked back over his shoulder, Tate was dead on his heels, running hard. Lil' Keith scanned the block as he put the burners on, spotting some of his partners down by Angel's Bar. He did the hood call, getting their attention. "Aww, aww!"

His partners were on point. As Lil' Keith shot past them, a youngin' they called Big Shays slid and caught Tate with a knock-out blow to the side of the head, using the ass end of a half-full fifth of Bombay. Big Shays got his nickname from pulling stunts like this. He wasn't but sixteen and only weighed about 150 pounds, but the youngin' barred none. He dipped off laughing and

Born to Die

did the hood call, happy to have put that work in for his partna. "Aww, aww!"

Lil' Keith rushed through the front door of Angel's, his eyes scanning the faces in the crowd, looking for any one of his partners. He spotted Jay Bey at the end of the bar and quickly passed him the .40 cal from off his hip, never losing a step. He shot out the back door and into the alleyway, only to be met by a swarm of plainclothes detectives, each with their gun drawn and ready to down him if he didn't give it up.

Lil' Keith stopped and slowly raised his hands with a cheap smile on his face. *Fuck it, I got my yeah up off me. They ain't got shit on me*, he told himself.

Out of nowhere, Lewis bullrushed Lil' Keith from the back and toppled him down onto the ground. "You son of a bitch! I ought to kill your ass." He was fuming about what happened to his partna, Tate, who was going to need at least twenty stitches to seal the gap Big Shays had put on his wig.

Angel, the owner of the bar, followed by a host of customers, spilled out the back door, making for witness."Is all that really necessary? He's already in handcuffs," snapped Angel. "I'ma report y'all asses, 'cause y'all trifling back here, jumping on this boy like this."

Lewis was forced to cease his assault for the moment until he could get Keith out of there. He snatched Keith to his feet like a rag doll and steered him toward the waiting backseat of his unmarked Impala.

With blood covering his gold teeth, Lil' Keith was still wearing a smile as Lewis threw him across the back seat and slammed the door shut. Angel warned Lewis one more time as he got behind the wheel of the Impala that if anything happened to Keith, she'd report his ass.

"Good. I'll be the one assigned to the case," he told her through the window from the driver's seat. He then

24   Dorian Sykes

kicked up a dirt cloud as he punched the Impala down the alley.

Marcus was at his condo inside the Clearwater Creek complex. He was lying in bed with his hands laced behind his head with a smile on his face, enjoying the full view of his wifey's voluptuous, flawless honey-beige skin tone. She stood under the morning's sun out on their terrace, modeling the new bathing suits she had bought for their trip to Miami.

"What you think about this one, baby?" asked Jasmeen. She turned to face Marcus, but his eyes were lost somewhere between her luscious, thick thighs and tiny waist. She shifted her stance and was now bow-legged, teasing him because she knew how much he liked staring at her gap. "I take it, then. You like this one?"

Marcus stroked his manhood from under the satin sheets, and with lust in his eyes, he told Jasmeen, "Come 'ere."

She seductively crawled up from the foot of the bed and pulled the sheets from over his body. She took his manhood from him and began stroking him up and down while she looked deep into his eyes. She loved pleasing him more than anything else.

"That's all you gonna do is tease me this morning?"

Jasmeen smiled and then licked her sexy, pouted lips. She threw her long, black, silky hair over her shoulder and went down on him. Marcus gasped and closed his eyes as Jasmeen took him on a ride of pleasure as only she knew how. She was the total package from top to bottom, and she knew it, too. Jasmeen was Creole mixed with Black, so she had this exotic look about her.

Marcus first met her downtown in the French Quarter, where she was working as a waitress at her family's restaurant. After she waited on him the first time he dined there, he went back five more times, until finally, Jasmeen agreed to go out with him.

What Marcus liked about Jasmeen right off the bat were her mannerisms. She wasn't like the chicken heads in the hood, all loud and always scheming on a dollar. Jasmeen was different than other women. She was polite and knew how to cater to her man, which was why Marcus had fallen head over heels in love with her, and vice versa, after just four months of kicking it. He moved her into his condo permanently, and even though they weren't officially married by law, Marcus didn't let that stop him from calling her his wifey. He could definitely see her being his wife in the future, especially if she kept her head game tight, like how she was putting it on him right now.

Jasmeen felt Marcus's nut brewing and on the brink of busting, so she concentrated just on the head of his dick until she caught the first burst of pre-cum against the roof of her mouth. Then she pulled him out and started jacking him off from the base of his dick to the head, while torturing him with that freak talk she knew would make him explode like never before.

"You like that, daddy, hmm?" she asked in a little girl's voice. "You gonna cum for me, daddy, hmm?"

Just then, Marcus shivered and clutched the bed sheets with a death grip as he started shooting off. Jasmeen took him back into her mouth, deep throating him down to his balls and sucking him soft. Jasmeen finished with a smile, knowing that she'd just put it down on her man and that the hoes in the streets would have a hard act to follow.

She sat up and kissed Marcus's bare chest, then rolled out of bed, leaving him panting. He called after her on her way into the bathroom, "Baby, fix me a blow, would you?"

Always willing to please Marcus, Jasmeen stepped over to her vanity and started fixing up Marcus's dope for him. She boiled the 911 over a flame using a candle and a spoon, then sucked the dope into a syringe, tapping the sides of it as she made her way back over to the bed.

"Here, hold this while I grab a belt," she said, handing Marcus his first morning wakeup. She returned with the belt and tied it around his arm tight. While looking for a vein, she traced her manicured fingers over his skin until she found one good enough to take the hit.

"Okay," she said, taking the needle back and shooting up the dope quickly before she lost that vein.

Marcus's eyes fluttered a bit, and his body sank further into the silk beneath him. That 911 was almost as good as Jasmeen's sex game. It was taking him on a mellow trip. "Thank you, baby, " he managed in a whisper.

Jasmeen undid the belt from his arm and for a long moment, she just stared down at him, wondering how and why he'd allowed himself to get on heroin at eighteen.

"Why you lookin' at me like that?" Marcus asked, pulling back a weak smile. The dope had him on the verge of nodding off.

Usually, Jasmeen would've felt it her place not to speak on her man's business, but she couldn't help but see what the heroin was doing to him. She was 25, but he was starting to look older than her as the days passed. She didn't want anything to happen to Marcus, like him dying from an overdose. She had noticed he was starting to need more dope with his fixes.

"I was just wondering how a young man like yourself got hooked on using heroin, that's all."

Automatically, Marcus's defenses went up hearing the word "hooked." He knew he had a habit, but hearing it coming from someone else, especially Jasmeen, was another story. He wondered just how bad he looked in her eyes.

Born to Die

He took a deep breath as she caressed his hand in support. "Well," he began, recalling the first time he had ever snorted dope. "The first time I snorted some dope was when I was fifteen years old. One of the big homies out the hood got smashed. He used to fuck with dope, so after the funeral, I snorted a bag with my niggas in memory of him instead of pouring out some liquor, ya feel me?" Marcus tried making light of the conversation. "And you know when a nigga off that dope, it's like he on Viagra, so when I saw that, I started getting a bag every time I fucked something, and before I knew it, I had a habit. Back then, bitches would tell you 'I want that dope dick,' and niggas was still getting money, so it was cool. I started shooting, though, 'cause the high is better and it hits you faster."

Marcus let his words trail off, as did his eyes. He was wondering if that was too raw for Jasmeen. But she didn't judge him. She was just glad that he had opened up and shared with her, because she knew he had grown up hard with no family except for the streets, unlike her, who had always had both parents in her life and siblings who loved each other. So, she figured, who was she to pass judgment on him?

Jasmeen ran her fingers through Marcus's dreads, soothing his scalp with her soft touch. "Baby, just promise me that when we come back from Miami, you'll slow down." Her eyes were sincere, as were her words. She wasn't expecting Marcus to leave the streets and dope alone altogether, but she needed him to slow things down, because at the rate he was moving, she knew that she'd have to bury him before they could ever get married and provide him with the family and love she longed to give him.

"You unique?" she again begged him to promise.

"Uniques are meant to be broken, baby . . . but I'ma give you my word instead, ya heard me?"

A smile stretched across Jasmeen's face from ear to ear. She leaned in and kissed his soft lips because she knew one thing for certain: Marcus was a man of his word. He had never given her any reason to doubt him once he gave his word on something. That's what it was.

"Thank you," she said, then kissed him once more before slipping out of bed. She said over her shoulder, "I'ma take a shower, 'cause our flight leaves in a couple hours. I'll get you up when I'm finished."

That sounded like a plan to Marcus because the dope was kicking in, and he needed a little doze. He watched with his eyes half slit as Jasmeen undressed in the bathroom, then climbed into the running shower. *Life is good for once*, he thought, closing his eyes shut and drifting off to sleep.

Marcus thought he was still dreaming when he heard the door come flying off its hinges and men shouting throughout the condo. He reached for his .40 cal, which he usually kept on the nightstand right beside him, but he came up empty. *Fuck is my yeah?* he thought. The footsteps were closing in on the bedroom quickly. *Jasmeen*, he thought as he snatched the sheets from over him.

"Police! We have a warrant!" a man yelled out just before he opened the bedroom door.

Marcus froze at the foot of the bed where his .40 cal lay on the carpet. He didn't know if it was the actual police or some niggas pretending to be the law so they could down him.

"Got 'im!" the first officer called out as he entered the room, seeing Marcus in plain view of the gun. "Down on the floor, now!" ordered the white officer.

Marcus's instinct of them being the real deal was confirmed when his archnemesis walked through the door. Lewis.

Born to Die

"Get him down and cuffed," Lewis said, immediately taking control of the situation.

Two more plainclothes detectives came rushing into the room to assist. They cuffed Marcus on the floor and did a thorough search of him even though he had on nothing but a pair of boxers.

"Get him up," ordered Lewis.

Jasmeen came rushing out of the bathroom, dressed in a towel. "What's going on? Do you have a warrant?" she demanded.

Early in their relationship, Marcus had sat her down and told her how to deal with the police if and when they came.

"Yes, we have a warrant for your little boyfriend's arrest and to search everything at this address. . . . Everything," Lewis said, looking Jasmeen over from head to toe.

"We'll see about that when my attorney gets here," said Jasmeen as she headed for the cordless phone on the nightstand.

"Better get the best in town 'cause he's being charged with two counts of capital murder, among other things," Lewis said to her back, which he was enjoying. "Get him outta here and straight over to The Parish."

Marcus didn't speak a word as the two officers steered him out in his boxers. He was confident in his woman. She was strong, smart, and knew the score. She'd call his lawyer and then get word to Tank A.S.A.P.

The only thing that bothered Marcus wasn't him being charged with murder. It was the trip down to O.P.O.— also known as Orleans Parish Prison, but the convicts who it held had long ago started calling the dump simply The Parish. It was a trifling experience, no doubt; one that Marcus wished he would never have to go through. But then again, he reminded himself that it was all part of the game he played.

CHAPTER FOUR

From the back seat of the unmarked Impala, Marcus could make out the murky images of The Parish in the nearing distance. It was connected to the courthouse and was the city's main jail, where they housed everything from capital offenses to federal inmates down to petty misdemeanors. Marcus knew he'd be classified as a capital offender, earning him a red band upon his arrival as a means to distinguish him for his charges of capital murder. Marcus had been down to The Parish too many times to remember, along with his right hand, Lil' Keith, and they wore red bands each time. The convicts called them Rolexes, giving them the highest esteem to be earned within the jail.

The rookie plainclothes detective riding shotgun turned halfway in his seat, flashing a cheesy grin toward Marcus as the Impala descended underneath the jail's parking garage. "Welcome home, sweetheart. I'm sure they've missed you," he wisecracked. He'd been trying his damnedest to initiate a conversation with Marcus since they'd left the condo, but Marcus kept the code of letting his lawyer do all the talking for him. This only pissed the red-faced rookie off even more, seeing that he couldn't break Marcus despite his belief that all niggas would fold under enough pressure.

"Fine, have it your way," the cop said, snatching Marcus out of the back seat and steering him into the registry.

32 Dorian Sykes

With a final nudge in his back, Marcus was handed over to a black female correctional officer down in R&D, Receiving and Discharging. She was most definitely from the projects. Marcus could tell by the way she kept looking him up and down and smacking at her gum.

"Where's his clothes at?" she spat in the direction of the detectives.

"I'm sure they've got something in his size," the rookie shot back over his shoulder, slapping a high-five with his redneck partner.

"They know they're wrong," said the female C.O. "Come on and follow me. Let's get you some clothes on."

Marcus followed behind the woman, trying to recall where he knew her from. He never forgot faces, and it was always good to know somebody when you found yourself in places as bad as The Parish.

Marcus caught a glimpse of her gold-plated nametag pinned against her breast pocket. *Kindle . . . where I know a Kindle from?* Marcus thought as the orderly working inside the change-out room quickly sized him up, then tossed him a dingy jumpsuit, two sizes too small, and a pair of mismatched sandals, along with a bedroll.

After quickly dressing, Marcus followed C.O. Kindle out for fingerprinting and to take three mugshots. He had pinned where he knew her from. She was some kin to his partna Eugene. She used to be on the set every now and then, hanging around Eugene's house, which he had converted into a full-fledged barbershop. *It's her for sure,* Marcus thought as she wrapped the red band around his wrist and cut the extra clipping with a pair of scissors. She just looked a little different without all of her gold jewelry on.

She looked up into Marcus's eyes as she finished his band and asked, "You see something you like, do you?" There was a trace of a smile on her sexy full pout.

Born to Die 33

"Maybe," Marcus said in a hushed tone. "You some kin to my homie Eugene, ain't chu?"

Her eyes went down to a slit, as she too tried placing where he knew Marcus from. His last name didn't ring any bells. "Where you be knowing my nephew from?"

"We grew up together on V.L. That's the set."

"And what they call you around there?"

"Just tell him his partna Marcus is in here."

"We'll see. Come on and follow me, " she said.

"I ain't get ya name," Marcus said as he followed her to an awaiting bullpen. She stopped with one hand on the cast iron bars and looked up into Marcus's eyes. "It's C.O. Kindle for now," she said, then slid the gate shut behind Marcus.

Marcus turned from the bars to face the hundred-plus bodies scattered about the musty holding cell. Dope fiends lay sprawled across the floor, staking their claim in every corner. The heavy stench of raw ass hung in the air like a rain cloud, a smell that Marcus had become oh-so-familiar with over the years of coming to The Parish. He quickly did an inventory of every face inside the tank, searching for any nigga he had beef with from back in the day to the present, 'cause in New Orleans, whether on the streets, jail, church, or wherever, it was beef on sight.

Marcus didn't see anybody who posed any threat to him, so he tried to relax a little. He looked around for a place to sit but decided not to, and instead, he posted up against the front of the bars, anticipating the many hours he was sure to wait until they moved him upstairs with the rest of the capital-offending "Red Bands."

When Marcus finally made it upstairs, he was too tired to argue or question why he was being held in isolation from the rest of the jail. As he was led down the pissy, pitch-black tier, he figured the order had to have come

34 Dorian Sykes

from none other than Lewis. It was his way of not only fucking with Marcus, but also a means to deny him access to the phone because the prisoners being held within isolation were restricted from using the phones.

Marcus heard the iron gate slam shut behind him as he stepped inside the tiny cell. *Home sweet home*, he thought, still able to hear the rookie's laughter ringing in his mind.

A roach nest was nestled at the foot of the stone slab bed made into the cell wall. Marcus stood in the center of the cell for a moment, watching the roaches scurry about the sink and walls, wondering how he'd sleep when he heard a voice from across the way. Up until then, he was certain that he was alone on the tier.

"Say, round, is that you over there?" the voice called again. It was low and meek. Marcus set his bedroll down on the bunk, then stepped closer to the bars. "Keith, is that you, round?"

"Yeah," said Lil' Keith with a heavy grunt. He struggled to get himself up to the bars. The lone lamp hanging down the hall illuminated the blood-stained turban of gauze wrapped around his head.

"Fuck happen to you?" asked Marcus as he stood there taking in all of Lil' Keith's injuries.

"Ain't shit, ya heard me? That bitch Lewis and coupla his flunkies call theyself doin' a nigga dirty, ya heard me?"

"We gone down that bitch, ya heard me?" said Marcus. He was fucked up to see his partna standing there with a pumpkin head, looking like the Elephant Man.

Lil' Keith flashed his gold teeth, smiling. "That bitch just mad 'cause what happened to his partna, that bitch Tate."

Keith gave Marcus the rundown on how their partna Big Shays had stretched Tate out on the set. They both shared a laugh, but Marcus was waiting on Lil' Keith

Born to Die

35

to fill him in on why they were there to begin with. He knew Keith knew why because out of all their trips to The Parish, it had always been on the account of Lil' Keith somehow or another.

"But say, round, what this chea all about, ya heard me?" Marcus asked.

Lil' Keith let his eyes fall to the floor of his cell as he started shaking his little head from side to side. "They talkin' 'bout some shit out in the Lake Chateau Estates, ya heard me?" he said, talking in code. "They ain't said nothing else though, round. Guess we just gonna have to ride it out, ya heard me? You know how we do."

Suddenly, Marcus didn't feel like talking anymore. "Say, round, I'ma kick back for a minute and try to piece this shit together, ya heard me?" said Marcus as he took a seat on the edge of his bunk.

"Nigga, don't start that stressin' shit on me now," said Lil' Keith. He hadn't left the bars, and his gold grin was still shining under the lamp's light. "You know we done been through this chea a hunnid time before, ya heard me?"

Marcus lay back against the thin mat with his eyes to the ceiling. He knew they'd been down this same dark road many times before, but the truth was that the shit was getting old, and it was starting to wear thin on Marcus. It was different when he and Lil' Keith were out there just thuggin' it and not giving a fuck whether they lived or died, but things were different now that Jasmeen had come into Marcus's life. He now had a reason to live and to care if he'd wake up the next day. Before Jasmeen came into Marcus's life, he couldn't have cared less what his future had in store for him, but this time around, the red band on his wrist didn't symbolize a Rolex as it had in the past, but the potential death sentence it was meant to embody for capital offenses.

36   Dorian Sykes

Marcus closed his eyes for a moment and tried thinking of Jasmeen, wishing they'd caught an early flight down to Miami. At least they'd be safe in each other's arms there.

Marcus's brief escape from the grim reality was broken when Lil' Keith tossed a balled-up wad of toilet paper across the hall from his cell, landing at Marcus's feet.

"That's fucked up. You gonna leave me standing at the bars, ya heard me? But uh, that yeah should help you get up outta chea."

Marcus unraveled the knot of tissue, revealing about two grams of his favorite pastime. He looked up from the dog food to see Lil' Keith nose-diving in a gram himself.

"In the morning, round," Keith said with a cheap grin as he thumbed his nose and grunted on his way to his bunk. He kicked off his sandals and balled up under the half sheet and blanket as if he had not a worry in the world.

Marcus did about a half gram, then returned to his nook on his mattress with his eyes locked to the ceiling and his thoughts wandering. *How'd I get caught up in this bitch again?* he thought. The answer to his question was snoring across the hall from him. Marcus couldn't help but laugh as he recalled what his grandma used to tell him about Lil' Keith before she passed away. She'd always say, "That boy ain't nothin' but the devil. He's gonna have you and him both in a world of trouble. You watch and see." Before Lil' Keith's momma started getting high, she used to say the same thing about Marcus.

Maybe they both were right, thought Marcus. Maybe he and Lil' Keith had led each other down the wrong path, but one thing Marcus knew for sure was that they'd always been partners, no matter the circumstances.

The 911 kicked in, and Marcus started to nod. He nodded off while remembering their first trip to The Parish.

Born to Die 37

***

The year was 1992, and Lil' Keith and Marcus were supposed to be in their sophomore year at Fortier High School, but they hadn't attended class since they first arrived, so they were stuck in the ninth grade. They didn't care, though, about being held back a grade, as neither had any aspirations of graduating or going off to college. For them, school had become nothing less than a fashion show and a meeting grounds where wards and sets settled on their ongoing beefs. Fortier sat directly on the corner of Freret Street in the 13th Ward. That's where all scores were settled Monday through Friday on the way to school and on the way home.

The 13th Ward had been beefing with the 17th Ward ever since the beginning days of Fortier and probably even before then. The 17th is split between three sections: Hollygrove, Pigeon Town, and Gert Town, making the 17th the deepest, because that's one of the biggest wards in the N.O.

Coming up, the 13th had encounters with all three sections. It started out with "ward banging" after school, then graduated to pistol play and niggas getting killed. Lil' Keith and Marcus hailed from the 13th Ward, so they pretty much knew every day after school that they had a fight on their hands with the niggas out the 17th. Their homies off the set lived by the old law: don't rat, don't snitch, don't bend, don't fold "under no circumstances." That included standing your ground and fighting no matter how many niggas you had to go up against. "Under no circumstances" were to not show fear and turn your back, and you better not have your partners fight by themselves unless you wanted that pumpkin-head-style beat down.

Lil' Keith never broke camp and left his niggas hanging, but he tired of the many ass-whoopings they had been

38   Dorian Sykes

taking on the daily after school, sometimes by grown men out the 17th, who were up at Fortier helping their youngins fight.

One day after school, Lil' Keith was the first of his clique down on the cement slab of steps leading to the corner of Freret Street. There was a mob repping the whole 17th posted on the corner, some parked at the curb in stolen cars, but all waiting for the midday brawl that occurred every day after school.

"Say, round, y'all fall back a step, ya heard me?" said Lil' Keith over his shoulder at Marcus, Samuel, and the rest of their clique. "I got this," Lil' Keith said to himself as he touched the last step down to the sidewalk. He was met by the smoldering hot sun and then by a swarm of 17th niggas.

"There go my ho. I been lookin' for you all day," one of the youngins said to Keith. It wasn't a full two seconds before the drama kicked off. All that could be heard were punches being thrown and sneakers screeching against the concrete.

Marcus and his clique jumped in to help Lil' Keith, but everybody scattered at the sound of gunshots . . . *Boom! Boom! Boom!*

The niggas from the 17th scattered like ants, with some jumping in cars while most took off on foot. When Marcus looked back over his shoulder, he saw Lil' Keith standing over a young nigga, who was lying on the ground, clutching his stomach in the fetal position. Lil' Keith was waving his chrome .38. Special from side to side toward the fleeing backs of their rivals. Marcus watched Lil' Keith then point the gun down at the young man's head and fire twice. *Boom! Boom!*

Marcus rushed back to grab Lil' Keith, who had blacked out. He was still cursing and daring whoever else wanted some to run up, and they'd get the same. Marcus was

Born to Die 39

able to get him out of there and back to the hood, but not before a parent who was waiting to pick up her daughter was able to I.D. him and Lil' Keith.

The Jump Out Boys rode the hood for two days, looking for Lil' Keith and Marcus because the shooting and murder had made headlines in the *Times-Picayune*. They needed a suspect in custody and charged because the victim was said to be an honor roll student and star athlete on Fortier's football team.

The Jump Outs caught Lil' Keith and Marcus coming out of the Chinese on Valence and Magnolia early in the morning. It was their first time riding in the backseat of Lewis's unmarked Impala, but with many more trips to follow. Even back then, though, Marcus and Lil' Keith stuck to the G-code by refusing to make any statements and demanding to see their attorney—not that they had any mouthpiece on retainer, but they knew what little rights were afforded to them by law.

At the age of fifteen, they were being charged with capital murder and were held at The Parish as adults for the first time. If convicted, they'd face the death penalty or life at Angola, the Louisiana State Penitentiary, at the very least. The latter option was the only deal prosecutors were offering as Lil' Keith and Marcus held out for trial. The D.A.'s office let it be known through Marcus and Keith's court-appointed attorneys that they'd seek the death penalty if the boys lost at trial.

Two weeks before their trial was set to start, Lil' Keith and Marcus got called for an attorney visit at the jail, but to their surprise, it was Tank, along with two high-powered lawyers they'd never seen before. Tank introduced everyone, then excused the lawyers from the room while he talked to Marcus and Lil' Keith alone.

Tank turned around, flashing his twenty gold teeth at the youngins, and said, "Money is like a master key, ya heard me? It opens all doors."

40 Dorian Sykes

Unimpressed with this nigga's presentation, Lil' Keith started him wondering just what the nigga's angle was because he was sure Tank kept one.

Tank took a seat on the small steel bench across from Marcus and Lil' Keith as he went into his spiel. "Look, youngins, I been following y'all case ever since they swooped y'all up, ya heard me? And I see the way they getting ready to do y'all dirty up chea in these white folks' courtroom, ya understand me? Now, I'm here 'cause I knew both y'all fathers. Comin' up, they both was Gs in the hood and two respected niggas that I looked up to as a youngin, ya dig? So, in they memory, I can't stand by and watch these white folks have they way with y'all, 'cause I'm knowing what the outcome gone be: either the needle or life in Angola, ya understand me?" Tank let his last words soak in for a minute.

"So, what chu want from us, ya heard me?" asked Lil' Keith, cutting to the chase.

Again, Tank flashed them with his gold teeth, then said, "I want for y'all to come be a part of my family."

"You mean work for you, right?" asked Keith.

"Youngin, everythang in this world ain't always gonna be cut and dry. Everythang doesn't come with a price, like y'all's freedom, ya heard me? But let them sell-out lawyers y'all got tell it, y'all life is over. Y'all ain't but what—fifteen? Y'all ain't even did no living yet, and these white folks wanna hang ya before ya life even begins. But with me, y'all stand a fighting chance. See, right outside that door is two of the best murder trial lawyers in all of New Orleans, and they're here to help y'all come home . . . if we're family. I know y'all both came up hard, but let me show y'all what family is, youngins. I'm tellin' you that amongst y'all selves, and then y'all let me know what it is."

Born to Die 41

With his spiel complete, Tank stepped out into the hall, confident that they had no one else but him. After he sprung them from jail, he'd be one step closer to sewing up the dope game throughout the N.O. with his new head bussas ready to down anybody, anywhere. Tank was set on bringing Marcus and Lil' Keith into his crime family because, as he said, he grew up under their fathers and witnessed the gunplay that they were about, and he knew that the apples didn't fall too far from the trees. With the right molding, they could be as feared and respected as their late fathers.

"What chu' think, round?" Marcus asked Lil' Keith.

"I think the nigga's full of shit, ya heard me?"

"Why you say that?"

"Cause the nigga's a creep, ya dig? Why he wanna help us for, huh? All that shit he kickin' 'bout knowing a nigga daddy from back in the day, that shit don't hold no weight with me, ya heard me?"

"Come on, Keith. Ain't like we got nobody else tryna help us. I think we should fuck with the nigga. I mean, what's the worst that can happen, ya heard me?"

"It's all on you, round. But all that family shit, I don't owe a nigga shit when this chea is all over with, ya understand me?"

"Round, our word is all we got."

"Then give the nigga yours. I got my yeah, fuck a word." Marcus figured Lil' Keith would come around once he saw Tank hold up to his end by helping them get out. He stuck his head out into the hallway, where Tank stood conversing with the two silver-haired mouthpieces.

"So, what y'all come up with, family?" Tank asked, extending both arms.

"Family," answered Marcus as he embraced Tank.

Lil' Keith reluctantly joined them in a brief embrace; then, it was down to business. Tank stepped aside, tak-

42   Dorian Sykes

ing up a perch by the mantel of dust-covered windows overlooking the city's skyline, while the lawyers scribbled notes down as they interviewed Marcus and Lil' Keith. Tank could see his family taking form. With the two young thoroughbreds now with him, the sky was the limit. What he liked most about Marcus and Lil' Keith was that they never once showed any signs of folding under pressure. He could only imagine what they'd be like with a force behind them.

The lawyers Tank hired for them were indeed some of the best out of N.O. They ate the D.A.'s case against Marcus and Lil' Keith alive. The witness against them all of a sudden couldn't recall all the facts and statements made prior to their arrest, thanks to Tank greasing some palms. The jury returned with not-guilty verdicts on all counts for Marcus and Lil' Keith. They made the front page of the *Times-Picayune* as Two murderous teens charged in Fortier's slaying are set free by jury.

Waiting for them outside the courtroom was Tank in a stretch white Lincoln limousine. He took them on a shopping spree, then to their welcome home party he had planned at Latina's, with everybody from the hood in the spot. To top the night off, when they finished partying, two Eddie Bauer Broncos—triple black—were outside, waiting at the curb. Tank proudly handed over the keys to Marcus and Lil' Keith in front of a crowd of spectators, making it official that they were a part of his family now.

"It only gets better. . . ." Marcus recalled Tank telling them that years ago, that summer night. Since then, they'd had their ups and downs going to jail, but each time, Tank was right there, lawyers paid up in advance. This was just the latest trip to The Parish.

CHAPTER FIVE

Marcus was awakened by the rattling of keys running across the iron gate of his cell. It was Lewis. "Wake your piece of shit ass up. You've got court in ten minutes!"

Marcus was still trying to gather his bearings as he swung his legs around to the floor and stepped into his slippers.

"Court?" he questioned as he stepped closer to the bars.

"Yes, court. You know, your second home besides this place," said Lewis.

The three detectives he had with him all shared in a hearty, redneck laugh.

"You, of course, don't have to have court this morning if you . . ." Lewis said, approaching Marcus at the bars, "if you've got something to tell me."

"Yeah, suck this dick, ya heard me?" Lil' Keith said from across the tier as he snorted the last of the 911.

"Grow one, you little shit," Lewis shot back over his shoulder, then focused back on Marcus. "Don't be like that piece of shit over there 'cause his ass is done. Help yourself, son. Allow me to tell the DA when we go in there that you're willing to turn over a new leaf. I know you're tired of all this. I know you'd rather be at home with that pretty girlfriend of yours."

Marcus looked Lewis dead in his eyes and asked, "Let me ask you something. Would you ever do anything to jeopardize your career?"

"No." Lewis shook his head.

44   Dorian Sykes

"Then what makes you think I'd ever do something that would jeopardize mine's, ya heard me?"

"Is that what you call this?" A smile took over Lewis's face until he flushed beet red. He raised his hands to the ceiling, pointing. "You call this a career?"

"It is what it is," Marcus told him.

"You're right about that. And your sorry black ass going to the gas chamber or spending the rest of your life in Angola is what it is, too, I guess. Hell, ain't no skin off my dick."

"You been sellin' that same shit since '92 when we beat ya white ass at trial, ya heard me?" Lil' Keith joined in. He got a kick out of making Lewis's blood pressure rise.

Lewis spun on his heels and rushed the bars of Keith's cell with both hands. "You won't be so lucky this time, you lil' maggot. You can bet that scrap metal in your mouth that your ass is mine on this. Jesus Christ couldn't save you if he wanted to. You know that gold Rolex you were wearing when we picked you up? It belonged to the victim. And what about the two grams of dope you dropped next to the body? It's got your little dick-beater fingerprints all over it. Not to mention, we have a witness that puts you with our second victim, Monay Adams, at the time of her death. Yeah, I'd say that ass is mines this time, ya heard me?" Lewis said, mocking Lil' Keith's slang.

"Bring the fight, cracker," spat Keith.

Marcus could only shake his head as the detectives clasped the cold steel metal bracelets behind his back. They slid his cell open and escorted him and Lil' Keith over to the courthouse attached to the jail. On the elevator ride up to the courtroom, Lil' Keith couldn't even look at Marcus because he knew that he had fucked up yet once again. Marcus couldn't understand his partna sometimes. Why on earth would he keep the vic's Rolex

Born to Die

and be wearing it? How were they going to explain that alone in front of a jury? Those were questions their high-paid attorneys would figure out. They'd come from under what seemed worse circumstances before.

Marcus pulled back a closed smile, instantly feeling better about the odds against him, as the detectives escorted him inside the courtroom, and he saw his mouthpiece, Ronald Crenshaw, standing beside the defense table, talking to the love of his life, Jasmeen. They both turned and gave Marcus assuring smiles that everything was going to be all right.

"Court starts in about five minutes. I'll leave you two alone to talk a minute," Mr. Crenshaw said, tapping Marcus on his shoulder as he excused himself. Jasmeen quickly embraced Marcus and slipped her soothing tongue in his mouth before the bailiff could say anything.

"Step back. Let me look at ya," said Marcus, as he took in Jasmeen's flawless frame head to toe. "Damn, you lookin' good, baby."

"You know I'm here to represent my man," Jasmeen said, blushing. "But how you holding up, baby?"

Marcus took a deep breath and then exhaled. He could never lie to Jasmeen, so he shot the real to her. "We're in for the long haul on this one, baby."

Jasmeen's soft hands turned to stone inside Marcus's. Her back stiffened as she asked, "What do you mean by the long haul? You are coming home to me, aren't you?" Her eyes were getting wet as she stood there contemplating the worst.

Marcus caught the lone tear with his thumb as it streamed down her cheek. "Of course, I'm coming home to you when this is all over with, but . . . but that's gonna be a minute, okay?"

"What's a minute?" Jasmeen asked, sounding like a little girl.

"It can be months, or a couple years while we fight this thing. You with me tough, right?"

"Yes, you know I am."

"Then that's all that matters." Marcus lifted Jasmeen's chin up and kissed her softly on the lips. "I'ma need chu' to be strong for us, baby."

Mr. Crenshaw was signaling that court was about to start. "I'll see you over at the jail tonight," said Marcus. He took his seat next to Lil' Keith and his lawyer Douglas Cummings. Cummings and Crenshaw had been representing Marcus and Keith since their first body and had beat every case for them since.

Marcus nudged Lil' Keith to wake up because he was nodding off from the dope.

"Wake up, round, the judge 'bout to come in," Marcus whispered.

"Fuck that bitch, ya heard me? She ain't 'bout to give us no bond, ya dig?"

All rose except Lil' Keith as Judge Victoria Curtis took her seat behind the bench. She grunted at the presence of Lil' Keith and Marcus being in front of her court yet again. Looking down over her spectacles, she promptly denied bail and set their next court appearance for two weeks in the future.

"Next!" she said with finality, hammering down her gavel.

"I told ya so, round," said Lil' Keith as he and Marcus stood to be cuffed and then escorted out of the courtroom.

"I love you," Jasmeen mouthed. She had tears in her eyes as she blew Marcus a kiss.

Back at the jail, Marcus was pacing his cell and doing push-ups every other time he reached the bars. He was

Born to Die

47

listening to Lil' Keith's theory on why they would beat the charges.

"I'm telling you, round, that watch don't mean shit. I could've bought that off any crackhead running around the hood. And that bag of dope they say got my prints on it doesn't hold no weight. For all the jury knows, Lewis planted that shit. He's got a bunch of complaints on him for planting shit on niggas, plus ain't no secret he's got a hard dick wanting to fuck since '92, ya heard me?"

Marcus dipped down to another set. "Yeah, I hear you, round . . . but what about this witness?"

"Can't be but one motherfucker, round. That boot-mouth bitch, Sasha. Who else can put Monay with me, let alone even knew that we was fuckin'?"

"It's all gonna be in the paperwork, and we'll go from there, ya heard me?" said Marcus.

They froze the game at the sound of keys coming down the tier. To Marcus's surprise, it was C.O. Kindle, who had processed him the other night. Lil' Keith shot a look of "who dat," as she stopped in front of Marcus's cell.

"You have a visit. Actually, two visits. One's your attorney, and the other is a young woman claiming to be your wife?" Her last statement was clearly a question, which Marcus left unanswered.

"See you in a minute, round," said Marcus, as he straightened himself as much as possible, then allowed C.O. Kindle to put the handcuffs on.

"Which one would you like to see first?"

"My lawyer," said Marcus, figuring he could make things quick with Mr. Crenshaw. It wasn't like he was there to tell him they were free to go. Marcus walked shoulder to shoulder with C.O. Kindle as she escorted him around to visitation. He couldn't help but bask in her strawberry-scented lotion, which he was sure came from Bath & Body Works.

48   Dorian Sykes

Marcus particularly liked the way her uniform hugged her every curve. He figured her to be in her early forties, but she still had the body of a schoolgirl. The only thing that threw Marcus about her was the way she wore her hair—long, crinkled burgundy-and-black weave down her back—with matching long fingernails.

"Just ring the buzzard when you're ready," she told him before shutting the door.

Mr. Crenshaw waved his hand at the steel gray chair before him. He was shuffling through some papers with his reading glasses hanging on the bridge of his nose. "Here it is," he said, finding the document he'd been searching for. "Do you know a young woman by the name of Sasha Carter?"

"What about her?" asked Marcus.

Mr. Crenshaw sat down the paper, then took off his glasses, setting them on his closed briefcase. He began massaging his temples with his eyes shut as if it had been a long day.

"I'm not supposed to have this information just yet, nor am I supposed to be sharing this with you, but as your lawyer, I must."

"I got you. What's understood need not be said."

"Good. 'Cause the D.A. is treating Ms. Carter as a surprise witness out of fear something might happen to her. You follow me?" said Mr. Crenshaw. His face was firm.

Marcus merely nodded but said nothing.

"Ms. Carter can put your co-defendant at the murder scene of victim Monay Adams. She claims that the victim called her hours prior to being found dead, stating that she'd be with him all night. Ms. Carter further claims that the victim confided in her weeks prior that she had been helping your co-defendant stalk the first victim for the purpose of robbing him."

Born to Die 49

"And what does all that have to do with me? She never once mentioned my name."

"I know, but then there's a second witness from the murder scene behind the Lake Chateau Estates who picked you out in a lineup."

Marcus's stomach dropped as he flashed back to him and the old white woman locking eyes in the alley. The old bitch had remembered his face.

"But I haven't been in no lineups," Marcus stressed to Mr. Crenshaw.

"It was a photo lineup with your mug shot."

"Were you present?"

"No."

"Then the shit's illegal!"

"Don't you think I know that? I've already got a motion in court to dismiss her as a tainted witness. If the judge tosses out her statement, you walk. It's that simple."

"What about Keith?"

Mr. Crenshaw ran a hand over his face and sighed. He knew how close Marcus and Keith were and that they were all the family they'd ever really known, so he was delicate with his response. "Unfortunately, there's a lot more evidence tying your co-defendant to those homicides. Not saying that he won't beat them both at trial, but he's in this for the long haul. You just let me worry about getting you in the clear for now, okay?"

"All right, but still send over all my discovery soon as you get it," said Marcus.

"Will do," said Mr. Crenshaw as he stood, placing everything back into his briefcase. "I saw your lovely fiancée come up on the elevator. Hope we didn't stay too long. Wouldn't want to keep her waiting."

Marcus pressed the buzzard on the wall for the C.O., and with a half-smile, he asked Mr. Crenshaw, "She told you we were engaged?"

50   Dorian Sykes

"No, I just figured with a young woman as nice and cultured as she is, you would have enough sense to want to marry her and start a family together." Mr. Crenshaw gave Marcus a pat on the back before stepping out. "You know, this life gets old sooner than later, son. Trust me, I know."

Marcus knew that this was Mr. Crenshaw's way of giving him some fatherly advice. He's always felt it his duty to drop a jewel here and there on Marcus because he'd been around so long and seen so much that he knew how the movie would end.

"You ready?" asked C.O. Kindle. "She's waiting in booth number three."

"How long do I got?"

"Take as long as you need."

"Thank you."

Marcus found Jasmeen waiting for him in booth three. She was beaming with a smile as Marcus came in. The booth was no bigger than the cell Marcus slept in at night. The four walls were cloaked with steel barriers, and there was another steel metal wall separating the prisoners from their visitors, which had a slender piece of plexiglass in the center to see through, with eight holes drilled through both sides so the visitors may talk through.

Marcus hated for Jasmeen to see him like this, but he did his best to mask his feelings as he met her hand against the glass. "Sorry 'bout the wait, baby. That was Mr. Crenshaw."

"It's okay. I figured you were with him. What did he say?"

"That he's filing a motion to suppress a witness statement and that if the judge grants it, I'm outta here."

"That's good news, right?"

"'Bout the best thing I heard all day."

"When will the judge rule on it? Will it be soon?"

Marcus sighed, then said, "That I don't know, but Mr. Crenshaw got pull over there in them courts, so I know they're not gonna drag me on it."

"I just want you home," Jasmeen whined.

"And I'm coming home to you. That's my word, okay?"

Jasmeen pulled back a smile and said, "Okay," because she always trusted Marcus at his word.

"But look, baby girl. In the meantime, I still want you to take that trip down to Miami, ya heard me?"

"And what, just leave you here? I'm not going to leave you in here by yourself."

"You wouldn't be leaving me. My next court date ain't until two more weeks. That's plenty of time for you to go and relax and enjoy yourself. Everything is already paid for."

"I wanted us to take that trip together."

"I know. Me too. But this won't be the last trip, baby. That won't be the last plane to Miami. We've got a lot of living to do, ya heard me? It would just mean the world to me if you went 'cause at least I'd know you ain't just stressing 'bout my situation."

"I don't wanna go by myself, baby."

"You've got two tickets. Take ya moms or ya sister, Lisa."

"Okay, I'll make you a deal."

"What's that?" Marcus braced himself for the catch.

"I'll go on the trip, but only if you agree that when this is all over with, we're leaving New Orleans."

"What you mean, like on vacation?" asked Marcus. He knew she couldn't be talking about leaving the N.O. for good. She was crazy; that's all he knew!

"I'm talking about moving someplace else and us starting a new life together. 'Cause the way I see it, I'ma be either burying you in the next year or so or coming to see you behind a metal wall for the rest of our lives. Is that what you want for us?"

Here we go, thought Marcus. "Jasmeen, you know that's not what I want for us."

"Then tell me, what is it that you want for us?"

Marcus knew that Jasmeen loved him, but he couldn't understand why she was suddenly bombarding him with deep questions that he felt she knew he didn't have the answers to.

"I see you thinking," she said. "That's good, 'cause you don't have to answer me right now, but I do want and deserve an answer soon."

She had a legitimate beef, and Marcus knew it, so he assured Jasmeen that he'd think about their future together and what that meant to him. The remainder of the visit was a blur. It ended with Jasmeen letting Marcus know she'd dropped two grand on his commissary account and made sure the house phone accepted collect calls for when they might move him to another unit, where he could use the phone. Undoubtedly, she was on point, and Marcus told her so and how much he loved her.

C.O. Kindle let Marcus rock out until they announced visiting hours were now over on the P.A. system. Jasmeen promised she'd be there Thursday, on his next visiting day.

"Have a good visit?" asked C.O. Kindle as she escorted Marcus back to lock up.

"Kinda sorta. It wasn't bad, though," said Marcus, still feeling the emotions stirring from the visit.

"Oh, one of those understanding visits?"

Marcus looked down at her. "Exactly. . . ."

"I got you. I've been doing this here a long time, so I done seen every kind of visit a prisoner can get in here, from death in the family, the understanding, the divorce, you know the cheating ones, and the dagger of 'em all—the 'it's over between us' visits. I think them the worst ones right there," she said with a chuckle.

Born to Die

Marcus was starting to see that she was cool. He knew most C.O.s only saw prisoners one way: as inmates, never as people. But she had compassion. And she was a flirt who shot straight from the hip.

As they rounded the corner out of earshot of anyone working in the near distance, she said, "And you never did answer my question of whether that's your wife or not."

Marcus smirked at her boldness, then shot back, "Nah, she's not my wife, but she's the closest thing to it."

"Um, well, what you need is a certified bitch like me on ya team."

They stopped outside the exit door leading to Marcus's isolation range. Marcus looked her up and down, knowing what must have piqued her interest.

"You holla at Eugene yet?" he asked, already knowing she had.

"Yeah, and he says that y'all are his peoples and to look out for y'all on whatever y'all may need."

Marcus knew that wasn't the only thing Eugene had told his aunt. Surely he had stamped him and Lil' Keith as head bussas and told her they were riding foreign out there and living a dream. But he'd play along with her for now.

"As a matter of fact," she said, digging down her panties. She came up with a brown package and handed it to Marcus. "Eugene told me to give this to you. I don't know what it is, and I wanna keep it that way. And I ain't even gotta tell you if they catch you with it, I ain't give you nothing. Just letting ya know now, 'cause I needs my lil' job."

"You know better than to even come at me like that. You see what type of charges they got me on. I ain't no rat, ya heard me?" snapped Marcus.

"I'm just making sure that we're clear, 'cause like I told you, I done seen every kinda visit there is, including them

54 Dorian Sykes

ones when these walls start closing in on a motherfucker's ass, and he starts singing, ya with me?"

"I respect that, but at the same time, we one hunnid on this end." Marcus looked at the package in his hand, then asked, "What I owe you for this?"

"Like I say, that's from my nephew. But, uh, if you just insist on paying me for it, I'm sure we can work something out," she said, rubbing her hand against Marcus's dick.

"You something else, ya heard me? What they call you?"

"Vicki," she said while boldly slipping her hand down Marcus's boxers.

"While we're making things clear, you gotta know that wifey comes first, and she's to be respected while she's up here to see me."

"Calm down, big daddy. I just wanna taste it from time to time," she said, stroking his full length.

"So we clear then?"

"We good," she said softly.

"A'ight, so when's the next time I'ma see you?"

"I'll be up here all day tomorrow, so if it's good enough, I'ma see about switching my post five days a week. Can you handle that, daddy?" She hadn't stopped jacking him off.

"We gonna see what it do, ya heard me?"

CHAPTER SIX

Lil' Keith was laid back in his bunk with his feet crossed at the ankles, deep in thought, reminiscing about the streets and all the dirt they'd done. He hadn't heard Marcus come back from his visits.

"You sleep, round?" Marcus asked, peeping across the darkened tier into Keith's cell.

"Nah, just thinking, ya heard me?"

"You, thinking?" Marcus said with a laugh.

Lil' Keith rolled over and sat up on the edge of his steel rack. "You know what these cells do that to a nigga. Have a nigga out there in them streets. Every time we came in here, that's when the dreams start happening, ya heard me?"

Marcus knew just what dreams Lil' Keith was referring to because he'd only have them when they were in jail, too. He knew what would get his partna's mind right. "Catch," he said, tossing Keith the package he'd gotten from C.O. Kindle.

"What this here is, round?" Keith asked, opening the package with a half-grin.

"The homie Eugene sent that for us. Ol' girl is his people."

"Yeah, I kept lookin' at her, and I knew she had to been familiar, ya heard me?"

"She gone be lookin' out, ya understand me?"

"Yeah, I saw the way she was eyeing a nigga too."

"Oh, you saw that, huh?" Marcus laughed.

56   Dorian Sykes

"You know, round, don't too much get past me," Lil' Keith said before sampling some of the heroin. He grunted a few times as he waited for the dope to hit him.

"This off P-N-C, ya heard me?" Lil' Keith had snorted so much dope from around the city; one hit, and he could tell you where it came from. "We need to get her to bring us that 911, ya heard me?"

"I'ma holla at her, but gone take you half of that here 'cause I know you 'bout out by now."

"Yeah, this here was right on time," Keith said, folding the package closed and then tossing it over to Marcus. "But what ya lawyer talking 'bout?"

"Shit, you called good money on that bitch, Sasha."

Lil' Keith kicked back on his bunk while he nodded in and out, listening to Marcus run down everything. Before long, Keith drifted off to sleep. Those dreams he spoke about were really the demons riding his soul for all the dirt he'd done and witnessed.

Lil' Keith was playing Nintendo in the back room of his father's dope spot out in St. Thomas Projects, while he waited for his pops to handle some business with his play uncle Sherman. Big Keith and Sherman had been hustling out of the same projects and around the city, but they'd always kept things separate. Big Keith had some dope stamped "Crazy Horse" that was known around the city to be the best heroin going, next to none. Big Keith had the St. Thomas Projects sewed up, while Sherman's spot usually caught whatever traffic Big Keith's spot couldn't handle due to demand. Sherman had been pushing some dope stamped "Wild Willow," but he could never match the clientele Big Keith was seeing, so he set up shop downtown in St. Bernard and the Iberville Projects.

Born to Die

Lil' Keith would sometimes ride with his pops to pick up bags of money, and sometimes to help him mix up the Crazy Horse because Big Keith didn't trust anyone when it came down to what he called "his recipe" or "his life." He'd always tell Lil' Keith that, "If a nigga ever kills me, it'll be somebody close to me. . . ." And for that reason alone, Big Keith always tried to keep his circle small and his enemies close. He was a G in the streets and always instilled loyalty and respect into Lil' Keith. He used to tell him, " You can't have one without the other."

Lil' Keith wanted to be like his daddy coming up and nothing else. Big Keith saw the makings of a young G in his son, so he always gave him the game raw and uncut. He figured it was better for him to give it to him than some nigga out in the streets. At least with him, he knew he'd be getting the real.

Lil' Keith paused the game because he thought he'd heard his pops and uncle Sherman arguing in the front room. They were arguing because Sherman had lost his heroin connect and needed Big Keith to turn him onto his supplier.

"Nigga, I do that, and then we both got the same dope. Nah, round, I ain't gonna do it!" said Big Keith.

"So you're just gonna sit back and watch all my spots go down the drain?" argued Sherman. His voice was desperate.

"If it was money you needed, maybe I'd be there for you, but I'm not turning you on to my peoples and I'm not scoring for you neither."

"I see what this is about," said Sherman, his voice rising. "You want my clientele. You want it all for yourself, don't you, nigga?"

Lil' Keith then heard a punch being landed and furniture moving around. He'd never before heard his pops and uncle argue, let alone fight. He rushed out of the back room and into the small living room. Big Keith and Sherman were locked together against the wall, tussling over the 9mm between them. Suddenly, the gun went off. Boom!

Big Keith jerked a bit, then stopped tussling. He had lost his fight, and as he slid down the wall, he locked eyes with his son . . . but said nothing. Sherman was still in a blind fury of rage. He raised the gun to Big Keith's forehead and, without hesitation, shot him three times at point-blank range. Boom! Boom! Boom!

On instinct, Sherman turned with the gun pointed dead at Lil' Keith's chest. He hadn't known that Lil' Keith was in the back room the whole time. Sherman knew that he should've killed Lil' Keith, but something inside of him just wouldn't allow his finger to squeeze the trigger.

"I'm sorry you had to see this," Sherman said, reaching down to clip Big Keith's pager from his belt. He scrolled through it frantically, looking for Big Keith's connect number. Finding the number, he began to backstep out of the apartment, still holding Lil' Keith at gunpoint. "That's all he had to do was give me the number," Sherman said before slipping out of the apartment.

Lil' Keith stood there in the living room, unable to move or say anything. He couldn't believe the sight before his young eyes. His father's brains were blown all over the walls, and he was lying in a pool of blood, dead.

It wasn't until one of the dope fiends came to the apartment that anyone else knew what had taken place inside. The woman rushed next door to call the police after she walked in and saw Big Keith lying dead. When the police got there, Lil' Keith was still standing in the same spot. It wasn't until they tried to move him from the room that he snapped.

Born to Die

He couldn't fathom the idea of his father being taken away from him, especially at the hands of a nigga that he called his uncle. Lil' Keith didn't speak a word for three months solid. Social workers thought that he'd been traumatized to the point he couldn't speak, but really, he just didn't want to talk. There was nothing to talk about, he figured. Almost every day, detectives would come by the house he shared with his mother and sister, Etta, asking if he was ready to help them catch the man who had killed his father. It was the first encounter he'd ever had with the then-young Homicide Detective Lewis. He was fresh on the unit and had a hard-on for wanting to solve ghetto murders.

To this day, Lil' Keith never told a soul who had killed his father. He wanted to be the one to catch Sherman and show him the same amount of mercy he had on his daddy.

In Lil' Keith's eyes, Sherman destroyed his entire family because after his father died, his mom turned to crack, and his sister ran away when she was fourteen, never to be heard from again. That's why every time Lil' Keith killed somebody, he imagined that it was Sherman's face in front of the bullet.

No one had heard from Sherman since Big Keith's funeral, where he had the nerve to come and place roses on Big Keith's casket and hug the family. Word was that he'd died from an overdose, while some say he was out of state getting money. Lil' Keith felt that one day, wherever the creep was, their paths would cross again.

CHAPTER SEVEN

"What you gonna do, just sleep all day?"

Marcus came from under the sheet and peered through the bars. It was Vicki, C.O. Kindle.

"Get up now. I brought y'all something to eat from home 'cause I know y'all butts 'bout tired of eating this mess they serving," she said, moving about the tier.

"What time is it?" Marcus asked from the face bowl as he washed his face and hands.

"Almost one o'clock," Vicki called from down by her officer station, where she popped their food in the microwave. "Hope y'all like gumbo."

Lil' Keith was at the bars, cheesing and rubbing his fat little stomach in anticipation. He made his hand into the shape of her ass over at Marcus, signaling that she had a fat ass. "I'm tryna hit that too, round."

"Fall back, ya heard me?" said Marcus, smiling.

Vicki came back with two styrofoam trays. "Watch 'em now, they're hot." She handed one to Marcus and one to Lil' Keith.

"Thank you," said Lil' Keith. "You made this?" he asked, wasting no time digging in.

Vicki stood on one leg and cocked her head matter-of-factly, and said, "I sure did. Is it good?"

Lil' Keith closed his eyes as he bit into a piece of succulent shrimp. "Yeah. This yeah."

"And how about you, daddy? You like my cooking? " asked Vicki as she turned and stepped closer to Marcus's bars.

62   Dorian Sykes

"You think you're slick. Gone feed a nigga first, ya heard me? I know what you on."

Vicki smiled. "Gotta make sure you've got ya energy up. We do have a date tonight, remember?" she teased in a low, sexy voice.

Marcus's dick grew four inches as he looked her up and down. She teased him even more, turning to give him a side view of what was in store. He could see that she wasn't wearing any panties underneath those tight uniform pants.

"I see your energy level is just fine today," she said, noticing what she was doing to Marcus.

"After I finish this, ya heard me?" said Marcus.

Vicki bit down on her bottom lip and said, "I won't be able to pull you out until all the shift supervisors go home, but definitely tonight."

"It's all on you, baby. I got something I need to holla at you about later anyways, ya heard me?"

"Okay, well, let me make my, rounds, and I'll be back to check on y'all a little later." She dug into her shirt pocket and handed Marcus a folded note sealed with tape peeled off of a deodorant stick.

"What's this here?"

"I don't know. Some nigga over in Templeman had gave that to me last night before I left. Says that y'all peoples and needed to get word to you."

"A'ight, good lookin' out, ya heard me?" Marcus finished crushing the rest of his gumbo, then peeled back the tape from the jail kite. *Who this here is*, he wondered.

What's up bitches? Look, we gonna make this short. I know you two bitches downed my lil' sister, ya heard me? Ya better hope these white folks get you 'cause you know what it is with me on sight, wodie, believe that!
—Deeco, 17th Hollygrove

Marcus stepped to the bars, laughing. "Check this here out, round," he said, tossing the kite over to Lil' Keith.

"Who this from, ya heard me?"

"Just read it. You gone see. Funny nigga there, boy."

"Man, this nigga faking like shit, ya heard me?" said Lil' Keith after he finished reading the kite and seeing who it came from. "You want this here back, round?"

"Fuck nah. Flush that shit, ya heard me?"

Lil' Keith came back to the bars with his morning fix in his hand. He snorted about a quarter gram, then pulled back a victorious grin while remembering the nigga Deeco and how they used to beef back in the days. He had to admit it, though; Deeco was about his yeah. The nigga was an official head bussa out the 17th Ward.

"Say though, round, who he talking 'bout . . . his sister?" asked Marcus. He barely remembered the nigga, except from Fortier.

"Guess?" asked Keith, cheesing from ear to ear.

"Who, round?"

"The bitch Monay, ya heard me?"

Marcus could only shake his head at his lil' partna. The nigga was devious for real. He now realized why it wasn't nothing but a thang for Lil' Keith to kill Monay and dump her body on the set of Hollygrove. She was Deeco's little sister, and they'd had beef with Hollygrove ever since they caught the body at Fortier High School on the little nigga out the 17th Ward. In retaliation, some niggas from Hollygrove came through the set on Valence and Magnolia, and they caught the big homie Remy getting in his car and smashed him. With blood spilled on both sides, the beef turned into a never-ending war that would last until the end of time.

When Lil' Keith and Marcus came home on the body, they dove head-first into the ongoing war, laying down demos left and right. They felt that big homie Remy got

64   Dorian Sykes

smashed because of them, so they'd handle it. Maurice was Remy's younger brother's murderer, so Marcus and Lil' Keith took him along when they went through Hollygrove looking for Deeco.

Word had gotten back that Deeco was bragging about being the one who smashed Remy, so Maurice wanted his blood on his hands above anyone else's out the 17th. The night before they were to go through Hollygrove, they got a couple of dope fiends from around the hood to go up in the neighborhood gun store Chet's to buy three brand new SKSs and had them flipped to 30-round clips. Back then, they sold choppers over the counter; all you had to be was eighteen with an I.D. and no record, so everybody had cutters. They nicknamed the hood "Down in the Dirty" because all they had around there were assault rifles. Niggas rode with them like they were .38s or 9s. That's how hard niggas was going.

The mentioning of Deeco sent Marcus and Lil' Keith back down memory lane. They stood at the bars, remembering that night they'd lost their lil' partna.

Lil' Keith was behind the wheel of the stolen sapphire blue Dodge minivan as they crept through Hollygrove in search of Deeco and his niggas. Marcus was riding shotgun, while Maurice was slouched down across the backseat, cradling his chopper. They passed by a little hood bar called Black Magic, and there was a mob of niggas hanging out by the curb, hollering at females and drinking as the bar let out.

"That was my hoe right there, round," Maurice said as he peered out of the back window, spotting Deeco talking to some girls.

"Yeah, I'ma bend back around the corner, ya heard me?" said Lil' Keith. He, too, had spotted Deeco and

Born to Die

wanted to hurry up and catch him while he was slipping. Not another word was exchanged in the van. They all knew what it was: hit everything out there, but down that nigga Deeco for sure. Lil' Keith cut the headlights off as he turned up the street with Black Magic in full view. He let off the gas and let the van ease against the curb behind a parked El Dorado. Deeco was still rapping with the girls.

Maurice was the first one out of the van. He didn't even bother pulling the ski mask down over his face, as he didn't want it to be a question as to who downed Deeco. He took off full speed at the crowd standing near the curb. He had Deeco in his sights as he upped the chopper, ready to bust, but a woman getting in her car screamed, putting everybody on point that something was about to go down.

Maurice let off a series of rounds, but he missed Deeco by a mere inch and killed one of the young girls instantly instead. Deeco dipped behind one of the parked cars and came up busting back with his .40 cal. Maurice took aim on the car and riddled it front to back, figuring he'd hit Deeco somewhere, but as he fumbled to reload the chopper with a fresh clip, Deeco sprung from around the back of the Chevy Corsica and filled Lil' Maurice with everything he had left in the clip.

Marcus and Lil' Keith were in the midst of a shootout of their own at the rear of the club next to the parking lot. The Hollygrove niggas were yanking back with Ks of their own, and they outnumbered Lil' Keith and Marcus, so the two started making their way back to the van.

"Maurice!" Marcus yelled his loudest over the gunfire. "Let's go, round!" he said, trying to hold them off while Keith got the van ready. He looked to the front seat for Keith and said, "Where's Maurice, round?"

66   Dorian Sykes

Lil' Keith pointed at the body lying out in the middle of the street, shaking with the SKS lying at his side. For a moment, it seemed as though time had frozen, as Marcus and Lil' Keith had a decision to make. Bullets tore through the van from both sides, causing Lil' Keith to slap the van in reverse and gun them out of there. The decision was a hard one, but it was the only one. They left Maurice to die out on the cold concrete.

No one had ever known except Marcus and Lil' Keith what happened that night. Up until now, they had never talked about it.

"Say, round, I hope this bitch does win his appeal, 'cause I'ma spank this nigga, ya understand me?" said Lil' Keith. He was heated that the nigga had the balls to write them, selling death and bragging about killing Maurice and beating the charge on the sly. *We'll see*, thought Lil' Keith.

CHAPTER EIGHT

Meanwhile, Tank was at his three-story mansion, which he had built from the ground up within the gated community of Eastover. The homes out there started around $200,000 and went all the way up to 6 zeroes. It's full of doctors, lawyers, pastors, athletes, rappers, and ballers. Tank had been out there since the developers announced the community would be built and began selling lots. Tank was a nigga who had a ghetto pass in almost every hood, but he preferred the finer things in life, like laying by the pool at his mansion while he watched five or six naked, young dime-pieces run around chasing each other.

Such was the scene today. Tank was perched underneath the white canopy stemming from the lawn table beside his Olympic-style swimming pool. He was draped in his pure white house coat, eating fresh crab out of the bucket while listening to his underboss, Dinyell, run everything down to him about what was happening in the streets. There was a slight problem over in the Calliope Projects. Four of their dope spots got robbed, and Dinyell was in fear that more would come if they didn't do something fast.

Tank set the silver bucket on top of the table and took a long swallow from the open bottle of Cristal. He took his time before answering Dinyell's dilemma, always wanting to seem in control of things and never wanting to let on whether he'd been rattled by the news.

"You see, round, the streets are talkin', ya heard me? Niggas is just like these here crabs in this bucket, always ready to pull a nigga back down to the bottom, ya dig? These niggas know youngins is in on them bodies, so they gonna keep tryna see how far they can go until one or two thangs happen. Either I punish they ass, or we fold, 'cause we ain't strong enough, ya heard me? See, round, you gotta know ya history, ya dig? New Orleans is a dope city, always has been and always will be. And with dope, you gonna always have mo' murder than money, ya understand me? In other big cities, it's 'bout that bread, ya heard me? But down here, it's always gone come down to that murder game, so what I'm tellin' you, round, is this here. Bring me some young, thorough niggas who I can put on them streets as head bussas, ya heard me?"

"But what about Marcus and Lil' Keith?" asked Dinyell. He'd been with Tank as long as they had, and he had watched them smash niggas all over the city.

"Them gone always be my youngins, ya heard me? But sometimes in this here life we livin', round, we as a family often outgrow each other, ya dig?"

Dinyell wasn't quite sure he followed Tank because it had always been loyalty over everything when it came to them as family. Dinyell was only 21, a few years older than Marcus and Lil' Keith, but Tank saw the making of a young boss in him, so he made him his right hand and underboss in the streets. Tank was good at picking up on a niggas' strengths and weaknesses, and he knew Dinyell's all too well. Tank was hip that Dinyell was a hustler and not a head bussa, and that he was a follower, not a leader, so he never feared not being able to control Dinyell's moves.

Tank lived by one rule, and it took him all the way to the top. He believed that if you can't control someone, keep them from around you . . . and lately, with every-

Born to Die 69

thing Lil' Keith and Marcus had been into, Tank was starting to feel he could no longer control them—especially Lil' Keith. It was always something extra with him. Tank would always try and mold them into playing their positions as just head bussas, putting in work for the family, but he never could keep them out of the streets. Every time there was a beef, their names would come up, and he'd try to school them on how beef and money don't mix, not to mention them getting high. Tank never approved of them messing with anything stronger than weed, but again, it was a clear sign and symbol of why he could no longer control them and why it was time to part ways. The timing couldn't have been more perfect.

"Hit the streets and find me some youngins, ya heard me? I'll meet y'all at the club," ordered Tank.

Dinyell stuffed the half-smoked blunt into the ashtray, then slid his chair back from the table, leaving Tank to his thoughts . . . and a serene view of the naked women splashing in the pool. Tank took another swallow from the bottle of Crist, resting it between his thighs as he stared off into the horizon of his gated haven. He knew that replacing Marcus and Lil' Keith wouldn't be easy. He laid back while remembering when they first came home, how they had wasted no time putting the murder game down.

For the longest Tank had his eyes set on The Bricks, which is what niggas call the Melph Projects in the 3rd Ward. In the early '90s, The Bricks had been the biggest dope spot around the city, doing a hundred stacks a day easily. It was run largely in part by this old nigga named Mike Lowry. He came from the old school, back when niggas used their whole government name instead of a street handle. He'd been pushing dope through the city since the '70s and was an old, filthy rich nigga, who, in Tank's eyes, was in the way. Tank watched the ol' nigga cake up millions after millions, but yet, Lowry wouldn't move around and let the next nigga in line eat, so Tank put the hit down on him.

The ol' nigga was really a sitting duck because he rarely left the projects, except on Sundays when he drove his elderly mother to her church for morning service. Lil' Keith and Marcus were young and wild enough at the time that they would've downed the ol' nigga inside The Bricks, but it would've been a suicide mission trying to make it out of there alive. So, they stalked the ol' nigga one Sunday as he left the Melph Projects with his mother riding shotgun in his Lincoln Town Car.

Lil' Keith and Marcus were parked directly across the street from the First Baptist Church of Christ in Keith's Bronco. They watched Mike Lowry ease up to the church and get out to help his mother to the front door. As Mike was on his way back to his car, Lil' Keith and Marcus slipped out from the black Bronco dressed in all black, wearing ski masks and gloves, looking like angels of death as they came from both sides, catching Mike with his back turned, about to get in his car. The screams of warning passers-by were muffled by the hail of gunfire they let off, ripping through Mike Lowry's fragile old body and tearing through his Lincoln parked at the curb.

Marcus and Lil' Keith left Mike's body out on the street, steaming from the burning hot 223s. They had riddled him with bullets from top to bottom. They slipped away from the scene as quickly as they'd come, leaving the streets blood-stained, scattered with spun shells, and a thick cloud of gun smoke hanging in the air. The murder made breaking news for days in the N.O. and was followed by daily headlines in the local papers as Marcus and Lil' Keith continued putting down the murder game across the city for Tank. Every time, it was the same scene: a hundred shell casings and dead bodies.

Tank took a swig from the bottle of Cristal, content that he was making the right decision. He was never a nigga to get caught up on feelings and emotions. He appreciated all that Lil' Keith and Marcus had done to help the family, but he didn't love them for it because he knew that with love came obligation and niggas feeling like you owe them something. That's why he always showed his appreciation through gifts and money. That was a fair exchange and would never be a robbery. Tank would never allow himself to owe a nigga shit, only the other way around. And if anything, he reasoned, they owed him for all the times they went down on the bodies and he paid their lawyer fees. They hadn't gone to jail because of him. Instead, they always got picked up because of some stupid shit they'd done. From the first hit on Mike Lowry, they had gotten snatched up because they were in Lil' Keith's truck, and now, Lil' Keith got caught wearing Brett's Rolex. In Tank's eyes, they'd become more of a liability than assets.

Tank decided he needed to relieve some stress, so he stood from the table and selected two naked women to his liking from the swimming pool. He turned up the rest of the Cristal as he watched on in lust as the two model-built imports climbed from the pool, dripping in water. They both smiled seductively at Tank, then led the way up the stone granite walk inside the mansion, giving Tank a full view of their sculpted backsides.

Life was indeed good to Tank, and he'd do whatever was necessary to keep it that way.

CHAPTER NINE

Back at The Parish, Vicki had snuck Marcus out of his cell after shift change and had him on the floor inside the officer's station, sucking the life from his dick. She had that old-school platinum head that'll make a young nigga fall in love. Marcus was indeed enjoying her blessings, but he wasn't thinking about falling in love with Vicki. What they had was a clear understanding. They'd sneak off and fuck, and in return, she'd look out for him and Lil' Keith while they fought their bodies.

Marcus lay back with one hand cradled behind his head, dick stiff from the dog food he'd snorted before coming out of his cell, but his mind was only half there in the moment. Two things had been bothering him the past couple of days: his last conversation with Jasmeen about leaving New Orleans, and then there was the case. Something about this one didn't feel right. He knew to trust his lawyer because they'd come from under what seemed to be worse, but something about this trip to The Parish felt like it would be his last. Marcus looked at the red band on his wrist, and it felt like a death sentence staring him in the face.

Vicki slurped on the tip of Marcus's head and asked while she jacked him from the base up to the head, "Are you gonna cum, baby?"

"Why don't you put that pussy on me, ya heard me?"

She stood and peeked down the tier as she unfastened her tight uniform pants, then seductively stepped out of the legs. Her body was immaculate. She turned, modeling all that ass for Marcus's enticement.

"You like what you see, daddy?" she teased as she stepped from the lavender lace Victoria's Secret panties, then straddled all of Marcus's nine inches. "Ahhh, shh," she gasped, throwing her head back and closing her eyes as she raked her fingernails under Marcus's T-shirt.

She started rolling her hips as Marcus dug his hands deep into her soft, plush ass cheeks, spreading them so she'd take every inch. Marcus couldn't front, the pussy was all that. She fit him like a glove, and she had that wet wet. She found her rhythm and started throwing that pussy on Marcus while grinding her swollen clit against his pelvis.

"Ahh, fuck this dick, baby," said Marcus. He could feel his nut starting to brew. "Cum on this dick, baby. Cum for me," he said, digging balls deep.

Vicki clawed into Marcus's chest and exclaimed, "Oh, I'm cumming . . . I'm cumming . . . ohh, shit!"

Marcus froze, then came with Vicki. She collapsed onto his chest and then rolled off him to the floor, where she lay stunned.

"Mm-hmm, all that mouth," teased Marcus as he rolled over and slapped Vicki's ass.

"Boy, you need to get circumcised, 'cause I don't know what I'ma do with you," she said, reaching for her panties and pants.

"That wasn't nothin' but a sample there, ya heard me?"

"I'd bet," she said, rolling her eyes with pleasure.

Marcus stood up and started fixing himself. "Did you bring what I asked for?"

"Don't I always?" Vicki dug inside her thermal and pulled out a Motorola cellphone and an ounce of 911, along with two needles. "And I'm not even gonna ask what those are for," she said, nodding down at the two syringes in Marcus's hand.

Marcus had heard her but he was too preoccupied by the brick flip phone. "How long does the battery last?"

"Probably a day, but I'll bring you an extra one when I come back in on Tuesday."

"Tuesday?"

"Yes, I do have a life outside of this place, thank you very much. I'm off the next two days, so try and make the battery last . . . and that shot of ass I just put in you," she said with a smirk.

Marcus laughed as he followed her out of the booth. "That you put on me?"

"Yes . . . you know you loved it," she said, looking back over her shoulder.

"Yeah, I'ma let you get that one, ya heard me?"

Meanwhile, Lil' Keith was standing at the bars of his cell, looking like a raccoon in heat. The swelling in his head had gone down, but he had two black eyes.

"What's up, round?" Marcus said, flashing his golds. He had that glow only a nigga fresh out of some pussy could ever have. Marcus slipped inside his cell and winked at Vicki, sealing their next date.

She waved over at Lil' Keith, then threw her ass every which-a-way as she headed off down the tier.

"Damn, round, that's how you play it? Why you ain't crack on her 'bout letting me hit that, ya heard me?"

"It ain't that type of party, ya heard me?"

"Yeah, 'cause you hand cuffin'," laughed Lil' Keith.

"Nah, never that. I'm doing what I do best, and that's working her, ya understand me?" Marcus tossed over one of the needles and a bag of dope. "Break me off half, ya heard me?"

Lil' Keith's fingers tore open the package. "This that yeah, ya dig?" he said, cheesing from ear to ear.

"Where you get the phone from?" he asked, seeing Marcus kicked back, dialing away.

76   Dorian Sykes

Marcus locked his feet at the ankles and smiled as he waited for Jasmeen to pick up.

"What's up, baby?" Marcus said, happy to hear wifey's soft voice on the other end.

"Nothing. I'm tired." Jasmeen sounded sapped.

"From what? It's only two o'clock."

"I've been running around with my mom all day, helping her with my dad. You know he had to go back to the emergency room last night."

"Nah, what happened?"

"He had another stroke. Yep, they say he may be permanently paralyzed on his left side, so . . ."

"Damn, baby, you know I hate to hear that. How's your mom holding up?"

"She's doing okay, I guess."

There was a long pause in the conversation as Marcus really didn't know what he could say, if anything, to help lift Jasmeen's spirits. She was close with her family, so he knew she was hurting on the inside.

"Listen, baby, don't worry about coming down to see me today, all right? Spend this time with ya family."

"But we need our time too, baby," said Jasmeen.

"Come check me out on Saturday. I'll be fine. That's my word, ya heard me?"

"Okay. . . ." Jasmeen relented.

"And don't sound so down. Everything's gonna be all right."

"It's just that you're in there, and now this."

"Well, hopefully this here will all be over soon once my lawyer gets the judge to grant our motion."

"That reminds me. I spoke with Mr. Crenshaw yesterday." Jasmeen sighed and paused.

"And what he say?"

"He didn't say anything about the motion, but he says that he hasn't been paid yet. I thought you said everything with him was paid up, baby?"

Born to Die

Marcus wondered if there was a mix-up because Tank always took care of their legal fees.

"He says that he's owed $35,000 to take on your case and another $50,000 if you went to trial."

Marcus didn't like all these numbers flying around. If anything, he felt Mr. Crenshaw should've come to him and not to Jasmeen about any money situation.

"Baby, I could take him what we have left, and I'll just—"

"No!" Marcus said, not letting Jasmeen finish. There was only close to $30,000 left in their safe, and there was no way he was going to leave Jasmeen out there on E.

"I'ma make a few phone calls, all right, baby? I want you to get some rest when you can, and I'll see you on Saturday, okay?"

"All right. I love you."

"Love you too. Bye-bye."

The phone clicked off.

Lil' Keith was standing at the bars, high as a kite. "*I love you too. . . .*" he teased Marcus.

Marcus was in no laughing mood, though, as he stabbed the numbers to Mr. Crenshaw's office into the phone.

"What's up, round? Why ya grill all tore up for?" asked Lil' Keith, peeping the look on his partna's face.

"Do you know this nigga ain't paid my lawyer yet?" Marcus threw up a hand for Keith to hold up as Mr. Crenshaw's secretary answered.

"Law offices of Barbara, Anderson, and Crenshaw. How may I direct your call?"

"Can you put me through to Mr. Crenshaw?"

"He's not in his office at the moment. Would you like to leave a message on his machine?"

"What time will he be in?" Marcus felt his blood boil over.

"I'm not sure, sir."

78   Dorian Sykes

"I'll try again tomorrow," Marcus said, closing the phone. He went into thought for a moment.

"That's probably why I ain't heard shit from my lawyer, ya heard me? Bitch ain't dropped that money bag yet."

"Still, though, round, how long these motherfuckers been our lawyers? They know Tank gone pay 'em," said Marcus.

"That shit don't hold no weight, my nigga," said Lil' Keith. "All them crackers care about is that check, ya understand me? They ain't letting no nigga slide and owe shit 'cause they're afraid once they open up that door, a nigga gonna always come late and last with theirs. I can't do nothing but respect they hustle, ya dig? But who you need to be calling is this nigga Tank. Tell 'em to get that money together A.S.A.P., ya understand me?"

Marcus found himself slowly dialing Tank's cell number. He didn't want to make it seem like he was pressing the big homie because he trusted Tank and knew that he'd never leave them hanging.

Tank was up in Saks Fifth on Canal Street with a Gucci duffle bag full of big faces tucked between his legs as he played the part of a street boss out to trick some loot on his latest acquisition, a Colombian student by the name of Krystal. He picked her up at a Saints game the weekend prior. Tank was lounging in front of the dressing room in one of those high-back wicker chairs as Krystal modeled all of the items Tank was buying her. They'd been up and down Canal Street all day, splurging on new things for Krystal.

As Krystal popped back into the dressing room, Tank snatched his cell phone from his hip. "What up, playboy?" he said, answering and feeling himself all the while.

"Big homie, it's me, Marcus."

Born to Die

"How you holdin' up in there, youngin?"

"We coolin', ya dig? You know, usually I wouldn't even be callin' you unless it was an emergency, ya heard me? But uh, my mouthpiece ain't handlin' the B.I., and he acting shady with my girl, talkin' about he ain't been paid yet and if we go to trial, he gonna need this and that, ya heard me?"

Tank smiled at Krystal, approving the sexy lingerie.

"I'ma straighten all that out with both y'all lawyers, ya dig? Just gimmie a few days, 'cause I'm outta town right now, ya heard me? But I want you to call me on Saturday, youngin, and we'll straighten up then, ya understand me?"

"Say no more."

"Let me get back to handling this business, though, ya heard me? And tell my youngin I send my best."

"A'ight, big homie."

Click.

Tank wasn't thinking about Marcus and Lil' Keith. *Fuck them and they lawyer fees,* he thought. The last meal had been served, and he was the chef. He had at least $150,000 between his legs that could've covered them both in full, but Tank would rather trick it off on Krystal then piss it in the wind by fucking with Lil' Keith and Marcus, because one thing he was certain of was that this wouldn't be their last time going to jail and needing him for a lawyer.

CHAPTER TEN

The *Times-Picayune* dubbed Deeco as "a murderous thug with nine lives." This came following the announcement by the Court of Appeals that they were vacating Deeco's conviction due to prosecutor misconduct and violation of due process rights.

Deeco was bum-rushed by his family and friends as he stood in Superior Court following the judge's decision to set him free. It had been a long, hard fight with the courts, prosecutors, and Detective Lewis over the past four years, but it was finally over.

Val, Deeco's baby momma, slid up under his arm and hugged his muscular frame against her petite self. "Can I take him home now?" she asked of Deeco's attorneys. She'd been riding through it all.

"Yes, and I may suggest you keep him there," the female of the two replied, smiling.

"Y'all the best, ya heard me?" Deeco said, expressing his thanks and gratitude for his two lawyers, whom he nicknamed "The Dream Team" because they'd beat every case against him since he was a juvenile.

Val led Deeco out of the court building to her new Dodge Stratus.

"I'ma get up with y'all on the block. Gotta spend some Q.T. with wifey, ya heard me?" Deeco told his partners out in the parking lot.

His right-hand partna, Courtney, slipped him a brand new .40 cal with dick dripping from it. He couldn't have his man out there naked on the streets, 'cause it was beef on sight, as usual.

82   Dorian Sykes

Val saw the whole thing and rolled her eyes at Courtney, then at Deeco, as he ducked into the passenger seat. She smacked her lips, getting in behind him. "Do you have to bring that with us?" she asked with an attitude.

"You know it's a must, ya heard me? Not everybody's gonna be as happy as you that I'm home, ya feel me?" said Deeco as he leaned his seat all the way back.

"No, I don't feel you . . . but I guess," Val said as she pulled from the courthouse parking lot.

Deeco and Val had two boys together. They'd been high school sweethearts since the days of Fortier. Since then, Val rode out two bids with Deeco and took care of their boys, all the while keeping his books phat and going to nursing school full-time.

Deeco was a street nigga, and that was all that he'd ever be. He knew it, and so did Val. That's why he never stressed her about seeing other men while he was down because deep down, he knew she was a good girl that deserved a nigga much more than he could ever be. But until his number was up, they'd always be together, inseparable.

Deeco reached for Val's hand as she drove. He locked their fingers together and kissed the back of her banana-yellow hand. She was his ride-or-die chick for real.

"Where you taking me?" he asked as they drove through downtown.

"You know I gotta get my man in something fly, so first we're going shopping, then feeding you, and then we're going to our suite at the Hyatt . . . just you and me," Val said, looking away from the road and over at Deeco.

"So you got everything figured out, sounds like, ya heard me?" Deeco was just happy to be home.

"Yep, so all you've gotta do is lay back and let momma handle the rest." Val shot him a smile.

Deeco had no doubts that his wifey would have everything in order when he got out. She was riding in

Born to Die
83

something new, going to school, and damn, she was still looking good. She had kept her figure together, with a small waist and phat ass, just the way Deeco left her the day he got arrested. He was proud of her, no doubt.

She took him to Lakeside Shopping Center and let him pop the tags on all the latest gear. It was the end of 1995, so niggas were on their Girbaud jeans and Soulja Reeboks real hard. Deeco copped a few other outfits and some fresh Ts to go, then Val took him out to eat at Red Lobster, where they dined and drank wine while reminiscing about the old days. Val suddenly went quiet at the table. She was moving her fork around her plate of grilled shrimp aimlessly.

"Lovey, what's on ya mind?" Deeco asked, reaching for her hand.

"I don't know, I was just thinking. . . ."

"About what?" Deeco soothed the back of her hand so that she'd maybe open up.

"As much as I love you, it's like all we have between us is the old days and the boys. I want us to make some new memories, baby. Good ones this time."

"I'm with you, lovey. You know that."

"'Cause the boys need you. I need you, Raymond."

"Okay, baby, I'm here, and I'm not going nowhere. Okay?" Deeco said, raising Val's hand to his lips and kissing it.

"Okay," she agreed, hoping she could believe in him.

"Now, can we get outta here so I can see what else my queen has in store for her king?"

"Yes," Val said, pulling back a wide, beautiful smile. Val had booked them a suite at the Hyatt overlooking the city of New Orleans. She had rose petals leading from the double doors of the suite into the French décor-style bath, where she ran a soothing bubble bath with scented candles burning throughout the bathroom. She stripped Deeco down to his boxers, admiring and kissing his chis-

84   Dorian Sykes

eled body from head to toe with each piece of clothing she shed. She climbed into the whirlpool behind Deeco and bathed him, giving him a sponge bath and then a shoulder and chest massage.

Deeco lay between Val's legs as she cupped handfuls of water over his skin.

"What you thinking about, baby?" she asked.

"I was just thinking 'bout Monay. I still can't believe she's really gone."

"Yeah, me too. I'm sorry, baby. I know you and your sister were close."

Monay was the female version of Deeco. She was hot-headed and would fight anybody, chick or nigga; she held no punches. And she would butt her gun. Deeco loved his little sister to death, and there was nothing he wouldn't do for her. He blamed himself for not keeping her out of harm's way. When he first got word in the joint that she was fucking with Lil' Keith, he flipped, 'cause not only was Lil' Keith a creep in his eyes, but he was also an enemy to the casket drops. Monay wasn't trying to hear any of that jail talk from her brother. She'd told him off and to stay out of her business because she was just as grown as he was.

That was the last time Deeco heard his little sister's voice alive. She had died at the hands of a vicious creep nigga, thought Deeco. His blood boiled just from the thought of Monay lying out against the curb with her brains blown out. He'd be waiting with guns cocked for Lil' Keith and Marcus to come home. He had a feeling they were going to beat the bodies because they were like him when it came to fighting cases. They would fight until they found some loophole and crawled through it. And when they did, he'd be right there holding a fully automatic chopper.

CHAPTER ELEVEN

Down in New Orleans, they've got what they call "Super Sunday," which is really like one big picnic that usually goes down in a park. It's more or less a car and fashion show. The traffic is backed up for miles, and the bitches are coming out from all over the city, no matter if it's in a park uptown or downtown. Niggas come for the simple fact they can't resist being where the bitches at, but also to see if they can catch a nigga they beefing with slipping. Sometimes the shit ends peacefully, but nine times out of ten, somebody out there is going to get smashed.

The first Super Sunday of the year was going down at Shakespeare Park, right across the street from the Magnolia Projects on Washington and LaSalle Street. Super Sunday was just the spot Deeco wanted to make his first public appearance after coming home. His crew had a nice-sized section of the park. Niggas were riding through on their new motorbikes, while others played their whips, putting on a show for the ladies.

Deeco was enjoying the scene and just being free around family and friends. They had broiled crawfish jumping, among other seafood dishes. It was all love. But still, Courtney and Deeco had them cutters on deck just in case a nigga ain't want to go home to their family for some reason and felt like getting stretched. Val was keeping tabs on Deeco, though, because she knew that things could easily go from cold to hot in the blink of an eye. Plus, she was watching for the many hood rats she was certain wanted to sink their claws into her man.

"What's up, round?" Deeco asked Courtney after noticing everybody had sort of slowed up. They were all looking in the same direction, indicating that something was about to pop off.

Courtney and Deeco were on point, though. They played the back, with their cutters but at an arm's length away.

Everybody was focused on the red fleet of exotic whips creeping down the strip. Everything from Benzess to Lexus, Jeeps, and custom Suburbans were amongst the fleet, with everything sitting on chrome and tinted windows. The convoy stopped in the middle of traffic, and one guy got out of the front of a 500 Benz.

"Who this nigga is, round?" Courtney asked as the man climbed the curb and came their way.

"I don't know, but I'ma smash him if he on something, ya heard me?" said Deeco.

It was Dinyell. He was met by a host of mean mugs and grunts as he inched his way through the mob of unwilling-to-budge Hollygrove niggas, who were looking for any old reason to get on his helmet.Dinyell wisely kept straight ahead, saying "excuse me" with each step.

Courtney stopped him dead in his tracks, though. "Hold up, wodie, who you, ya heard me?" Courtney was blocking Dinyell with his elbow, shielding him from Deeco.

"I came to holla at ya partna right here," Dinyell said, nodding to Deeco.

"Nigga, I asked you who the fuck you was, ya heard me?" snapped Courtney, his free hand sliding underneath his T-shirt for his yeah.

"They call me Dinyell, round. I got somebody that wanna meet you, ya heard me?"

"Who?" asked Deeco.

"The big homie, Tank."

Born to Die

Deeco looked past Dinyell out at the fleet of whips lining the curb. He knew who Tank was. His name had been ringing all the way from the streets to the pen. "What the nigga want to meet me for, ya heard me?"

"Business," said Dinyell.

Courtney let it be known that he wasn't feeling the whole situation, and he was ready for Dinyell to be out.

"It's straight, round," Deeco told him.

"You sure, round?" questioned Courtney.

"Yeah, I'ma see what's up with this nigga, ya heard me?" Deeco had his yeah on him, so he wasn't tripping. He followed Dinyell to one of the Suburbans, and its back window rolled down.

"What's up, playboy?" It was Tank. "Come take a ride with me, ya heard me?"

Dinyell opened the back door for Deeco to get in. Deeco threw up his hand at Courtney, letting him know that he'd be back, then climbed inside the truck. Tank signaled for the fine young yellowbone he had driving to go around the convoy, and they dipped through traffic.

"You smoke?" Tank asked.

"Nah, I'm straight, ya heard me?" Deeco was a little uncomfortable and wanted to know what was up. "Say, round, what this here all about?"

"You know who I am, right?"

"Yeah, I heard of you."

"All right, well, listen, wodie. I'm a nigga that's 'bout respect and loyalty, ya heard me? And I respect how you stood up and fought them bodies like a G, ya heard? I heard you was home, and from one real nigga to another one, I wanted to reach out and extend my hand to you, 'cause I know what it's like just coming home."

Tank pulled a stack of hundreds out of his pocket, holding it out for Deeco to take.

88 Dorian Sykes

"What this here is?" Deeco said, looking at the money in Tank's hand. He knew that nothing in life was ever free. *What is up with this nigga?* he thought.

"Like I say, it's a blessing, no strings attached, ya heard me?" Tank pulled back a thin smile, showing his gold teeth.

Deeco slowly took the money and looked at it, still waiting for the punch line from Tank, which he was sure was coming.

"Like I said, youngin, I respect ya gansta, ya heard me? And I could use a solid nigga on my team."

Deeco cut him short. "I don't work for no nigga, ya heard? So if this what this here is 'bout, then—"

"I ain't never had a nigga working for me. When I say team, I mean family, ya heard me? Everybody you seen back there, all them cars, that was all family, ya understand me? Everybody eatin' and breakin' bread as a family. I'm hollering at you 'cause prison ain't no place to be spending all of your life in and out of, ya heard? You come fuck with ya boy, and I got you, youngin." Tank was laying down his favorite spiel on family.

"And what I'ma be doin for you, ya heard me?"

"What you know best, ya understand me? I know you got some official partnas and that y'all 'bout that murder game. And like I said, I need some head bussas."

One thing didn't sit well with Deeco about the whole pitch Tank was throwing his way. He had heard that Lil' Keith and Marcus were rolling with him, and now he was wondering why Tank would be pulling up on him.

"Let me ask you something," Deeco said, turning from the window. "What's up with you and them niggas Lil' Keith and Marcus, ya heard me?"

"I know what they done to ya lil' sister, and I don't condone or respect that shit, ya heard me? I was feeding them niggas, but we ain't never been family, 'cause they

Born to Die

don't know how to be. It's always some shit with them, ya heard me? They're not smooth like you, ya dig?"

Tank was saying all the right shit. Deeco was hearing that he could not only get money with this nigga, but that he had the green light to smash Lil' Keith and Marcus. "Let me think about it, ya heard me?" Deeco told him, not wanting to seem pressed.

"I respect that, playboy."

CHAPTER TWELVE

Jasmeen was on her way to meet Tank out at his Eastover mansion. Marcus had spoken with Tank, and Tank told him to send his girl out to pick up the money for his and Lil' Keith's lawyers. But what Tank was really on, he was going to try Jasmeen once she got out there. He knew that his spot usually got a broad's interest piqued and her panties moist once they stepped foot inside the marble décor. Tank had been wanting to get with Jasmeen since Marcus brought her to the grand opening of his Club 360.

Jasmeen pulled up to the security gate and smiled at the guard as she told him her name and who she was there to see. The guard opened the black iron gate and pointed Jasmeen in the direction of Tank's lot. Jasmeen parked Marcus's Benz behind the array of foreign whips that lined the circular driveway. She thought with a closed smile as she got out of the car, *How ghetto,* at all the cars. She was met at the front double doors by three scantily-clad women as they spilled out of the mansion, laughing amongst each other. They never even acknowledged Jasmeen as she passed them.

Jasmeen stood in the white-marbled foyer, unsure if she should wait or just go in. People were coming and going as though it were an open-door policy. Tank bent the corner draped in gold and diamonds with a fresh cold bottle of Cristal in his hand. He pulled back a thin smile, showing his gold Aarons.

"I wasn't sure whether I had the right home by all the activity. Are you sure now's a good time, or should I come back?" said Jasmeen.

"Don't be silly. Come on in, please, and make yourself at home," said Tank as he took Jasmeen in from head to toe. She was killing it in her low-rider jeans, stilettos, and wife beater, with her hair pulled back into a long, silky ponytail.

Tank gave her a tour around the mansion, hoping to blow Jasmeen's mind because he could tell she had never been exposed to the type of living he was about. Jasmeen was cordial, and she had to admit that Tank had done really well for himself. But she still secretly thought to herself that he was an over-the-top type of nigga.

Tank led Jasmeen outside by the pool, where they sat, and he ordered his personal chef to grill them some shrimp and lobster tails.

"You do eat scallops, don't you?" asked Tank.

"I'm from New Orleans. What do you think?" Jasmeen said matter-of-factly.

"I'm just asking now, ya heard? What part of New Orleans you out of?"

"I'ma downtown girl. Yeah, I'm from the French Quarter. My family owns a nice little Creole eatery on Bourbon Street. That's actually where Marcus and I met. Yeah, he kept coming in like he was there for the gumbo, but he was stuck on the idea of us going out."

"How long did you make him wait 'til you went out with him?"

"I think after, like, his fifth time coming in, I finally said yes."

The chef arrived with their food. They ate and ended up talking for hours. Jasmeen had noticed the sun descending against the sky and realized she'd been there half the day, but she didn't want to seem rude by coming

Born to Die

93

out and asking Tank for the money. She decided to do it in a more subtle way by looking at her watch, then acting like she'd let time get away from them.

"I'm supposed to be down at the jail to see Marcus in twenty minutes," she said.

Tank was unmoved by her apparent rush as she gathered her handbag and stood.

"You know that life gets old after a while," he said, then took a sip from his champagne.

Jasmeen was at a loss for words, so Tank went on to say, "That ain't no life for a woman like yourself, running back and forth down to them jails, going to court. All that comes with stress, and really even more so once they make it to prison. That ain't the life for a young, beautiful woman like ya self."

"What do you mean, prison? I thought Mr. Crenshaw was the best and that he planned on filing a motion that would set Marcus free." Jasmeen was nervous now after hearing "prison."

"I don't know what all Marcus done told you, but ain't no motion. 'Bout to cut him loose. He's going to prison, and for a long time, ya heard me? Now, I'm tellin' you this here 'cause you don't deserve to be dragged along on a one-way trip to prison. You deserve—"

Jasmeen cut him straight off because she saw where Tank was going. "What I deserve is of none of your concern. I am here on behalf of Marcus. Now, you were supposed to have the money so I can take it to their lawyers. Do you have it ready? 'Cause I have to get going." Jasmeen was curt now.

Tank was a boss nigga who hated rejection. He felt that he had a shot with every pussy under the sun because he was that nigga, so he got mad, not knowing how to stomach Jasmeen shutting him down.

"I'll take care of it myself, ya heard me?"

"And when might that be? 'Cause their next court date is within a few days." Jasmeen was standing over him.

"I'ma handle it," Tank said, flashing his gold Aarons as he stood to escort Jasmeen off his premises.

Something told Jasmeen as she climbed into Marcus's Benz that Tank was going to leave them out to dry. She couldn't believe he had the nerve to try to crack on her. She knew how much Marcus loved Tank and how he looked to Tank as a father figure.

Jasmeen wrestled over whether she should tell Marcus as she drove to the jail. She was running late, but she hoped that they'd let her in so she could see Marcus. She decided that it would be best not to tell Marcus because she knew it would only do more damage than help. Besides, it wasn't like Tank had made it too far out there with his intentions. She had shut him down how she was supposed to.

CHAPTER THIRTEEN

Marcus and Lil' Keith were both pissed when their lawyers didn't show up for their court date. The judge asked them in open court if their attorneys were still representing them.

"Why wouldn't they be?" snapped Marcus.

He had no idea Tank never got the money to their mouthpieces. The judge rescheduled them for the next week, but not before warning them that they'd better have their attorneys in court ready to proceed next week, or she'd appoint them attorneys herself from the Public Defender office and proceed with the case.

Marcus wanted to throw a chair up at the bitch for having talked down on them like they were some broke-ass niggas who needed a public defender. He was even more so pissed that he hadn't seen Jasmeen sitting in the courtroom. She hadn't been to see him in over a week, and he couldn't get her on the phone.

Back at The Parish, Marcus paced his cell while trying to convince himself that Jasmeen would never play him. There had to be a good enough reason behind her absence. *Maybe she's with her father,* Marcus considered. But he still couldn't get past why neither Tank nor Mr. Crenshaw were taking any of his calls. Every time he tried to reach Mr. Crenshaw, his secretary would say that he was out of the office, and Tank's cell would just ring.

Lil' Keith held no punches on what he felt was going on. "That bitch nigga done said fuck us, ya heard me? He ain't

96   Dorian Sykes

dropped that bag on our lawyers. That's why they cracker dog asses ain't show up, ya heard me?"

Marcus heard his partna, but none of it made any sense to him. Why would Tank want to leave them hanging? He had always come through for them, Marcus reasoned.

"I'm telling you, round, that nigga playing games and leaving us in here, and I'ma spank his ass, ya heard me?" Lil' Keith saw things for what they really were.

"Just chill out, round," said Marcus. "Let's see what the day bring."

As they stood talking, Vicki came down the tier. "You know you've got a visit waiting on you," she said, stopping in front of Marcus's cell.

"Who is it?" Marcus asked from the face bowl.

"It's your wife."

Marcus dried his face and left the cell. When he walked inside the visiting booth, he almost didn't recognize Jasmeen. Her hair was in an unkempt ponytail, and she had grease stains around the collar of her shirt. Marcus put his hand to the glass, matching Jasmeen's. She could barely look at him, and she had tears in her eyes.

"Baby, what's wrong?" asked Marcus.

"Everything," Jasmeen said, bursting into tears. Jasmeen began wiping her tears. She was trying to decide if she should tell Marcus everything.

"Jasmeen, where have you been?"

"I've been helping my mom at the restaurant. I moved back home last week."

"Why would you do that when you've got the condo?"

"Baby, we can't afford that place right now. I had to take the money you saved to get you a new lawyer."

Marcus's blood pressure skyrocketed. "Why would I need a new lawyer, Jasmeen? What's going on with Mr. Crenshaw? I thought you'd got that money from Tank?"

Born to Die   97

Jasmeen dropped her eyes to the floor. "I went to pick up the money from Tank, but he kept me out there for hours, trying to push up on me. When I shut him down and asked for the money, he told me he'd handle it. But I knew he wasn't going to, so I went and got you a new lawyer. Her name is Lori Morris. She should be out to see you tomorrow."

Marcus had zoned out. He hadn't heard anything past Tank trying to push up on Jasmeen. Marcus had no question whether Jasmeen was telling him the truth. He knew she would never lie to him. But still, Tank, why?

Marcus needed to get back to his cell. He couldn't stand to see Jasmeen like that and not be able to do anything about it. Marcus told her that he'd figure something out, but he was really not sure what that meant. He ended the visit early, telling Jasmeen that he needed to get his head around this whole thing.

"I love you," she said with tears welling in her eyes as Vicki cuffed Marcus and pulled him out.

Marcus was stone silent as Vicki walked him back from visitation.

"Is everything okay?" she asked.

"Nah, it's not," Marcus said dryly.

"Anything I can help with?"

"Nah, but I appreciate you asking."

"All right, I'm here if you need me," Vicki said as she put Marcus back in his cell. "I'll come check on you before I go home tonight," she said, leaving Marcus to his thoughts.

Marcus felt like he had a knife stuck in his back. Never in a million years would he have seen that coming from Tank. He had always been a solid nigga in Marcus's eyes, a nigga of principles and loyalty.

"What's up, round?" Lil' Keith asked from his bunk. He had been asleep when Marcus came back in. He sat up to see Marcus stressing.

98 Dorian Sykes

"You was right, round." It almost killed Marcus to admit this, but it was what it was.

"Right 'bout what?"

"The nigga Tank, ya heard me? My girl just told me he wouldn't give her the money, and she say the nigga tried pushin' up on her."

Lil' Keith came to the bars. "We gone smash that nigga, ya heard me? That's on everything I love, round."

Marcus wasn't even thinking that far ahead. He was wondering how he and Lil' Keith were going to come from up under the bodies now that their lawyers and Tank had said fuck them. Marcus had never heard of this lawyer Jasmeen hired for him, so he doubted if she had any pull in there with them white folks like Mr. Crenshaw did. He felt bad for Lil' Keith, knowing that he'd have to take a public defender.

"Round, we gotta put our heads together, 'cause right now as it stands, we in bad shape, ya heard me?" said Marcus.

He and Lil' Keith stood at the bars, trying to come up with their game plan. The odds were against them, but one thing that they'd never do was lose sitting down. It was all or nothing from that moment forward.

CHAPTER FOURTEEN

Two days after Deeco and Tank talked, Deeco got up with Tank at his Club 360, letting him know that he was down for the family. This was like sweet music to Tank's ears because his dope spots were getting knocked off left and right with Lil' Keith and Marcus not there to protect them. But all that was about to cease because Tank not only got word from the streets about who was behind the capers but also had a certified head bussa to take over the problem.

Tank gave Deeco and Courtney his famous family sermon, swearing that it was them against the world. They partied hard that night, but at the end of the night, Tank dropped a name on Deeco and Courtney.

"Orlando," he slurred after drinking Cristal all night.

"Yeah, I heard of the nigga. Tenth Ward, right?" asked Deeco.

"That's the one, ya heard me? I want that bitch casket in the dirt by Sunday, ya understand me?"

"Say no more." Deeco assured Tank that the problem would be solved A.S.A.P. He and Courtney stumbled out of the club with two broads each under their arms, courtesy of Tank.

Tank was setting it all out for his new hitmen, and he had every intention to spoil them just like he'd done with Marcus and Lil' Keith. Tank would do anything to keep his ghetto empire. It was all like one big chess game, where he was the only king, and everyone else a mere expendable pawn.

100 Dorian Sykes

***

The next day, Deeco and Courtney were parked across the street from Club Tiger's in a stolen black Chevy Tahoe. They were stalking Orlando, A.K.A. Lando. It wasn't hard to find Lando in the N.O. because every time he and his nigga hit a lick, they went to a strip club to buy the bar out. Everybody in New Orleans knew their M.O. Duck was a part of a ten-man crew of Jack Boys from the 10th Ward. They were notorious for robbing, pulling kick doors, and kidnapping. They had pulled so many capers over the years that anytime something happened, they would receive the blame because the streets knew that nine times out of ten, they were responsible.

One thing the local strip clubs could count on was the Jack Boys coming through and making it rain whenever they hit a lick. Tank had got word that they were out balling around the city, parading in Caprices and Impalas all on one hundred spokes and tearing down the malls. On their last caper, they didn't even bother using masks, letting it be known that they were the culprits. To Tank, this was a clear sign of disrespect, and he knew that they'd only grow bolder unless he put some head bussas out there to see about them.

Deeco and Courtney were both cloaked in black army fatigue suits and black soulja rags tied around their faces. It was almost two o'clock in the morning, so the parking lot outside of Tiger's was jumping. That wouldn't deter Deeco and Courtney from their mission, though.

When they saw Duck and his crew spill out the front door of the club, they slipped out of the stolen vehicle unnoticed, crossing the street with their AK-47s in full view. They started busting before anyone had even seen them.

Courtney dropped three Jack Boys as they stood under the valet canopy waiting on their cars, while Deeco gunned for their main reason for being there: Lando.

Born to Die

Deeco chased Lando around to the back of the parking lot. He shot him twice in the leg and thigh, causing Lando to skid down against the concrete.

Deeco was merciless as he stood over Lando, who was crawling slowly and moaning from the burning hot sensations filling up his body. Deeco stabbed the barrel down into the back of Lando's head and pulled the trigger twice, rocking him to sleep eternally.

Courtney pulled the Tahoe up at the alley of the club, and Deeco jumped in. They made it out of there just as the police were pulling up. From the rear-view mirror, Courtney could see that they had blocked off the street leading to Tiger's. Red and blue lights flickered, with more sirens blaring in the distance.

They rode in silence, anticipating any would-be car chase or shoot-out with the law. They'd both had their share of high-speed chases and shoot-outs with the police, so they knew not to take anything for granted until they were all the way in the clear.

They made it to Tank's club without incident. Tank was waiting on them upstairs in his office. He greeted them at the door with a wide grin. He'd already got the word on Lando.

"They say playboy up outta here," Tank said, nodding at the television. The news was shooting live outside of Tiger's. Five bodies had been reported dead, and seven others seriously wounded.

Tank pointed out that they had no suspects and no witnesses, something that never happened with Lil' Keith and Marcus.

Tank rewarded them with another $20,000 and went into his sermon on family as Deeco and Courtney lounged on the sectionals, sipping on the private stock. Tank told them that there was more work to put in, and he wanted them to waste no time getting to it.

CHAPTER FIFTEEN

Meanwhile, Marcus and Lil' Keith were in for the fight of their lives. They had come up with a game plan on how best to proceed, and it wasn't with the two low-budget lawyers they'd been stuck with.

Marcus called on their lil' partna Big Shays. The men knew that Big Shays was about his yeah and really was their only chance at ever seeing the streets again. Marcus gave Vicki a kite to take over to Eugene's barbershop, where he knew Eugene would get it to Big Shays with no problem. At the end of the kite, Marcus left the number of his smuggled cell and told Big Shays to call him as soon as he got it.

Big Shays was out on the block when Eugene came out of the shop and gave him the kite. Big Shays read it right quick, then walked up to the pay phone at the Chinese store.

"What's up, round?" he said as Marcus picked up.

"Youngin, we need you, ya heard me?"

"Say no more, big homie. I got y'all's message, and I'm dead on top of that, ya understand me?"

"Good, because that's the only way we're walkin' outta here alive, ya heard me?"

"What's up with Lil' Keith?"

"Ah, he right here. We good for the most part, ya dig? Niggas working out and tryna come from up under this shit, ya heard me?"

104 Dorian Sykes

There was a long silence.

"Big Shays, you still there?" asked Marcus.

"Yeah, I was just thinkin', ya heard me?"

"What's up?" Marcus asked, noticing the distance in Big Shays' voice.

Big Shays didn't want to add to his partnas' stress, so he wasn't sure he wanted to tell them.

"You know the nigga Tank done hooked up with the niggas Deeco and Courtney."

"What you mean hooked up?"

"He got 'em rolling with him now. I guess to take you and Lil' Keith's place. They out here smashing shit and everything, ya heard me?"

The line fell silent again.

"Big homie, you want me to see 'bout them niggas, too, ya heard me?" asked Big Shays.

"Nah, leave them bitch-ass niggas to me, ya heard me? Just take care of that business in the kite A.S.A.P."

"A'ight. Let me go to it, ya heard me? See y'all niggas when y'all come home."

Click.

Marcus stood at the bars of his cell, fuming. Not only had Tank left them stankin', but he now was fucking with the enemy.

"What's up, round?" asked Lil' Keith, seeing that look of murder in his partna's eyes.

"You won't believe what Big Shays just told me, ya heard me? He say the nigga Tank out there fuckin' with Deeco and Courtney ho ass."

Lil' Keith could see the hurt and pain in Marcus's eyes as he stared down the tier. He knew that it wasn't a good time for an I-told-you-so moment. There was nothing really that could be said. They both knew what this meant if ever they saw the streets again. It was murder.

Born to Die

***

Big Shays was a young, solid nigga. He had mad love for his two partners. That was why when he got Marcus's kite, he wasted not a single minute going to work on trying to see his niggas free.

Big Shays took the keys to his momma's Delta 88 and bent out with his .40 cal in hand as he drove. He stopped downtown in the French Quarter outside of a two-story white historical building. He peered at the gold-lettered address painted above the building awning, then back at the kite from Marcus. It was the right address, so he pulled the car around the corner and walked back to the building, entering its cool central air that only white folks had the luxury of having where he was from. He found a somewhat startled old white secretary sitting at her desk with her ear pressed into the phone. The smile on her face turned to stone when Big Shays pointed the .40 cal at her forehead. He put his finger to his lips, warning her not to scream as he looked both ways down the empty halls of the law office.

"Hang it up," he ordered in a hushed tone.

"We don't keep any cash here," the woman said, figuring this was a robbery. She slowly stood from her desk.

Big Shays snatched her up by the arm, steering her down the hall while looking at the brass name plates on the closed doors.

"Where's Crenshaw's office?" he demanded.

"He's in the office next to our right."

Big Shays kept the bitch moving at gunpoint. He stopped briefly outside of Crenshaw's office, then ordered her to open the door. Big Shays rushed her inside and closed the door behind him. Mr. Crenshaw sat motionless behind his desk, looking up from a stack of documents sprawled before him. He was like a deer caught in headlights.

106   Dorian Sykes

"What is this?" he asked.

Big Shays pushed the old bitch down to the floor, then took aim at Mr. Crenshaw.

"Look, we can make this here ya funeral, or you can give me what I came fo', ya heard?" Big Shays said, laying down the law.

"And just what is it that you're wanting?"

"I want a copy of Marcus's discovery."

"I can't give you that. Besides, I'm no longer representing him," said Mr. Crenshaw in a clipped tone.

"I know. I am. And you will give me that here, or I'ma push ya shit, ya understand me? Now, get ya bitch ass up and get it," ordered Big Shays.

Seeing that the youngin meant business, Mr. Crenshaw reluctantly slapped his hands down on his desk as he stood and walked to the file cabinets. "You're never going to get away with this," Mr. Crenshaw said, pulling the file out and handing it to Big Shays.

Big Shays quickly flipped through the file to ensure he had the right one. Satisfied that he'd gotten what he came for, he turned cold and sparked Mr. Crenshaw's dome with three shots. *Boom! Boom! Boom!*

He stood over Crenshaw's slumped body and pumped five more shots into the back of his skull, then turned on the secretary, who was crying and trembling.

"Please . . ." she tried to say as Big Shays stood over her, feeding three shots into her temple.

Over the ringing of the gunshots, Big Shays could hear people screaming outside in the hall and the running of heels and loafers against the granite flooring.

Think! he told himself, locking eyes on the back window.

Big Shays snatched the air conditioning unit from the pane and leaped out into the alley. He made it around the corner to the Delta, where he made a smooth getaway.

As he drove to his next destination, he thumbed through the discovery material in search of two names and their addresses. He found Sasha's home address in the 17th Ward in Hollygrove. Marcus ordered her dead on sight, as well as the old white woman who had identified him from the night of the murders.

"I got you, big homie," said Big Shays as he drove back toward the hood. He knew that the .40 cal he was toting wouldn't do anything but get him killed in Hollygrove. He had to get his hands on a chopper.

CHAPTER SIXTEEN

Vicki pulled Marcus into the officer's station for what she was hoping would be another one of their fuck sessions, but Marcus hadn't been in the mood to do anything besides think since he'd learned the crosses his once big homie Tank was putting down on him and Lil' Keith.

"What's wrong, boo?" Vicki whined as she slipped under Marcus's arm and began soothing his chest.

"I want you to help me kick this habit."

"You're serious?" she said, seeing the look in Marcus's eyes. "I mean, of course, I'll help you. What do you need me to bring you that'll help kick it?" she asked.

"Nah, I'm doing this here cold turkey. Just give me ya word that no matter how sick I get or how much I beg. I need you not to bring me nothing, ya heard me?"

"Okay," Vicki said. Her voice was meek because she didn't want to ever see Marcus sick and going through withdrawals.

But for Marcus, kicking his habit cold turkey was the only way. He felt that if he went through all the sickness, then he'd never want to get high again. He decided to kick the habit because he realized that the dope was taking a toll on him. He wanted to be the man Jasmeen deserved when he got out. And he wanted to be on equal grounds with a clear mind and no weaknesses when he went after Tank. He knew that Tank was a treacherous nigga firsthand, so he and Lil' Keith would have to not only slang that iron, but they'd have to be able to think on Tank's level because he was playing for keeps.

Lil' Keith was standing at the bars, fixing his needle and tripping on Marcus at the same time. "Nigga, I don't know about you, but I'ma die high, round." Lil' Keith had a sinister grin on his face as he tapped against the sides of the syringe. "Fuck I wanna be sober for, ya heard me?"

Marcus hadn't done his morning fix, and he was already starting to feel the sickness knotting inside his stomach. He balled into a fetal position and pulled his blankets over his head. He had spoken with Jasmeen the night before and told her not to come visit him. She cried into the phone, thinking Marcus was pushing her away, but really, he didn't want Jasmeen to see him as he suffered. He needed to take care of this now, while he was at the lowest point of his life. Jasmeen cried and wept, but she had understood and respected Marcus's wishes that she was not to visit him for two weeks.

Two weeks was about what Marcus figured he'd need to kick. It would be a brutal fourteen days, no doubt, but he was tired of what his life had become. And really, he didn't know how much more he could stand. He wished that his father had had the courage to kick his habit before he was killed. Marcus's father was a certified street player, an all-around hustler, and well-respected. He was also known for all the bodies he'd put in the dirt. His only weakness was that he let Marcus's mother turn him out on dope. Just like Marcus, his father started off snorting, then eventually graduated to banging. He was found shot dead in his Coupe de Ville with his eyes open and a needle stuck in his arm.

Four days later, Marcus's mom was found shot in the head execution-style. Her body had been thrown in a dumpster naked. Those were the haunting memories Marcus had of his parents. He didn't want to end up like either of them, but instead, to raise a family with Jasmeen. He was still thinking about whether he'd leave the N.O. for good, as suggested by Jasmeen.

But where would they go? And what would he do for money? Those were the two questions he struggled to answer. But he knew that he had to make a change, the first being to kick his habit.

CHAPTER SEVENTEEN

"Let me hit the yeah," Rasul said from the back seat of the Delta 88. He was leaning forward with his lil' fingers held out, anticipating the blunt Big Shays and Damon were blowing between them.

"Nah, ya heard?" Big Shays said, pulling the blunt down to a roach, then flicking it against the wind. He looked back at his partna's tight face. "You know what happened the last time we put some work in and you was high," said Big Shays.

"Nigga, I ain't see the bitch crossing the street," spat Rasul.

"That's 'cause yo' ass was high," Damon said with a half grin, remembering the fatal night when Rasul struck a woman as she was crossing the street and killed her.

"I got something for you, round, as soon as we put this here work in, ya heard me?" Big Shays said from behind the wheel.

Damon and Rasul were his niggas. They were down for whatever, just like Big Shays. That's why it wasn't but a thing for them to suit up and grab their cutters when Big Shays told them what Marcus and Lil' Keith were up against. They had mad love for their big homies and would do anything to see them back on the streets.

They all sat low in their seats as they made it into Hollygrove because, knowing that they were out of bounds, beef was liable to spark before they even made it to their destination. Big Shays searched the address painted against the curbs as he brought the Delta 88 to a slow creep.

"There that bitch right there," Damon said, nodding toward a group of women standing in the driveway two houses up.

"Yeah, that's that bitch," Big Shays said, spotting Sasha amongst the women.

Marcus had always taught Big Shays about the power of surprise, so he did something not even Damon or Rasul was expecting to happen. He pulled against the curb and slapped the car into park, jumping out in broad daylight with his AK in hand. Damon and Rasul were right on his heels, though.

Somehow, a snitch knows when it's their time to go and that the gunmen are there for them. Sasha froze stiff, with her mouth open and eyes wide with fear. Big Shays upped the chopper and confirmed her worst fears. He riddled her frame from the neck down until she was on her back. He walked up and gave her a single dome shot to put her out of her misery.

Within a short time, niggas from Sasha's block came running out from around the sides of the houses on both sides of the street, busting back with everything from choppers to .40 cals. Damon and Rasul held up the slack as Big Shays drove behind the wheel to get them out of there. He hit the horn hard for them to come on!

"Let's ride!" he shouted.

They all ducked as Big Shays gunned the Delta 88 down the street. Bullets ripped through the car on both sides, sounding like rocks banging against metal. At the end of the block, Big Shays sat up and made a hard right turn, side-swiping two parked cars and nearly hitting two little girls as they crossed the street. Big Shays looked back at the little girls in the cracked side mirror, thanking the street gods he hadn't struck them. His attention then turned to his partnas.

"Y'all straight?" he asked, looking over at Damon, who was riding shotgun.

"Yeah, I'm straight, ya heard me?" said Damon as he sat up and checked his mirror to make sure no one was following them.

Rasul was quiet. He hadn't said a word, when usually they couldn't pay him to shut up.

"Round, you straight back there?" asked Big Shays. He stole a glance back at Rasul and nearly lost control of the wheel. Rasul's eyes were closed, and his little black fingers were soaked in the blood that was seeping from his side. His eyes flickered open, then shut again.

"Rasul!" Damon yelled as he leaped into the back seat.

"Wake up, round. Not like this. Don't go out on me like this. Come on, wake up for me, round." Damon was cradling Rasul's limp body, searching for any signs of life. But there was none.

Tears welled in Damon's eyes as he accepted the fact his partna was gone. Bit Shays felt it, too, because Rasul was their nigga from the dirt. Seeing him go like that wasn't the way Big Shays ever wanted to watch any of his partnas go out. He made Rasul a promise that he was going to smash all them niggas in due time. If one of his niggas had to die, then he'd match them with at least two of their niggas. But one thing for sure, the shit wasn't going to go unpunished.

"Rasul!" Damon was in tears.

Big Shays drove back toward the hood while trying to think what to do with Rasul's body. He couldn't bring himself to drop him off at his mother's crib because he knew Ms. Bertha would lose her mind, not to mention have them implicated in her son's murder, with downtown asking a bunch of questions.

"What we gone do with Rasul?" Big Shays asked Damon.

"I say we take him to Memorial," said Damon.

It wasn't ideal, but it was better than anything Big Shays could come up with. He drove over to Memorial Hospital and pulled right up to the emergency door, parking near the entrance. Big Shays hopped out and helped Damon carry Rasul's body to the sliding automated doors, where they laid him down, then headed back to the Delta 88 in a rush.

Two medics on their smoke breaks sprung into action. One of the white men was trying to hold up Big Shays from driving away.

"What happened to him?" the man asked as he stood at Big Shays' window.

Big Shays peeled out of the parking lot, hoping the cracker wouldn't remember his face as he was trying to catch the plate number. But Big Shays wasn't tripping on him writing the plates down because it was a dummy plate he stole. He just couldn't afford to be identified. Not now, anyway, because he still had some work to put in for his homies. He had given Marcus his word that all would be handled, so that's what it was. On to the next mission.

"We gotta switch cars, ya heard me?" said Damon.

"Yeah, I know," Big Shays said, thinking of the bullet holes all throughout his O.G.'s whip.

CHAPTER EIGHTEEN

Entering Jefferson Parish was enough to make any gangsta's stomach sink, especially when riding dirty or on the way to put some work in. The crime rate out there was almost nonexistent, making the police response ten times faster than in the city of New Orleans.

The sun had started to descend. Big Shays thought it best to slide out to the Lake Chateau Estates during rush hour traffic so that they'd blend in amongst the other motorists. He parked his mom's car in an alley downtown and then set it on fire to kill the evidence. He and Damon stole a new model Buick Regal and headed out to the suburbs. They knew that they were highly exposed going out there with all the white folks, but what kept Big Shays' foot on the gas was the fact he knew Marcus and Lil' Keith wouldn't hesitate to do the same for him. They wouldn't ask someone else to do something that they themselves wouldn't do or hadn't done. This gave Big Shays the heart to press on.

"How we 'posed to get in this bitch?" Damon asked of the black iron gate wrapped around the estates.

"There's gotta be a way in, ya heard me? The homie wouldn't send us unless he knew we could make it in."

Big Shays scoured the estates in search of any nook or cranny they could slip in at. There was an opening at the back end where the estates opened up to some woods and alleyways.

"We in through there, ya heard?" said Big Shays.

118   Dorian Sykes

"I don't know 'bout this here, round. How we 'posed to make it outta here?" asked Damon.

Big Shays had pulled the Regal deep into the woods and killed the engine. He smoked a cigarette while thinking about their dilemma. He knew that there was a good chance that after he let off a couple of gunshots, the police would be on the scene in minutes or even seconds.

"I'ma push by myself, ya heard? You just leave the car running, ya dig?" said Big Shays, figuring it would be less suspicious if he went by himself anyway.

"You sure, round? Because you know I'm down if you need me, my nigga."

"Yeah, I got it. But look, if I get jammed up, I'ma let off three shots for you to dip out, ya heard me?"

"I'm not leaving you out here, round."

"Look, ain't no sense in us both going down, ya understand me? Just dip if shit goes bad, and I'll get up with you on the flipside."

Without another word, Big Shays slid out of the car and started through the woods. Damon jumped behind the wheel and cranked the engine, leaving it in neutral in case he had to dip at a moment's notice. He watched Big Shays fade to black in the woods. He could only hope that his partna would make it back safely. He couldn't stand to lose both his homies on the same day.

Big Shays casually strolled through the manicured courts, discreetly checking the addresses of each estate against the one he had palmed on a small piece of paper. As he passed the homes, he could see families moving about inside the estates. The courts were deserted, with the exception of an old white man out watering his lawn. He eyed Big Shays sternly and suspiciously. There was no doubt that Big Shays was out of place. The old man must've known everyone who lived within the estates, so he was well within his rights to be leery of Big Shays.

Big Shays could feel the old man's eyes piercing through his back as he crossed the court, now in full stride because he knew the chances of the old bastard calling the police were almost guaranteed.

Big Shays stole a glance at the address cuffed within his palm, then thought, *This gotta be it*. After locking eyes on the two-story colonial estate, he cut across the lawn and climbed the single step leading to the front doors. He chimed the doorbell and clutched his .40 cal deep inside his hoody. Moments later, a woman's voice called out, saying that she was coming. Judging by the sound of her voice, Big Shays could tell she was an older woman. He hoped she was who he came to see.

The door swung open without her asking who it was. Her blue eyes froze in a hazy look of fear at the sight of the young black man standing before her. Her wrinkled lips pursed together in contempt for what she presumed to be a thug.

Big Shays flashed his gold teeth in an effort to disarm the old bitch. In his best put-on white voice, he kindly asked her if she was Darlene Harris. The old bitch, sensing some sort of danger, said no, and then hurriedly tried to close her door. But Big Shays had seen it in her eyes that she was lying; it was her. He forced his weight against the door and knocked the old woman back into the house. Big Shays heard the old man across the street holler over, "Hey!" But Big Shays was all business as he grabbed a pillow from the living room couch and cornered the woman, who was cowering at the foot of the crème chaise lounge.

Big Shays kneeled over top of her, jamming the pillow into her face, then firing two muffled dome shots. Blood splattered all over the crème décor and over Big Shays' pants from the close-range shots. As Big Shays stood up, he saw a silhouette inside the foyer. The old man had a shotgun in his hand.

"Darlene! Are you in here?" The man was slowly approaching the living room area. His head was on a swivel, ready to take down anything that moved.

Thinking on his toes, Big Shays grabbed a vase out of the curio and threw it high in the air toward the hallway. He watched the old man raise his shotgun and shatter the vase in a single shot, but that was all the time Big Shays needed. He swung from around the wall separating them and fed the old man from the neck up with ten hollow points. Big Shays didn't even stay to see the body drop. He bolted from the house, cutting across the court, the tool still in hand because he had downed a would-be hero. *Just make it back to the car*, he told himself.

The blaring sounds of sirens and home alarms had his adrenaline pumping hard and fast. He slipped back into the woods, running full speed through the darkness. Bugs and mosquitoes slapped against his face as he ran aimlessly without any sense of direction because of the darkness. He could hear the blades of ghetto birds winding in the near distance. Big Shays knew that he couldn't allow the helicopter to pick up his heat signal because once they did, it would be hell trying to shake them.

He kept one foot in front of the other, never looking back or thinking about getting tired. Much to his relief, Damon flicked the headlights on him.

"My nigga," Big Shays said, still running for the car. He dove into the passenger seat with a wide, open-mouth grin. He leaned back, out of breath, but still managed to tell Damon to get them out of there.

"Get us back to the hood, ya heard me?" Big Shays lay back and sparked a Newport while thinking how much Marcus and Lil' Keith owed him for all this. Really, he was just hoping that it would be enough to bring them home.

CHAPTER NINETEEN

At two o'clock in the morning, Lil' Keith and Marcus were snatched out of their cells and separated.

"You know what this means, round!" Lil' Keith yelled back at Marcus with a victorious smirk on his face.

Marcus knew exactly what it meant. Big Shays had come through for them, and now they were being separated just to make it seem as though the police were doing their jobs.

Lewis led a team of detectives into The Parish at this hour because he was certain Marcus and Lil' Keith were behind both witnesses' murders. And boy, was he pissed. Lewis got the first call on Sasha's death early in the day, and while he was still on the scene investigating, he got the call about Darlene Harris and her neighbor. What he thought to finally be a slam dunk case against them had vanished right before his eyes within a mere few hours.

Lewis was at his wit's end now. He'd tried playing it by the book, but all that ever got him was the law thrown back in his face whenever he watched Lil' Keith and Marcus walk away scot-free. He was determined to get a confession out of them by any means necessary.

Detective Sloan, a pot-bellied nigga who wanted nothing more in life than to be equal to the white man, was standing over Lil' Keith, bitch-slapping him hard across the face using the backs of his ashy, leather-like mitts. It was always the nigga police out to prove something amongst their colleagues at the expense of another black man.

The other white detectives formed a circle around Sloan, rooting him on in his relentless assault.

"Give him five minutes," Lewis said, calling off his sick and twisted dog for the time being. "Don't worry, your partner is downstairs getting the same tune-up," Lewis taunted Lil' Keith.

"Fuck you, ya heard me?" said Lil' Keith. He refused to bow out to a pussy like Lewis.

Lewis broke out into shoulder-shaking laughter. He shoved his hairy knuckles deep into the pockets of his tan cargo pants, then looked down from Lil' Keith over to his men.

"Fuck me?" he said, losing the grin and taking a step, closing the space between them. "No, fuck you, you piece of shit. You're not gonna walk on this, not this time." Lewis got in Lil' Keith's face and whispered to him, "I'll kill you myself before I let your black ass walk outta here."

"What's wrong with ya, killer, ya heard me? Gone and get it over with, cracker. Fuck you think, I'm scared to die? I'm not you, cracker. You kill me now, and I'll see you in hell, bitch."

Lewis couldn't stand Lil' Keith's disdain for him. He cocked back and punched Lil' Keith so hard that he fell out of the chair, and it knocked him out on contact. Just then, Sergeant Reed from The Parish stepped into the room, carrying the Motorola flip phone his team of officers had found in Marcus's bunk during their cell searches. He gladly handed it over to Lewis for his inspection and approval.

"Any idea who brought it in?" asked Lewis.

Reed's face tightened as if he had just been stabbed in the back with a dagger.

"Are you suggesting that one of my officers smuggled this into my jail?" asked Sergeant Reed.

Born to Die

"Smuggle is such a generous word, and I am not suggesting anything. How else would these perps come to possess a cell phone unless someone from the inside brought it? But we'll revisit this later. In the meantime, what I want from you is a full copy of every officer who's worked around these two since the day they arrived, from sergeants down. Do I make myself clear?" barked Lewis.

"We're clear." Sergeant Reed was flushed red. He couldn't believe Lewis's audacity.

"You can get to that now," said Lewis. He dismissed Reed and then began studying the phone's contents. There were only four stored numbers, but Lewis had a gut feeling that at least one of them would lead him to his killers.

He sent the phone back to the station crime lab to run a cross-check on the phone itself and the stored numbers. All four numbers came back with hits. Lewis recognized Tank's cell number and the second as being Jasmeen's line at her mother's. But there was one under the name of Vicki Kindle, and the other was to the payphone on the corner of Valence and Magnolia Streets.

CHAPTER TWENTY

The tier where they moved Marcus to reeked of feces and days old piss. They had moved him downstairs to one of the mental health wards, where he lay cold and shaking on the filthy concrete floor. He was in pain; the withdrawals were growing more intense with each day that passed. Marcus had broken out into a cold sweat as he dry-heaved from the sickness. He barely had enough strength to sit up. He was starting to smell almost as bad as the mental patients surrounding him.

Marcus, in as much pain as he was in, still managed to stretch a closed grin across his face and raise his middle finger at the sight of Detective Lewis staring down at him through the cell door's plexiglass. Marcus was smiling because he knew his lil' partna Big Shays had come through clutch, and it was only a matter of time before they walked out of there yet again.

Lewis turned beet red in the face. He'd be damned if he let those little fucks beat him again.

When Vicki walked in for work, her bags were seized by Internal Affairs at The Parish. Sergeant Reed stood flanked by two of his corporals. They watched as Vicki was thoroughly pat-searched by a female agent.

"Sergeant Reed, what's going on?" Vicki asked in her most innocent white-folks voice.

126   Dorian Sykes

After she was cleared, Sergeant Reed scolded her with his stare. "Officer Kindle, there are some people here who need to speak with you, and I suggest that you be truthful in the matter."

Vicki was led by the agents from Internal Affairs to an interrogation room. Waiting inside was Detective Lewis. He introduced himself as being from homicide, instantly causing Vicki's stomach to sink to the lowest pit of depth. She nearly lost her breath when Lewis pulled the Motorola cell phone from his back pocket. He was trained to study body language, so he picked up on Vicki's nervousness.

"Have you ever seen this phone before?" he asked. His voice was stern, and his speech short and clipped, almost accusing.

"Um, no. I don't think . . ."

"It's either yes or no, Officer Kindle. Now, have you ever seen this phone before?"

"No," Vicki said with an attitude. She didn't know who this redneck thought he was talking to, but she could assure his ass that she wasn't the one. She rolled her eyes and shifted her weight in her seat.

"Need I remind you that you're under oath here, Ms. Kindle?" said the female agent.

"I understand that," spat Vicki.

"Then maybe you'll explain why your home number was found on this cell phone," roared Lewis.

"I don't even know where that phone came from, or who it belongs to, so I have not the slightest idea as to how or why my home number would be in there."

Lewis wanted to slap her black ass hard across her face. She was lying, and she knew it.

"Look, this phone has been linked to two homicides already that we know of. It was used to order hits by two inmates being held in segregation, who also happen to be assigned to your unit."

Born to Die

"What are you accusing me of?"

"All I'm saying is that it sometimes happens. We all are human and are capable of making misjudgments."

Vicki stood abruptly. "Not me, okay? Now, seeing as though I am clearly a suspect, I will not continue this interview without my lawyer present."

Lewis wanted to punch her fucking teeth down her throat because he could no longer proceed in any line of questioning, simply because she had lawyered up. She was lucky for the presence of Internal Affairs. Otherwise, he'd have her ass downtown getting some of the same treatment Lil' Keith was in the midst of getting from his men.

Lewis and the two agents shared a knowing glance at one another as Vicki exited the interrogation room. They all felt she was guilty of sin. Why else would she need a lawyer unless she had something to hide? Not to mention an earlier interview with another officer, who had indicated that Vicki had approached him some weeks back about changing posts with him. Why else would she request a change of her post other than to be closer to Marcus and Lil' Keith?

For now, Lewis didn't have enough on Vicki to arrest her. However, she was put on leave pending an investigation.

Big Shays woke up to his mom's bitching still about her car being stolen. At least, that's what he told her happened to her Delta 88.

"I'ma find you another one, Ma," he promised, saying anything to get his O.G. off his case.

"Boy, please. You can barely take care of ya self. How I'm 'posed to believe you finna buy me another car? Get on my damn nerves. I swear yo' ass ain't shit, just like ya no-good-ass daddy." Ms. Bertha held no punches.

128 Dorian Sykes

Big Shays rolled out of bed and stepped into his fresh new black-and-red Air Max 95s. He stood and grabbed a loose Newport out of an ashtray.

"Where you think you're going?" his mother asked, dead on his heels. "Answer me, boy!"

"Out," Big Shays said, not looking back at his mother, who was still bitching him out from the doorway of their two-bedroom bungalow.

He stood near the curb as he smoked his morning square down to its filter. He put his hand over his eyes like a visor and looked up the block. Seeing Black Boy and Samuel posted up by the Chinese store, he fell in step. *It's hot as a bitch out here,* he thought. It couldn't have been any later than ten o'clock in the morning, and the sun was already cooking. Big Shays tripped on Black Boy and Samuel as he approached them. They'd be out there no matter what. Even if it was 110 degrees outside, they were going to be posted like a stop sign.

"What's up, round?" Samuel said, seeing Big Shays first.

Big Shays gave them both some dap, then posted up under the canopy with them. He scanned the passing cars and faces, nodding to some in acknowledgment.

"What the lick read, ya heard me?" asked Big Shays, knowing that if anything was going down, his two partnas most definitely knew the score.

"Them Impalas been sliding through all morning. I don't know who they looking fo', though, ya heard me?" advised Black Boy.

He was nursing a bottle of Wild Irish Rose and cradling a loosie at the corner of his mouth. He took a long pull from the square with his eyes glued on the passing cars. He spotted two white boys riding behind tinted windows in a black Chevrolet Blazer. The two white boys made eye contact with Black Boy but kept on in the direction of Valence and Freret Streets.

Born to Die

"Y'all see them crackers there?" Black Boy asked. Just then, the payphone started ringing.

"That bitch been ringing all morning, ya heard?" Samuel advised.

Big Shays pushed off the wall in haste. He figured that it must be one of the big homies calling. He rushed over and snatched the phone up to his ear. "What's up?"

A female voice came across the other line. "Yeah, I got a message from Marcus. Who is this?" the woman asked.

"This Big Shays. Who this here?"

"I'm Tavia, and I'm a friend of Marcus's. Are you the one he normally gets his messages to?"

Who is this bitch really? thought Big Shays as he turned to face the corner. He had never heard Marcus speak on no chick named Tavia. Something wasn't adding up.

"Are you still there?" the woman asked.

Big Shays placed the phone on the receiver and started walking toward the front store. He turned around at the sound of a car engine revving fast. It was Detective Lewis riding shotgun in a blue Impala.

Big Shays took off to run but was stopped in his tracks by another Impala coming from around the corner, followed by the Blazer full of plainclothes detectives.

The convoy of detectives came to a screeching halt along the curb.

"Get him down on the ground!" ordered Lewis.

His men got Big Shays down at gunpoint, then frisked him hard for any weapons. They cuffed him, then stood him up to face Lewis.

"You're the piece of shit who put my partner in the hospital," said Lewis as he sized up Big Shays.

"I don't know what the fuck you talkin' 'bout," claimed Big Shays as he stood in the clutches of two detectives. They were just itching for Lewis to give them the green light to beat the brakes off of Big Shays.

"I'm going to give you one chance to help yourself. Do you hear me?" asked Lewis as he took a closer step.

Big Shays stood firm, but he heard him out.

"Who's calling you on that payphone?"

"My lawyer. Wanna call him back for me?"

"Get him the fuck outta here. We'll see how smart your ass is in twenty-five years," cracked Lewis. His henchmen shoved Big Shays into the back of their Impala and headed downtown for The Parish.

As they pulled off, Big Shays' gut feeling told him that this was going to be his last ride through the hood for a long time. He nodded at Black Boy and Samuel as the driver barreled past the store. Big Shays could see his O.G. standing out on their front porch with her hand covering her mouth in fear for her only son's life.

Yeah, it's gone be a minute, he thought, accepting his fate. He slouched down in his seat and dreaded the trip to The Parish.

CHAPTER TWENTY-ONE

Three Weeks Later

When they wouldn't allow Jasmeen to visit down at The Parish, she automatically knew something was wrong with Marcus, so she called his lawyer, asking her to go to see about him. Marcus's lawyer had been informed of the two slayings of the state's witnesses, and she relayed this as being a turning point in the case because she doubted if the state had enough evidence otherwise to proceed. She went on to explain that in New Orleans Parish, the courts have a ruling known as 701, in which they have sixty-three days to either bring a suspect to trial or release them. And in Marcus's case, she foresaw him being released.

"How soon will this be?" Jasmeen asked, ecstatic that Marcus would walk free.

"I'd say in a couple of days, by the end of the week at the latest." She assured Jasmeen that she was on her way to see Marcus and that she'd call her later to talk about how he was doing.

Marcus had gained his strength back over the course of the past few weeks. He was no longer going through withdrawal, nor was he fien'ing for a hit. For the first time in years, he could wake up in the morning and not feel sick because he hadn't done a blow. He vowed to himself never to touch dope again. It was a weakness he

132 Dorian Sykes

didn't enjoy having. And besides that, he knew that dope and money didn't mix. While he was laying against the hard, cold concrete in his cell, throwing up and dry-heaving, Marcus told himself that if he could allow something like heroin to control his life for so long and bring him down to the lowest point of his life, then he could master selling it.

For Marcus, it was a challenge he wanted to meet. If a nigga like Tank could master the dope game and make millions of dollars, then so could he. He and Lil' Keith were the real reason why the nigga was able to sew up the N.O. Without them, Tank was a half-respected nigga who could have never reached the heights he'd seen with Marcus and Lil' Keith.

Marcus was over the fact that Tank had played them out; it was what it was. And that was murder—when the time was right. Marcus didn't want to just kill Tank and have it all be over with. He wanted to destroy him first because of what he tried to do with him and Lil' Keith. He needed Tank to see him at the top of his game while Tank was at his lowest point.

Those weeks of lying on the floor in his own vomit had caused Marcus's heart to turn cold—colder than it had already been. The only love he had left was for Jasmeen and his partnas Lil' Keith and Big Shays. That was who he now considered to be his family.

Marcus had also been thinking a lot about what Jasmeen had asked him about leaving New Orleans. She had family spread all over the map who were willing to do anything to help her. Marcus thought it would be a good look for him and Lil' Keith to go somewhere and lay low for a minute once they got out because they were coming home naked, and beef was still beef. They needed to come up on a bankroll before they started taking nigga to war.

Born to Die 133

When Marcus walked inside the visitation room, his lawyer rose from her seat and began flipping out on the two officers as they un-cuffed Marcus. She took one look at Marcus and knew that they'd been mistreating him. He reeked of urine, being over-ridden by a strong stench of feces. His dreads were matted to his scalp, and his jumpsuit was soiled. She demanded to see their shift supervisor and promptly wrote both their names down, threatening to file suit for cruel and unusual punishment.

"Are you okay? Are you hurt in any way?" she asked as the two officers disappeared from within earshot.

Marcus answered by pulling back a victorious grin. He knew she was there to tell him that the state had no case and that they'd soon walk.

"I have some good news," she shared. "I will be filing for a 701 release this afternoon. The, um, the witnesses against you were both killed, so really, the state doesn't have a strong enough case to proceed. I will also notify the courts of your ill treatment here, asking that you be released into my custody pending the ruling."

"What about my partna? They gonna cut him loose too, right?" asked Marcus.

"I am not his attorney, but this motion for release, I'm sure, would be granted for you both."

Good, thought Marcus. He couldn't leave Lil' Keith in there by himself.

"I strongly suggest that you keep a low profile once out because the D.A. and Homicide are working to build another murder case as we speak."

"On what?"

"They strongly believe you and your co-defendant orchestrated the slayings of both witnesses from your cell, using a cellular phone—which, by the way, they found inside your cell and that contained some questionable numbers stored in its memory."

134 Dorian Sykes

"I don't know nothin' 'bout no phone. Far as I know, they planted that shit, ya heard me?"

"Well, I have no reason not to believe you. I am just encouraging you not to fan any flames because they've made one arrest already," said Ms. Morris. She rifled through some papers, then read from an arrest warrant copy. "Do you know a Jason Williams?"

"Nah," lied Marcus. He knew who that was. It was Big Shays, but he wasn't about to tell her that he knew him. "What about 'im?"

"He was arrested during a sting that homicide detectives set up at the payphone on the corner of Valence and Magnolia Streets. The number to the payphone was found stored in the cellular phone. Anyhow, the detective team called the payphone, and Mr. Williams answered it."

Marcus scrunched his face up. "So, what does that prove?"

"It proves nothing as long as Mr. Williams doesn't decide to trade his freedom in exchange for a deal. He's been charged with critically assaulting and disfiguring a detective months prior. He's facing a lengthy sentence here."

Damn, Marcus thought. He had sent his little partna off and got him jammed up. He wasn't worried because his little nigga had been tried, tested, and approved. Big Shays snitching hadn't even crossed his mind. But still, Marcus wouldn't leave Big Shays hanging. He now had all the more reason to go hard and get money when they got out.

CHAPTER TWENTY-TWO

Jasmeen and Ms. Morris were waiting outside The Parish. They'd been informed of the court's decision to release Marcus and Lil' Keith due to lack of evidence. This came after sixty-three hard, long days of suffering the agony of the unknown.

Marcus pushed through the tinted glass double-doors leading out to the street. He was followed by Lil' Keith. They stood under the sun for a moment, looking the part of two niggas just released from jail.

Jasmeen sprang from the driver seat of her Acura Legend and bolted across the street with tears in her eyes. Marcus accepted her into his arms, hugging and kissing all over her tears.

"I missed you," he said.

"I'm so happy you're home," cried Jasmeen.

Marcus wiped Jasmeen's tears as she cradled under his arm. Ms. Morris smiled on from the sidewalk.

"You have a beautiful woman riding in your corner. I hope you're going to stay out this time," she said.

"I'ma do my best, ya heard me?" said Marcus, looking down at Jasmeen.

"He better," Jasmeen said, playfully punching Marcus in the stomach. She kindly thanked Ms. Morris, as did Marcus.

"Okay, call me if you need me. And remember what I told you," Ms. Morris said to Marcus. She nodded at the unmarked Impala parked near the intersection with two detectives.

136 Dorian Sykes

Lil' Keith was ready to get the fuck on because he felt naked standing out there without his yeah. They climbed into Jasmeen's Acura and pulled away from the jail. From the back seat, Lil' Keith let Jasmeen know that they had a quick stop to make. He needed to hit the block and grab a .40 cal from one of his niggas, just until he could hit up Chets' in the morning for some choppers and crates of bullets.

"Absolutely not," Jasmeen said, shutting Lil' Keith's murderous plans down. "I am taking you guys to my parents' house. They're in New York visiting my family there. You are to stay put until tomorrow. That's when our flight leaves for Detroit."

"With all due respect Jasmeen, I appreciate ya lookin' out for me and my partna, but I'm not going to no Detroit, ya heard me?" said Lil' Keith.

The N.O. was all he knew. Jasmeen wasn't hearing any of this from Lil' Keith because she knew he and her man were joined at the hip. The only way she'd be able to get Marcus out of New Orleans was if Lil' Keith came with them.

Jasmeen looked back at Lil' Keith through the rear-view as she drove. She said in a serious tone, "Lil' Keith, do you want me to turn this car around and take you back to The Parish? Because if you stay here in New Orleans, that's where you're gonna end up. Right back in there or in somebody's graveyard. Now, you're coming with us whether you like it or not."

Lil' Keith couldn't believe this chick. Hadn't she heard? Wasn't she scared to talk to him like that? *Detroit?*

What the fuck is in Detroit? thought Lil' Keith.

He tried to make eye contact with a smiling Marcus, who was pretending to be staring out of the window. He could have never convinced Lil' Keith to leave the N.O. Marcus was smirking because Jasmeen had laid the law down.

Two days before Jasmeen brought the news to Marcus that he and Lil' Keith would soon be released, she made him give her his word that he'd at least try out Detroit for a couple of months. Marcus felt as though he owed Jasmeen at least that much, so he gave her his bond that they'd try out the change of scenery—anything to make her happy.

Jasmeen's parents lived not far from where Marcus once had his condo out in Jefferson Parish. They owned a beautiful stucco ranch-style home tucked on four acres of rolling,/ty manicured lawns.

"Welcome to our humble abode," Jasmeen said, pulling through the circular driveway and parking beside the stone water fountain. "Come on, you guys," she said, getting out and walking toward the trunk.

Lil' Keith whispered at Marcus before they got out, "I'ma fuck you up, round. Get me out of here."

"Would y'all come and help me carry those bags in?" said Jasmeen. She had gone shopping for Marcus and Lil' Keith so they'd have some fresh clothes to put on.

"Just fall back, ya heard me? I got a plan, round. We comin' back to the N.O. a'ight? You with me?" asked Marcus. "You know I need you and can't do it without you."

Lil' Keith shook his head. "I'm tellin' you, round, if I don't like it, I'm on the first thing smokin', ya understand me?"

"That's understood, ya heard me? But as in everything else, we're in this here together, and I got us."

They dapped up, then got out to help Jasmeen with all the bags of clothes and shoes. Lil' Keith didn't know yet what his partna had planned, but he could see the seriousness in his eyes, so whatever it was, he was sure Marcus had thought it through. Secretly, though, Lil' Keith was proud of Marcus for having kicked his habit.

138   Dorian Sykes

He himself could've never kicked his habit, especially not cold turkey like Marcus did. He teased Marcus, telling him, "I'ma die high, round. It just is what it is, ya heard me."

Tank was in the midst of balling out. He was on the center floor of his office with a gold bottle in his hand and diamonds flickering at every point of his body as he put on for Deeco, Courtney, Dinyell, and a host of scantily clad women looking for a come-up. Tank was soaking up all the ass-kissing and dick-riding being thrown his way. He loved being the center of everyone's attention.

He was in a festive mood because his heroin operation was flourishing, and it was all thanks to the three men lounging on the Italian leather sectionals. They enjoyed themselves thoroughly, drinking the best grapes and aged Cognac and smoking only the best herb in the company of all dime-pieces. The after-party was going down at Tank's Eastover mansion, where they'd all have two women apiece. Life was good—until Tank's desk phone began to ring.

He excused himself, still smiling for the crowd as he walked around the back of his desk, snatching the phone up to his ear. It was his personal attorney, William Jeff, calling to inform Tank that Marcus and Lil' Keith had been released.

"How long ago?" Tank snapped into the phone. His lawyer was supposed to give him the heads up before they were cut loose. Tank wanted to have them downed as soon as they hit the streets.

But now Mr. Jeff was telling him that they'd been out since early afternoon, and there weren't any signs of them, according to his people.

"Are you there?" asked Mr. Jeff.

Born to Die

Tank had zoned out, thinking about the possibility of Marcus and Lil' Keith coming for his head. He knew they were no slouches and barred none when it came to playing the murder game. Tank slammed the phone down in Jeff's ear. Tank hated excuses, and that's all Jeff was feeding him—a bunch of excuses on why he'd fucked this up.

Deeco and Courtney caught the look on Tank's face. He had gone from being jovial to somber in a blink of an eye. Courtney ushered the girls out so that they could have some privacy.

"What's up, big homie?" Deeco asked Tank, who had taken a seat behind his desk.

"I need y'all to boot up, ya understand me? They done let Marcus and Lil' Keith out early today. My fuckin' lawyer was 'posed to give me a better drop so we could've caught 'em slippin'," said Tank.

"Where they at now, on V.L.?" asked Courtney.

"Ain't no tellin', ya heard me? But I want y'all to find 'em A.S.A.P. and down 'em, ya understand me?"

Deeco stood as he downed the rest of his Cognac. This was the moment he'd been waiting on since he got the word up in Angola that Monay had been killed. Now it was time for niggas to feel his wrath.

"I'ma have they asses downed by the sun up, ya heard me?" Deeco told Tank.

He nodded for Courtney, and they cut out on their way to the hood so they could suit up and grab their cutters. Deeco was willing to bet his life that they'd find them somewhere in the 13th, celebrating being home. And they'd catch them slipping and down their asses.

Meanwhile, Tank wasn't so convinced that killing Marcus and Lil' Keith would be easy. He had spent years around these young niggas, and he knew firsthand just how crazy they were, especially Lil' Keith. Tank was so paranoid at the thought of them being back on the streets that he called downstairs and told the manager to close the club. He didn't want to take any chances of them slipping inside the club undetected, so he sent everyone home early.

Tank watched from the monitors as the club's lights came on and the bouncers ushered people out through the exit. He thought it would be best if he went underground until his head bussas gave him the call that things had been handled.

CHAPTER TWENTY-THREE

Heat waves bounced across the airfield at the New Orleans International Airport. The temperature was a smoldering 102, but the cabin of the 747 Delta Airlines jet was cool as a breeze. Lil' Keith had never been on a plane before a day in his life, and neither had Marcus. Hell, they'd never left the city of New Orleans, for that matter. Their whole lives had been so far confined to uptown and downtown, beefing and killing. Neither ever imagined leaving their birthplace; it was what consumed them.

Lil' Keith nervously sat behind Marcus and Jasmeen, leaning forward and asking them questions every other minute as they waited for the pilot to take off. "If this bitch go down, they got them chutes for us, ya heard me?"

Jasmeen turned in her seat and tried assuring Lil' Keith that the plane was going to make a safe trip and landing. Marcus was just as nervous, but he was more preoccupied with having never left the N.O. and not knowing what to expect. Jasmeen clasped her hand into his as he stared off against the horizon.

"Sir, I'm going to need you to fasten your seat belt," a young white stewardess said to Lil' Keith. "We're getting ready to take off."

"I don't know how I let y'all talk me into this shit here, ya understand me? Got a nigga leaving the set, and for what? What's in Detroit, ya heard me?" Lil' Keith went on rambling about his discomfort for leaving the N.O. as the plane taxied around the take-off strip.

142   Dorian Sykes

Jasmeen pulled back a closed smirk, listening to Lil' Keith's rant. It humored her that he'd be nervous about flying when he was, in fact, a stone-cold killer in the streets. Lil' Keith stopped complaining as the pilot blasted full speed ahead. He braced himself as the plane began lifting against gravity. He closed his eyes in fear of seeing the ground below as they climbed into the clouds. Finally, the plane reached its desired height at 30,000 feet. Lil' Keith heard people now moving about the aisles, so he slowly opened his eyes to see Marcus and Jasmeen laughing at him.

"Y'all think this shit funny, huh?"

"We just fuckin' with you, round," said Marcus.

"Yeah, Lil' Keith, don't be salty," said Jasmeen, smiling. She motioned for one of the flight attendants and sent for some Tanqueray and club sodas.

"This will help you settle your stomach," she told Lil' Keith. "Just try and relax because we've got about a three-hour flight."

Jasmeen had brought on board two portable CD players, one for Marcus and Lil' Keith each. She also made sure she'd brought along their favorite CDs, mostly N.O.'s local artists and bounce music.

Lil' Keith started relaxing when he popped in "Uptown Thang" by Baby Gangsta. It was one of his favorite songs and always had him ready to smash something.

Jasmeen nuzzled against Marcus's shoulder as he stared down against the plains moving below. "You're not going to listen to your music, baby?"

"Nah, I was just thinkin' 'bout some things."

"You care to share it with me?" asked Jasmeen. She'd understand if he didn't. She knew Marcus was nervous about moving to a new place.

"Remember when we were at the condo lying in bed, and you made me give you my word that I'd slow down on using?"

Born to Die 143

"Sure, I remember."

"Well, I didn't tell you this because I wanted you to see it in my actions, but while I was in, I kicked my habit."

Jasmeen's face lit up. She sat up. "Really, baby?"

"Yeah, I went cold turkey for weeks. That's why I didn't want you coming to see me. I wanted to come home with nothin' in my way."

Jasmeen could sense there was more to be said. "In your way of what, baby?"

Marcus turned back toward the window. He spoke as he watched the tiny specks of life bustling below. "Baby, who am I fooling? I'ma street nigga, and gone always be one, ya heard me?"

Jasmeen squeezed Marcus's hand in support to show him she was listening and wanted him to go on.

"The one thing my father ever taught me was that it ain't what you do, but how well you do it. Guess that was his way of tellin' me to be the best nigga out here in these streets that I can be. So, that's what I'ma do. Because for five years, I been letting this dope run my life and keep me from becoming the nigga I should be, so now I'ma flip the game on 'em and take us to the top."

Jasmeen had known Marcus was a street nigga. It's what attracted her to him, but still, she didn't want to lose him to the streets either. She felt his plight, and she would have his back on whatever he wanted to put down as long as there was an end to the means.

"Baby, I'm with you, you know that. But tell me what you're going to be doing this for?"

"I'ma be doing it to make sure we're straight and that you can have all of your heart's desires," said Marcus.

"I already have all my heart's desires. Being together is enough for me. I'm not worried about the money, Marcus, but I want you to set an amount you'd feel comfortable with because you are getting out. We're not

144 Dorian Sykes

going to spend the rest of our lives in this. Now, give me your word on that."

Marcus hadn't thought that far ahead into things, only that he'd take over the dope game in the N.O. and live a lavish lifestyle with Jasmeen by his side.

"Fine, since you can't come up with a number, I will. Five million, and we're done," said Jasmeen. Marcus looked at her. "That's right, I said, *we*. If we're going to do it, then we're going to do it right and get out when it's time. Deal?"

She's amazing, Marcus thought. *Always down for her man no matter what.* He kissed the back of her hand and said, "Deal."

"Good, because I have an uncle in Detroit who's in the game. I'm sure he'll deal with you as a favor to me," said Jasmeen.

"How long you been sitting on this, ya heard me?"

"I keep telling you that I wasn't always this good girl you fell in love with," Jasmeen smiled and stole a kiss.

"Oh, no?" teased Marcus.

"Nope. . . ."

The truth was, Jasmeen had been down this road before with her last boyfriend, a nigga out of New York named Blue. She'd plugged him in with her Uncle Oliver back then on some grade-A China White heroin. Blue was doing life in the feds because he had let the money go to his head and wouldn't listen when Jasmeen tried to tell him it was time to pull out.

She nuzzled closer to Marcus, thinking about how she wasn't going to lose him to the dope game. She was going to see to it personally by handling the money and making investments so they'd be straight later on in life. She was really his ride or die chick, whether he knew it or not.

CHAPTER TWENTY-FOUR

India stood outside the Metro Airport terminal, waiting eagerly for her favorite cousin to walk through the sliding doors. Full of anticipation, she eyed every passing face. It had been almost five years since she'd seen Jasmeen. India rushed from the sidewalk at the sight of Jasmeen coming out.

"Jasmeen! Oh my God," she said, arms spread wide.

They rushed into each other's arms and hugged for what seemed like an eternity. Growing up, they were inseparable back in New Orleans, but India's parents moved to Detroit after her dad was given a position in the growing family business. But still, every summer, India and Jasmeen would hook up and city-hop, from South Beach to New York and Jersey. They hadn't really talked since Blue and India's then-boyfriend, Tatum, got indicted. The ladies were also implicated by the feds and were facing serious time in prison, but Blue and Tatum stood up and took the charges.

Marcus and Lil' Keith stood off to the side as India and Jasmeen reconnected. Lil' Keith was already scheming on India. She and Jasmeen could easily pass for sisters. They were equally pretty with long hair and flat stomachs and Coca-Cola shapes, except India had a little more ass. Lil' Keith watched as her luscious ass rolled inside her capri-style shorts.

"I'm sorry," apologized Jasmeen, ending their catching up. "This is my boyfriend, Marcus, and his best friend, Keith. And y'all, this is my cousin, India."

Dorian Sykes

India smiled as Lil' Keith took her hand and made pleasantries.

"Jasmeen, why you ain't tell me your cousin was this beautiful? Are all the women in y'all family this beautiful?" he said, shooting his shot.

India was blushing. "I don't know about that, but there's a lot of us."

"You got a man?" Lil' Keith still hadn't given her hand back.

"Keith, leave my cousin alone," said Jasmeen.

India was still blushing because she had always liked her men a little rough around the edges, and she could tell by looking at Lil' Keith that he was definitely a thug.

They started walking over to India's Lexus 300. Marcus and Lil' Keith walked a short distance behind them.

"I'm hittin' that, ya heard me?" said Lil' Keith.

"So, you're glad that you came then?" asked Marcus.

"If everything 'round here looks like that, then hell yeah, I'm glad I came, ya heard me?" Lil' Keith was lost in India's hips and walk. She was undoubtedly a bad bitch.

India opened the trunk for Marcus and Lil' Keith to put their luggage in. They piled into India's white Lexus with Jasmeen riding up front. Lil' Keith couldn't keep his eyes off India as they drove. She was that deal, and she knew it. She met eyes with him through the rear-view and pulled back a closed smile, then turned to catch up with Jasmeen. So much had changed since the last time Jasmeen had been to Detroit. Her family's business was at its peak, so her aunt and uncle had bought a new home out in West Bloomfield Hills. They left their first home in Gross Pointe Woods to their spoiled daughter and only child, India.

Two other cars decorated the exterior of India's five-bedroom brick. She had an X-type Jaguar and a 4-series BMW. She was, without a doubt, a boss chick, and at 27, she was on top of her game.

Born to Die

147

Jasmeen wasn't sure how long she, Marcus, and Lil' Keith planned to stay in Detroit, but India insisted they all stay with her. She claimed to be lonely in that big old house all by herself. India gave Marcus and Lil' Keith a tour of the house and the pool house, then showed them their rooms.

"Where's your room at?" quizzed Keith. "I mean, I might need something in the middle of the night, and I don't wanna just be walking in on you, ya heard?"

India looked him over with a knowing smile on her face. "If you need anything, my room is the only room upstairs. We're going to get something to eat in a little while, so I'll let you guys settle in."

India smiled and left Marcus and Lil' Keith alone in Lil' Keith's room. When she was out of the room, Lil' Keith commenced scheming.

"Round, why you been holdin' out? How come you ain't tell me ya girl had a rich and pretty cousin?"

"I ain't even know. Jasmeen never talks about her people." Marcus was starting to wonder why when she and India seemed so close.

"It don't matter because I'm on her line, ya heard me? And you already know what it is once I slap some of this dope-dick on her, ya understand me?"

Jasmeen and India were upstairs in her bedroom, both sitting Indian-style on India's queen-sized bed.

"I've missed you, Jasmeen," India said in a low and most sincere voice.

They hugged again. "I missed you, too," said Jasmeen, closing her eyes and remembering what had caused the long absence. For years after Blue and Tatum pleaded guilty, the feds were still watching Jasmeen and India, certain that they were co-conspirators in Blue's cross-country heroin operation. Jasmeen and India felt it'd be best if they cut ties for a while anyway, but years had slipped by, and life had changed.

148   Dorian Sykes

"How's your mom and Uncle Oliver?" asked Jasmeen.

"They're doing great. You know, just traveling and enjoying life. I wish that I could find someone to share the love that they have."

Jasmeen had grown up seeing that love within her own parents' marriage.

"You'll find someone," Jasmeen tried to assure her cousin.

"I sure hope so because it's not like we're getting any younger, you know?"

"Yeah, I know."

"Do you remember when we were little, we had our dream weddings all planned out?"

"I remember." Jasmeen smiled.

"We're two years behind schedule. We said that we'd be married by 25 with kids by 27. And look at us, Jasmeen. Tell me that Marcus is the one. At least one of us would be on the right track. Is he the one?"

"I think he is," Jasmeen said, unable to keep from beaming. Just the mere thought of Marcus could always put a smile on her face.

"I'm happy for you, Jasmeen."

"Thank you."

"He's cute. So much cuter than Blue ever was."

"Do we have to bring him up? Besides, I don't remember Tatum being something from out of *GQ* either."

"You know how I like 'em, ugly and hung."

"You're still crazy," laughed Jasmeen. "I think Keith likes you."

"Is he hung?"

Jasmeen was dying laughing with her hands covering up her face. "How would I know?"

"Well, he's definitely ugly, so he half qualifies."

"For?" Jasmeen asked. She knew full well what for, but she wanted to hear India say it.

"I haven't had any dick in almost four months, so . . ."

"You're too much."

They laughed and then changed the subject. India was still in the dark as to what brought Jasmeen back to Detroit. She was always welcome because she was family, but India sensed that Jasmeen had been trying to escape something.

"Anything I can help with?"

"Nah, not this time. I think that I got us both in enough trouble the last time," admitted Jasmeen. She secretly blamed herself for India's involvement with Tatum because she had introduced them, knowing what type of guy Tatum was.

"You didn't get me into anything. I knew what was going on," said India.

"Yeah, well, not this time because I can't stand to have your mom mad at me again."

India dismissed that notion by waving her hand. Her mother was like all other mothers, always looking to blame someone other than their own child.

"But I do need Uncle Oliver's help. You think he'll be willing to this time around?" asked Jasmeen.

"Jasmeen, you know that besides me, you're his favorite. He could never turn you down. You know that."

This brought a smile to Jasmeen's face because she knew her cousin was right. Uncle Oliver had always been there for her, and he'd never turned his back on her.

India snatched the phone from its cradle on her nightstand and punched seven quick numbers in.

"Who are you calling?"

"Daddy. I know he's going to want to see you."

The line picked up, and India turned into a little girl over the phone. She broke the news to her father that Jasmeen was in town, and he immediately told them to come out to the house for dinner. It wasn't a request, but a directive.

150   Dorian Sykes

"Okay, love you, bye."

"What he'd say?" Jasmeen asked, a bit nervous.

"He wants us to come have dinner with him tonight."

Jasmeen was ecstatic that she'd get to see her beloved uncle, but she was torn on whether to take Marcus with her or wait for another day. She decided not to take Marcus because she and Uncle Oliver needed to clear the air on some things.

Jasmeen left India to go get ready for dinner. She found Marcus enjoying a nice hot shower in their master guest room. He hadn't noticed Jasmeen as she undressed outside the fog-steamed shower glass. She surprised Marcus when she slipped into the shower behind him, running her soft hands up his back, around his chest.

Marcus's erection was instant. He turned around four inches harder, taking Jasmeen's mouth against his. They let the soothing water cascade down over their bodies while making passionate love. Marcus had picked Jasmeen up with her legs wrapped around his waist, leaning her back up against the wall for support as he dug deep in her guts, stroking all the right spots he knew would drive her crazy.

Meanwhile, Lil' Keith was on the prowl. He wasted no time in finding a reason to go upstairs and holler at India. He found her strolling through her walk-in closet, wearing only a bra and panty set. Lil' Keith was stuck in his tracks as he stood behind India from the bedroom. Her banana-yellow ass cheeks were spilling out the sides of her panties. Lil' Keith was in sheer lust. India turned around and put her hand on her hip with a sly smirk.

"And how long have you been right here?" she asked.

"Not long enough."

"You always walk around like this?" asked Lil' Keith.

"Just when I'm at home," India said, lifting her hands for emphasis.

Born to Die

Lil' Keith pulled back a smile, then changed the subject. "I thought we was going to get something to eat?"

"Oh, that's right." India thought for a second. "Jasmeen and I are going to have dinner with my parents, but I can order something for you guys and have it delivered here."

"Nah, I was hoping we'd get to sit across from each other and get to know 'bout each other."

Lil' Keith closed the space between them and put his hand up on the wall in full mack stance. India stood there, eating it all up and feeling the vibe as well.

"Tomorrow, I'll take you guys and show you the city. Deal?"

"That's a bet." "Lil' Keith said, looking her up and down from head to toe. He went on and let her finish getting dressed for dinner.

CHAPTER TWENTY-FIVE

The evening sunset glistened off Uncle Oliver's glass-front estate as India and Jasmeen pulled into the property.

"This is beautiful," Jasmeen found herself saying.

"Yeah, it is," India said, pulling into a space beside her mother's Rolls Royce.

Jasmeen was in awe of how well the family business was treating her uncle. She estimated the property to be worth in the tens of millions. It was definitely fit for a man of her uncle's stature.

They were greeted by Thomas, her parents' butler. He received them in the grand foyer dressed the part in a black and white tuxedo. Thomas was an elderly man from the islands.

"Hey, Tommy. I want you to meet my cousin, Jasmeen. She's visiting from New Orleans," said India.

Thomas nodded at Jasmeen with a closed smile, then instructed India that her father was in his study.

"Did he come with the house?" Jasmeen asked as she followed India through the white-on-white décor.

"Nah. Daddy brought him back from St. Thomas a couple of years ago."

"What the hell is a study?"

"It's his man cave, where he goes to not to be bothered."

I'd bet, Jasmeen thought as she recalled her uncle's wife, Renee. Jasmeen couldn't stand her ass only because Renee didn't like her. She'd always gone out of her way to make Jasmeen feel uncomfortable in her home. It had something to do with Jasmeen's mom. Jasmeen never took to Renee either, so back in the day, she tried to introduce Uncle Oliver to a friend of hers despite his relationship with Renee. Ever since, there had been bad blood, with Renee figuring Jasmeen was a product of her mother.

India slightly knocked on her father's study door, then pushed it open. Uncle Oliver was standing behind the wet mixing himself a drink. "Daddy, look who I've got with me?" said India.

Jasmeen stopped in the center of the floor atop the thrown Persian rug, fiddling her fingers like a nervous schoolgirl.

"My Jasmeen," said Uncle Oliver. He rushed from around the bar to embrace his favorite niece. He squeezed her tight and kissed the sides of her face, then cursed her in their native tongue for not coming sooner. "Step back and let me look at you," he said, holding Jasmeen by her shoulders. She melted back into a little girl, as only her father and Uncle Oliver could make her feel. "Still as gorgeous as your mother. How is she?"

"She's doing okay, I guess."

"Good. And your father?"

Jasmeen sighed at the mention of her dad. "He's been in and out of the hospital for minor strokes."

Uncle Oliver hated hearing this. He and his little brother hadn't talked in nearly five years, ever since the feds picked Jasmeen up. Jasmeen's dad blamed her Uncle Oliver for his daughter's troubles with the law for having supplied her no-good boyfriend with heroin. Jasmeen's dad wanted her to finish law school and go on to become a prominent lawyer, but she had chosen the same family business as her infamous drug lord uncle.

Born to Die

Changing the subject, Jasmeen asked. "But how have you been doing, Unc?"

He looked his usual regal self, dressed in all fine linen and handmade loafers, except he'd grayed around his temples. Uncle Oliver was a short but powerful man.

"Oh, we're doing just fine."

Jasmeen's skin crawled on her neck at the sound of Renee's shrieking voice. Jasmeen turned around with a thin smile for Renee as she pranced her way into the mahogany-wooded study, her lean frame crammed inside a white skirt that fit like a glove, with diamonds flickering from her neck, wrist, and ears.

"Hello, Renee," said Jasmeen.

"And to what do we owe this pleasure? I sure hope not another federal investigation."

"Mother!" India said as if ordering her not to start.

"Actually, I'm just visiting." Jasmeen smiled.

"For how long?" quizzed Renee.

Uncle Oliver sensed some old tensions rising and stepped in. "She'll be staying for as long as she wishes."

Over Renee's dead body. She grunted and excused herself rudely, saying she was going to check on dinner. She stopped on a dime and turned to Jasmeen. "And will you be joining us?"

Uncle Oliver answered for her. "Yes, so have Thomas set out another plate. Thank you, baby." He waited until his wife was out of earshot, then apologized to Jasmeen for her rudeness.

Jasmeen waved him off. "I'm used to it by now."

"So am I," Uncle Oliver joked.

India had left them alone so they could talk in private.

"Can I get you something to drink?" he asked, making his way back around to the bar.

Jasmeen leaned against its counter. "Sure," she said.

"What will it be?"

156 Dorian Sykes

"I'll have a gin and tonic."

"That's my girl. Always been a strong one to handle," Uncle Oliver said with a cool grin as he mixed Jasmeen's drink.

"Thank you," Jasmeen said, accepting her drink.

"To family," Uncle Oliver said, raising his glass for a toast.

"I'll drink to that." They clinked glasses and took a drink.

Uncle Oliver took a stool beside Jasmeen. Swirling his drink as he always did when in thought, Uncle Oliver put his arm around Jasmeen and pulled her close to him.

"I've missed you, Jasmeen," he said sincerely.

"I missed you too."

"What have you been up to?"

"Just working and helping my mother out with my father."

"You know that you can always come to me if you ever need me."

"I know. . . . I was kinda hoping you'd help me with something."

Uncle Oliver turned and set his drink on the bar top. "Anything, just name it." He meant just that. There was nothing in the world he'd ever deny Jasmeen.

She let her eyes fall to her lap because she really felt bad for coming to her uncle with this. Before she caught the flight, she saw things going much easier in her head. Maybe it was Renee's crack earlier about her being the cause of the last federal investigation. It was no secret she blamed Jasmeen for the heat on her husband and daughter. And the last thing Jasmeen wanted to do was bring more problems her uncle's way.

Uncle Oliver put his hand softly on the back of Jasmeen's. "Talk to me, Jasmeen. What is it?"

"I have someone I want you to meet."

Born to Die

Uncle Oliver took a deep breath, then reached for his drink.

"Forget it," Jasmeen said, picking up her uncle's discomfort.

"I didn't say no." Uncle Oliver took his time before continuing. He was wondering just who the thug was that had his niece back out there ready to take penitentiary chances again. "Who is he?"

"Someone very special to me," Jasmeen said in a low, sincere voice. Marcus was indeed special to her, and she'd go to the ends of the earth for him.

Uncle Oliver knew Jasmeen was a good judge of character when it came to the family business. She had introduced him to Blue five years ago with the same intent, and when the curtains fell, Blue stood up. And in the game, Uncle Oliver knew that loyalty and principles were almost extinct.

"When do I meet him?"

"Is tomorrow a good time?" Jasmeen hoped it would be.

"Tomorrow's perfect. We can meet at the yacht club."

Good, Jasmeen thought, hoping that Renee wouldn't be present. Uncle Oliver usually went to his yacht club either alone or to talk business. "Thank you, Unc."

"You can thank me by letting this be our last time, you hear me?"

Jasmeen nodded her head.

Uncle Oliver continued, "Get in and get out. Let's not make the same mistake we did last time."

He was speaking on Blue getting the big head and drawing heat down from the feds. Jasmeen understood, and she wouldn't have it any other way. Five million, and they were done.

"Let's get ready for dinner," said Uncle Oliver as he put his arm around Jasmeen, and they walked together. It felt good having her around again.

158   Dorian Sykes

***

Meanwhile, Lil' Keith grabbed the keys to India's Jaguar, and he and Marcus hit the city. Lil' Keith was never one to sit around the house bored, plus his veins were itching to try the dope in Detroit. They found themselves on Schoolcraft, right in the heart of the hood.

Marcus was leaning back, riding shotgun. "Don't get us lost, ya heard me?"

Little did he know, Lil' Keith was already lost. He hadn't a clue where they were at or how to get back to India's. But judging from the rundown surroundings, he felt right at home. Down in the N.O., the hoods looked different than Detroit because Lil' Keith was used to projects and wards, but the hood was still the hood.

Crackheads, dope fiends, street stalkers, and stick-up kids were all lurking in the avenues as Lil' Keith pushed through in the Jag. He pulled into a dimly lit BP service station after peeping two fiends posted up outside, apparently on their grind of panhandling. Lil' Keith rolled the window down and addressed the man as he stood beside his woman, both wearing Newport hats.

"Say, round, where they got the yeah at around here, ya heard me?" asked Lil' Keith.

"Say what now?" the old man asked. He hadn't understood a word Lil' Keith said. "Y'all not from around here, are you?" he said, looking at Marcus and Lil' Keith, noticing the dreads and gold teeth.

"We from New Orleans, ya heard me?"

The woman pulled back a toothless grin. "Is that right? I'm from New Orleans, too, baby. Been here ever since '89." She had followed her man up to Detroit with a dream of making it in the music business, but instead, she wound up getting turned out on heroin.

Lil' Keith would have loved to stay and kick the bobos, but he was trying to get right. They pointed him to a dope

Born to Die

stroll off Dexter. The man said that it was some of the best dope in the city.

When Lil' Keith pulled up on Monterey Street, he saw a mob of young niggas running from the curb up to cars making hand to hands. There was a line of waiting cars trying to catch the evening rush before the stroll closed up shop. As Lil' Keith and Marcus inched forward, they could see the youngins out there slanging couldn't have been any older than fifteen, but they were running the shit like grown men.

It was unlike anything they'd seen back in the N.O. These young niggas in Detroit were out there with gold chains and Cartier sunglasses on, with cell phones clipped to their belts. And all of them had on new gear with new high-end cars parked up the block. They called it "rolling fresh."

One of the youngins ran up to the Jag, ready to serve, but he stopped in his tracks at the sight of Lil' Keith behind the wheel.

"Let me get ten of 'em, ya heard me?" Lil' Keith said, holding out a hundred-dollar bill.

In Detroit, it's almost unheard of for niggas Lil' Keith's age to be copping blows, so the youngin was hesitant to serve them. "Where y'all from?" he asked.

Damn, everybody wanna know where a nigga from, Lil' Keith thought before telling him, "New Orleans, ya heard me?" Horns blew impatiently behind them, as Lil' Keith was holding up traffic.

The youngin reluctantly made the sale for the ten blows, then slipped into the darkness to serve the next customer.

"This here ain't bad, round," Lil' Keith said after nose-diving into one of the lottery ticket packs they used to keep the dope in. He held out for Marcus to try.

160   Dorian Sykes

Marcus kept his eyes out the window. "I'm straight, ya heard me?"

"Nigga, you keep actin' like you done kicked. Don't you know this here is for life?" Lil' Keith said, snorting down another blow.

"Says who?"

"Says the game gods. Ain't a nigga under the sun stronger than this shit here, ya understand me? All you doing right now is taking a break. You'll be back."

Despite his partna's doubts, this shit was over far as Marcus was concerned. It was about that bread now and nothing else. He wondered about how everything was going between Jasmeen and her uncle. If she could get him plugged, then the sky was the limit.

Lil' Keith was looking for something to get into. He had a nice mellow high going, and he just wanted to go someplace where some chicks were and chill. They ended up downtown, off Jefferson Avenue. It was like a car show; all the latest whips made up the avenue, as well as tricked-out old schools sitting on spokes.

"This where it's going down out here," Lil' Keith said, sitting up to floss the Jag for all to see. He and Marcus cruised around and nodded to a few cars full of females in traffic, but none fit the bill of what Lil' Keith was looking for. They ended up in a club off the water called 2000, and it was wall-to-wall with chicks—more ugly ones than bad ones. But still, Marcus and Lil' Keith were feeling the elements of the club and its music. It drew a younger crowd, so the music was more up-tempo.

They stuck out like a sore thumb as they strolled through the club, their dreads a dead giveaway that they weren't from around there—that and their gold teeth. Niggas in Detroit rarely rocked the dreads, and you'd only see the old heads with maybe one or two golds in their mouths, but never Aaroned out.

Born to Die

161

Marcus and Lil' Keith stepped close to the dance floor just to watch the style. The Detroit niggas had their own swag and dances they were doing. Lil' Keith leaned into the girl's ear who was watching beside him, and he asked, "What they call that?" He nodded at the niggas' foot-working and ticking.

"Jittin'," she said, then carefully looked Lil' Keith up and down, starting from his crispy white Air Ones. She liked his neatly oiled dreads and the tattoo of an an AK-47 on his neck.

"You're not from around here, are you?"

"If one more person asks me that tonight, I'ma. . . What, do I have a sign on my forehead that says 'I'm not from round here'?"

"No," the girl said, pulling back a pretty smile. "You have an accent, and the way you dress."

Lil' Keith hadn't noticed how cute she was at first, but a quick inventory of her flat stomach, phat ass, nice skin, and pretty smile had him wanting to know her name.

"What they call you?" he asked.

"Sin."

"I'm Keith, and that's my partna, Marcus." Marcus had stepped off to the bar.

"So, where are you guys from?"

"The dirty."

"Where's that?"

"New Orleans. You know, the dirty South. Ever been?"

"Can't say that I have. What brings you to Detroit?"

"Just visiting some of my partna's peoples."

"Eastside or Westside?" asked Sin.

"Uh, I think it's called Grosse Pointe, whichever side that is."

"That's the money side. Your people must have a couple of dollars if they livin' out there."

"Like I say, them my partna's peoples. Me, I'm from the dirt, ya heard me?"

Sin was from the dirt, too. She'd grown up poor in the projects with nine other brothers and sisters. On the weekend, she escaped to the clubs with her homegirls to find solace and get away from the madness of the Brewster projects and her crackhead mama.

She and Keith hit it off because they had a lot in common. She was definitely feeling his whole swag and approach. There wasn't anything phony or fake about him. And Keith took a liking to Sin right off the bat, and it wasn't even about him wanting to get with her. He was thoroughly enjoying her company and wanting more of her time.

When the club let out, Keith cracked for Sin's number, but she seemed unsure about letting him call her. Keith had thought they'd clicked and that she was feeling him. Sin shamefully pulled Keith to the side, away from her girls, as they stood outside the club. She explained that she didn't have a phone at her house, and that's why she was hesitant. Usually, Sin would just turn a guy down when they asked for her number, even if she liked them, versus coming clean about being an heiress to a worthless crackhead mother.

"But how I'ma see you again? I do wanna see you again, ya heard me?" Keith really was feeling Sin and didn't want to chance never seeing her again.

Sin turned and looked over at her girls. "Okay, I can give you my girl Tesha's number. I'm over her house a lot anyway."

"A'ight, that's a bet, but I'ma do you one even better, ya understand me? Let me drop y'all off. That way, I'll know where to find you worse come to worst."

Born to Die 163

"I don't know if my girls gone be cool with ridin' back with y'all."

"Ain't all y'all from the projects?" asked Keith.

"Yeah, so?"

"Well, then I know y'all can fight, and I bet y'all strapped up. Probably got razors and some mo' shit in ya purse, ya heard me?"

"You're funny." Sin was smiling. Keith seemed cool enough, she guessed. "Let me go ask my girls."

They were in because a ride beat taking two buses home any day. Plus, Sin's girl, Token, was feeling Marcus anyway and could use the drive to make her move. They piled into the butter-soft, leathered-out Jaguar with Sin riding shotgun, giving Keith directions on how to get to their project. She was feeling Keith even more, seeing what he was pushing. He had a thug appeal about him, so she could tell he was in the streets. This only heightened her interest.

Keith dropped them off in the Brewsters, and he had to admit that they were from the bottom like he and Marcus. He promised to call Sin soon to hook up, and then he and Marcus dipped out.

When they finally found their way back to India's house, Jasmeen and India were waiting on them in the living room.

"Where'd you guys go? We were worried sick," India said from the sofa.

"We hit downtown and rode around a little. Nothin' major. Why, you missed me?" said Keith.

India rolled her eyes with a thin smile. She wasn't tripping about them taking off in her Jaguar.

Marcus was snuggled up under Jasmeen on the other sofa.

"Tomorrow," she simply told him, letting him know that everything was a go. He never doubted her for a second. She was a boss chick. He'd seen it in her from the first moment he laid eyes on her. He was just glad that she was his. He clasped his hand around hers and kissed the back of it.

Tomorrow couldn't come soon enough. It would mark the start of a new beginning that could change their lives forever.

CHAPTER TWENTY-SIX

The next day, Jasmeen woke up early so she and Marcus could get ready to meet Uncle Oliver at his yacht club. Jasmeen dressed in some boat shorts and deck shoes, anticipating a nice cool breeze of a day out on the Detroit River.

She and Marcus were ready to pull out, but Jasmeen wasn't sure if India wanted to join them, so she went upstairs to India's bedroom. She knocked once before opening the door leading into the master. Jasmeen froze in her tracks at the sight of Lil' Keith sleeping beside India.

"India?" Jasmeen yelled with her hands on her hips.

India woke up and cradled the sheets over her breasts. Keith was awake now, lying there with a gold smile on his face.

"Never mind," Jasmeen said. The deed was done, and India was going to do her regardless of what anyone said.

"I'll see you when we get back," Jasmeen said, leaving the room.

"Where are you going?" India called out after Jasmeen, but she didn't answer her.

Lil' Keith rolled over and put his arm around India's naked body, pulling her closer to him.

"You got me into trouble," said India.

"She'll get over it, ya heard me? You enjoy yourself last night?" Keith asked while sliding his hand between India's creamy, soft thighs. She moaned and allowed him to explore her treasures further.

166   Dorian Sykes

Lil' Keith had slipped into her bed after midnight as she lay up watching *The Godfather*. Lil' Keith was buzzing good and had done a few blows, enough to put the dope dick game down on India. He fucked her so well that they went for hours nonstop. She came so hard that she had forgotten she could ever feel like that. Lil' Keith was moving in for round two of some early morning sex. He was trying to make sure he blew India's mind because he definitely saw her in the grand scheme of things. She was a spoiled brat who had access to her people's unlimited bankroll. There wasn't any way he was going to let he slip through his fingers. When he was done putting his G down, she'd be eating out the palm of his hands.

Uncle Oliver was a member of the prestigious Belle Isle Yacht Club, which sat on an island two minutes away from Downtown Detroit. He owned a 120-foot, three-level vessel, which he gave the name Chyna White. It was a nod to the China White heroin his family dealt that had made them rich beyond their wildest dreams.

Jasmeen and Marcus left the car with the valet and were then led inside the private club by a woman serving as a hostess. The club had been in existence since the 1930s. It was founded by the infamous Purple Gang, a Jewish Mafia clique who ran the rackets in Detroit during Prohibition. Initially, the name of the island was Hog Island because the mob used the island as a hub for the liquor they were running out of neighboring Windsor, Canada. They kept poisonous snakes around the island to ward off trespassers, but the feds unloaded boatloads of wild hogs onto the isle, killing the snakes and allowing them to seize the island.

Born to Die

Uncle Oliver was the only non-Jew or Italian member at the club, and his membership only came after years of bringing in millions of untaxed dollars to the mob. That was the one thing the mob loved: untaxed profits and longevity. They had been working with Jasmeen's grandfather since the late '60s, and when he retired, Uncle Oliver took his seat as head of the family. The position would have gone to Jasmeen's father, except he didn't want it. He instead wanted to lead a simple life with his wife and children.

The hostess stopped out on the back deck that faced the array of yachts docked against the pier. She pointed at Chyna White. Jasmeen could see him standing on the third level with his back to them, staring out against the river.

"Thank you," Jasmeen said to the woman, and then she and Marcus made their way down the pier. They climbed aboard her uncle's yacht as it peacefully swayed within the river. It had been years since Jasmeen had been on Ms. Chyna, as her uncle liked calling her. They had so many fond memories on that yacht.

Jasmeen smiled and put her arm around Marcus's back as they climbed the two flights of marble steps leading up to the third level.

"Uncle Oliver," Jasmeen called out as they touched the top of the vessel where he stood in thought.

He turned with a broad smile and stepped from the railing with arms stretched forward. He and Jasmeen embraced, and she nestled against him still. She looked up and made Marcus's introduction.

"Unc, this is my boyfriend who I was telling you about. And Marcus, this is my Uncle Oliver."

Uncle Oliver extended his hand unsmilingly. Marcus shook his hand firmly while maintaining eye contact. "Pleasure," said Marcus.

"No, the pleasure is all mine. Any guy my niece here claims is her boyfriend, I'm always happy to meet."

Uncle Oliver turned to Jasmeen and told her that there were some crabcakes and Moët downstairs chilling in the kitchenette. That was her cue to excuse herself so Uncle Oliver could screen Marcus more thoroughly.

"So, Marcus, is it?" Uncle Oliver asked, pulling his designer gold aviator shades from his shirt pocket and putting them on. He turned to the water and raised his hands, taking in a deep breath of air. "Ahh. . . . Ever been on a yacht before?"

"Nah, I haven't. This is the first."

"Well, I can tell you that there's nothing else like it in the world." Uncle Oliver hit a lever to raise the anchor, and then he turned over the engine. They pulled out into the river and headed toward the Ambassador Bridge, which led into Canada.

Marcus had to admit that this was nice. He watched as Uncle Oliver expertly steered them down the river with a closed smile of satisfaction. He seemed not to have a worry in the world, and to Marcus, this was living.

Uncle Oliver killed the engine down at Hart Plaza, where the Strawberry Festival was taking place. It was an annual event where Detroiters went for live music and good eating. Marcus and Uncle Oliver leaned against the top railing to watch the passers-by. "What brings you to Detroit?"

Marcus sighed first. "Honestly, Jasmeen. She's the best thing that could've ever happened to me."

"How so?" Uncle Oliver knew just how special Jasmeen was, but he wanted to make sure Marcus was sincere with his intentions and not just running the game so he could get plugged in.

"Let's just say she saved my life. When I first met Jasmeen, I was on a road going nowhere fast. I was

Born to Die   169

addicted to heroin since I was fifteen, and I was so far
gone in the streets that I stayed in and out of jail, facing
life in prison every time. And this last time, I kicked the
habit while I was in, and I gave Jasmeen my word that
when I made it out, I'd slow down and make a way for us."
    Uncle Oliver respected Marcus and all his honesty
because he knew firsthand how hard it was to admit
one's shortcomings, especially to someone else. Uncle
Oliver knew all about a life of addiction. He had once
been turned out on snorting cocaine to the point where it
was affecting his business. And just like Jasmeen, it was
his wife Renee who had stayed down with him, believing
that he'd bounce back and touch the sky when he did, so
he had no judgment to pass on Marcus. He could tell that
Marcus grew up hard, which was a good sign of loyalty.
Uncle Oliver had his theory on those who came up with
little to no family: give them a chance, and they'll be loyal
to you for life.
    "Has my niece told you what my family business is?"
    "Yeah, she told me a little about you."
    "And so tell me, what makes you think that you can
make it in the heroin business? I'm sure you do know it's
a very rough business and sometimes even deadly."
    Marcus was unmoved. He'd been downing shit before
he got his first piece of pussy. But to answer Uncle
Oliver's question, Marcus had a plan on how he and Lil'
Keith were going to set up shop and position themselves
back in New Orleans. It was the same way they'd made
a way for Tank to take over—by blood and by murder. It
was the only way in the N.O.
    Uncle Oliver knew when he was in the presence of a
gangster, so he didn't question Marcus's capabilities any
further once Marcus spelled out his game plan. He'd been
around dope his whole life, so he knew all the crosses to
be expected coming with the game.

Uncle Oliver only had two concerns: One, that if Marcus was ever to feel himself slipping and on the verge of relapsing, that he'd have enough respect for the family to pull out. Uncle Oliver knew what it would be like working with pure kilos of the finest heroin and the temptations Marcus would be under. And two, that he'd protect Jasmeen at all costs, even if it cost him his life. Uncle Oliver extended his hand for Marcus's.

"How soon do you want to get started?" he asked.

"In a couple of weeks or so. Right now, I just want to take some time to spend with Jasmeen and clear my head."

"Good. Because trust me when I tell you that peace of mind is hard to come by in this business."

Jasmeen had come back up. She was carrying a tray full of crab cakes and a bottle of Moët.

"There she is," Uncle Oliver said, smiling.

They ate and sipped bubbly while enjoying the warm summer sun as it bathed down on them. At that moment, life was goodm, and the future seemed even more promising.

Marcus couldn't believe his luck. He had stumbled upon the most beautiful person God could have ever put into his life. He wrapped his arms around Jasmeen from the back and kissed the side of her face. "I love you."

"I love you, too," she said, happy that everything had worked out between him and Uncle Oliver.

"When am I going to be a great uncle?" asked Uncle Oliver.

Jasmeen turned to Marcus and looked him in the eyes as she answered her uncle. "In five years, when we're done with this business. That's our plan. Right, baby?"

Marcus nodded, then kissed Jasmeen softly on her forehead. He wouldn't have it any other way.

CHAPTER TWENTY-SEVEN

Back in the city of New Orleans, Detective Lewis had yet to throw the towel in on bringing Lil' Keith and Marcus back in on the murder charges. It was personal with him and had been since '92 when they first beat him at trial.

His men had delivered the news that Marcus and Lil' Keith had fled New Orleans to Detroit, but Lewis trusted in his gut that they'd be back. All his years on the force had taught him one thing about fugitives: they all had to come back home. No matter what, they'd be back. It was like they'd be homesick and just had to come back. Lewis was sure the case would be no different with Marcus and Lil' Keith. They'd be back.

But in the meantime, Lewis was gung-ho on making things stick this time around. So far, Vicki hadn't broken down and snitched. She was still on leave and holding solid, and Big Shays was doing the same despite facing decades in Angola for disfiguring Detective Tate's face.

Lewis had one more trick up his sleeve, though, and he'd hoped it would be his ace in the hole. He always kept his ear to the street, courtesy of his underground network of snitches. He'd gotten word that Tank had a hit out on Marcus and Lil' Keith and that he was laying low at his high-rise condo uptown.

Lewis decided to drop in on Tank for a surprise visit. He had weight in New Orleans in every district and every ward. Everyone knew who he was, so no one dared try to stop him upon entering the supposedly guarded condominium. He knew exactly where he was going as he located the bank of platinum-colored elevators and rode one up to the 37th floor. On the top floor, only four penthouse suites sat perched, overlooking the city's skyline.

Tank was in his whirlpool-style tub with two Asian women he had sent over from his favorite massage parlor. He was craving the happy endings they always gave him after catering to him like the king he dubbed himself to be.

He was laid-back, with *Scarface* playing on the mounted 60 inside the master bath. He smoked a stogie as the women took turns petting his skin with soft, oiled sponges.

Lewis walked straight in through the gold-handled double doors. Tank's bodyguard was on his heels, trying to explain to Tank that Lewis had barged in.

"Nah, it's straight, ya heard me?" Tank nodded to his bathers, and the women stood naked, soaked in bubbles.

Lewis watched their breasts, then backsides, with a cheesy grin plastered all over his face as they climbed out of the sunken tub.

"Must be nice," he said to Tank.

The bodyguard waited on a cue from Tank, to which he nodded, signaling that it was cool to leave them. He shut the door, and Tank pulled on his cigar.

"You got a warrant for my arrest?"

"If I had a warrant for your black ass, you'd be drug out that tub by your balls and in the back seat of my Impala."

"So then, what the fuck you doing here?"

Tank knew that he ran a tight ship in the streets, so he wasn't worried about Lewis because he was federal material.

"We can help each other," said Lewis.

"What makes you think I'd ever need help from you?"

Born to Die

"Your shit-dick little hitmen—what's their names, Deeco and Courtney?—haven't been of much help in finding Lil' Keith and Marcus, now have they? I know you're hiding up here in your little slice of paradise while your flunkies try to find them. I know you're scared shitless, too, 'cause you left them hanging, and now they're going to kill you."

Tank tried to appear unmoved by Lewis's spiel. He said nothing. Lewis ran a hand over his five days of beard, then through his sweaty mane. He was studying Tank.

"Let's be frank here. You're a piece of shit. We know this. But Lil' Keith and Marcus are bigger pieces of shit, and I wanna bust their asses only God knows how hard!" Lewis's neck veins were showing, and his face flushed red. "The reason your men haven't been able to find them is because they're in Detroit. They left the next day after they were released."

Tank had underestimated them, but who could they have known up in Detroit? *That bitch*, Tank thought of Jasmeen.

"But they're coming back, and when they do, you and I both know they're going to come for you. And we both know how good they are at killing. But let me help you. Give me something that will put them away forever."

Tank was a businessman. To most, what Lewis was asking him would be considered some rat shit, but with Tank, it was all part of the game. He had plenty on Marcus and Lil' Keith since back in the day, but he wasn't about to jump just because Lewis said, "Jump!" If anything, things would be on his time and terms.

Lewis flicked one of his cards into the tub at Tank. "Call me when you're ready to deal." Lewis left Tank to his bath. He knew how Tank got down and that he was a creep who'd sell his own mama's ass if it meant saving his own. Tank would be calling sooner than later once

174 Dorian Sykes

Marcus and Lil' Keith resurfaced on a blood-thirsty mission.

Lewis would be right there to play them all against each other like the dumb niggers he figured them to be. He'd been making ten-dollar snitches out of niggas for years. Lewis smiled as the elevator door closed, thinking about the day he'd soon hear a jury say, "Guilty" and sentence Marcus and Lil' Keith to life in prison. That day couldn't come soon enough.

CHAPTER TWENTY-EIGHT

The plush coach leather seats inside Lil' Keith's new, white 740il BMW felt like something fit for a king. He pulled back a grin as he gripped the wheel with one hand, thinking about how open he had India. In just two days of putting his G down, she had taken him to her father's car lot, Exotic Motors, out in Orchard Lake, Michigan, and signed for the Beamer. After getting the car for Lil' Keith, she took him to the bank and pulled out $20,000, saying it was spending money for him.

Lil' Keith was living the good life. He had a bad bitch who didn't mind dropping that cake on him. Down in New Orleans, it was the other way around.

But even though India was a cold dime piece with plenty of money, Lil' Keith couldn't stop thinking about Sin. He was on his way to see her. She'd told him that her mother had been locked up, so she had to stay and watch her brothers and sisters, but he could come over if he'd like.

Lil' Keith was from the dirt, just like Sin, so the projects were home to him. He rolled up on the Brewster Projects, or the Jets, as they called them. They were abuzz with traffic going and coming; niggas posted up like a stop sign by the entrance. Little kids were playing in an open fire hydrant, trying to beat the summer's heat. And crackheads decorated the exterior of the Jets, expertly trying to swindle some credit from the hustlers. Yeah, it was home to Lil' Keith, all right.

He pulled the big body into the first court, catching a few stares from a huddle of niggas shooting dice against the curb. For the first time since he'd been in Detroit, he felt naked without his .40 cal on his lap. Lil' Keith pulled up to Sin's project and parked beside a rusted-out brown Ford Tempo that sat on four cinder blocks. The black metal screen door to the house was hanging off the hinges, and the front door was open, giving Lil' Keith a full view inside. There had to be at least twenty-plus bodies inside. A lil' nappy-headed nigga stuck his toothless face through the busted screen, peering out at Lil' Keith, then Sin appeared from behind the little boy. She waved for Keith to come in with a smile.

Keith hopped out, looking fresh to death in the new clothes India had splurged on him. She had oiled his dreads and trimmed the loose ends, making Keith look like new money in the D.

As he climbed the two steps up the porch, Sin gave him a half hug, then asked if he'd like to come in. Keith looked past her shoulder at all the kids running around in the living room.

"Can't we go someplace else? Somewhere close by?"

"I told you I have to stay here with my brothers and sisters. They feel more like my damn kids." Sin turned and hollered inside for them to stop running around.

Keith knew how it was for his own momma to be on crack. She'd been to jail a few times herself, so he knew what Sin was going through, and he felt her pain.

"I tell you what . . . I'ma shoot over here to this pizza spot I seen on the way over and grab us all something to eat, then we can kick it, ya heard me?"

"Ah, you don't have to do that," said Sin. But Keith had seen all her siblings, and he knew a hungry face when he saw one. They were all hungry.

"It's nothing, and besides that, I want to."

Born to Die 177

"You're gonna come back, aren't you?" Sin said, thinking maybe Keith had seen how bad she was living and was just saying anything to get out of there.

He started laughing, then assured her that he wasn't trying to play her.

"Of course I'm coming back. Give me twenty minutes, ya heard me?"

Lil' Keith put his hand around her bare waist, and Sin smiled. He couldn't front; she was as bad as the night he'd met her at the club, even standing there with her hair up in a scarf and thong flip flops on her feet.

Keith ordered ten meat lover's pizzas and Buffalo wings, figuring that should be enough for everybody. While the kids attacked the boxes, Sin was able to pull Keith into her room in the back for a bit of privacy.

Keith knew he was in the projects for sure when he watched Sin twist and turn a combination into the padlock she had on her bedroom door. He was surprised as to how neat and clean she had everything. It was like stepping into a whole different apartment: clean carpet, fresh linens on the bed, and a new stereo and television.

"Make yourself comfortable," Sin said, waving a hand toward her twin-size bed.

Keith flopped down and swung his feet off the edge while he watched Sin move about the room. She was digging through a couple of bags of clothes she had on the floor in the corner. Keith could see that most of the clothes still had price tags on them. He wasn't slow to the game. She was boosting clothes. That explained why she was so fly at the club that night.

"What you smirking at?" Sin asked as she turned around, holding a pair of Guess shorts and a matching shirt.

"Nothing, ya heard me?"

"No, what? Tell me," Sin insisted.

178   Dorian Sykes

"I was just peeping out ya hustle, but I respect it."

"Is that right? And what is it that you hustle, 'cause just the other day you were in a new Jag, and now today you show up in a BMW. How can I be down?" Sin joked.

"I'ma head bussa, not a hustla. I get mine's the hard way, ya heard me?"

Sin stood on one leg, looking at Keith. "And what's a head bussa, anyway?"

"Let's just say niggas pay me not to kill 'em."

Sin grunted and turned with the clothes. "Sounds like my brother Jamar. All he wanna do is rob somebody."

"If that's his hustle, then what's wrong with that? Maybe that's all he's good at."

"You're not too good at it if you get caught and end up in jail every time."

Keith thought about this for a moment and how many times he'd been to jail himself. Was he and Sin's brother one and the same?

"What's wrong? I ain't hit a nerve, did I?" she asked.

"Nah, it's all good."

"Good. 'Cause I respect ya hustle too, long as you're eating off it. And you seem to be doing just fine."

If only she knew that Keith was dead broke, other than the money India had just laid on him, and he'd probably been to jail more times than her brother.

Sin grabbed a nickel bag of weed from out of her purse, along with a Swisher Sweets blunt, then sat beside Keith on the bed. "You smoke?" she asked, rolling the blunt into her wet mouth to moisten the leaf.

"Better," Keith said, pulling out a few blows wrapped in lotto tickets. He opened one for Sin to see.

She scrunched up her face and grunted at the yellowish powder. "Ain't you too young to be messing with coke?"

Born to Die

"Who said anything about coke? This here is boy."

Sin wasn't hip to the street slang of drugs.

"Heroin," Keith said. He took a sniff, killing the paper.

Sin watched him. "How does it make you feel?"

Keith's eyes were glazed over as he pulled back a cheap grin, showing his fronts. "It's the best feeling in the world," he told her. "Here, try one and tell me it's not the best feeling you ever had."

Sin took one of the open blows and slowly lifted it to her nose. She closed her eyes and inhaled the whole thing in one snort. She gagged and coughed for a minute, then sat back as the boy took her on a beautiful ride, one that she'd never been on a day in her young life.

"Huh?" Keith said, smiling down at her. "Feels good, right?"

All Sin could do for a while was smile. The high was mellow and chill and had her feeling like a cool million.

Keith moved in for the pussy, knowing that it would be the best sex Sin had ever had in her life. He slid her from out the sky-blue capris she had tattooed to her fat ass and camel toe pussy. Keith grew five inches at the sight of Sin's hairless pussy throbbing in his face. She smelled like a fresh bath and scented oils. Her pussy was seeping wet with anticipation as she lay on her back with her eyes closed and one finger creasing her slit, inviting Keith to do the damage. They fucked themselves into a sweat. Keith finally came after two hours of raw sex.

Sin brushed back Keith's dreads from his face as she lay across his chest. "Let's do another one."

Keith smiled because he knew he had one in Sin. He'd turn her out, and she'd be his little ride-or-die chick while he was up in Detroit.

He set her up with another blow, and then they went for round two in the sheets.

CHAPTER TWENTY-NINE

Lil' Keith had been spending a lot of time with Sin, and he was learning something new about her every day, like the fact that boosting clothes wasn't her only hustle. She confided in Keith that she was at the club that night looking for a baller type nigga—one that her girls could trick someplace, tie their ass up, and then rob them for everything while they lay there, defenseless, thinking they'd be swimming in some pussy. That was their main hustle.

Sin told Keith that it took everything in her not to do him the same way because she was genuinely feeling him the whole night. She had told him that the reason her brother was in prison this time was because she had set up this balla for him. She'd lured him to a hotel room where her brother and two of his boys were waiting in the bathroom. She did her thing, tying the balla up, and had him thinking he was about to hit, but her brother sprang from the bathroom, gun in hand.

Sin left, figuring her brother and his boys could take it from there. The nigga she'd tied up shot her a death stare as she quickly dressed and left.

Her brother got greedy, though, and demanded one million dollars from the nigga's people instead of the $100,000 Sin knew he'd be good for. His peoples put the police on them, and now he sat in prison for kidnapping, serving a twenty-to-sixty-year sentence.

182   Dorian Sykes

To make things worse, the nigga she'd set up put a ticket on her head.

"How much?" Keith asked, figuring that if it was enough, he'd down her ass himself. Really!

"Ten thousand." Sin wept as she lay curled into Keith's lap. They were at Chene Park, sitting on a bench facing the Detroit River. "What am I going to do?" whined Sin.

Lil' Keith never failed to seize the moment. Here it was. She had let him know that she was pretty much living in fear for her life. The nigga she set up name was T. Roy, and he was heavy in the streets. A Mack Avenue nigga who was killing them on the weed, so dropping stacks on her head was chump change to him. It was only a matter of time before a head bussa came to collect the guap off her head. Keith knew she was in a vulnerable position, not to mention she had picked up a growing habit of messing with the heroin they had been snorting every time they freaked off, which was at least twice a day.

As much as Keith liked Sin, he still refused to let her into his heart. He had grown up so hard that he was cold-hearted to the point where he'd never allow himself to love another soul. He was secretly afraid of loving someone because the people who were supposed to love him always did the opposite.

Keith was looking for a reason to be his cutthroat self with Sin, as he was with everybody else, and her dilemma gave him that reason. And besides that, Keith couldn't get past her out slicking him that night at the club.

"I got you, ya heard me? Long as you with me, I ain't gonna let nothing happen to you, ya understand me?"

Sin believed him at his word. For some reason, she felt safe in Keith's arms. He was the gangsta missing in her life.

Sin must've been reading Keith's mind when she told him that she had another balla nigga who'd been sweatin' her that they could set up.

Born to Die

"I'm listening," said Keith.

Sin ran the lick down to Keith, and the shit sounded like a sweet, smooth come-up. Sin was a scheming bitch, no doubt. She had the nigga's whole steelo down to a science. She said that she'd been sitting on this lick for a while because she hadn't had anyone worthy of putting up on game until Keith.

The lick was supposed to be for $200,000. Sin told Lil' Keith that this nigga name E-Major had made love to her over a bedspread full of money that she watched him pull from his safe. He told her it was two hundred bands.

Probably a hundred bands, Keith thought, knowing how niggas always put ten on shit. But still, the lick sounded real good. Too good to pass on.

"Tell me everything you know about this nigga, ya heard me?" Keith wanted a full rundown—every detail—because he'd been playing the game so long that he knew it was always the smallest thing that made the difference on whether or not the lick went straight.

CHAPTER THIRTY

"Wesley! Move your feet! Side to side, just like I showed you." Uncle Oliver sighed out of frustration.

He and Marcus were standing ringside watching Wesley, Uncle Oliver's prize MMA fighter, work out with his trainer.

Uncle Oliver slapped his hand down on the ring for the action to cease. He climbed up into the ring and collared Wesley, a Brazilian flyweight. He was grilling Wesley to get his head together because they had a big fight coming up, which millions would be bet on.

Marcus stood watching the activities of the gym, which was owned by Uncle Oliver. It was all state-of-the-art; Uncle Oliver had spared no expense. Next to yachting, Mixed Martial Arts was his pastime—one that he took as seriously as a heart attack.

Uncle Oliver climbed back out of the ring, patting the sweat from his face with a towel he wore around his neck. His eyes hadn't left Wesley as he finally spoke a word to Marcus since his arrival two hours before.

Marcus was there because he was ready to get down. It had been two weeks since their first meeting. Marcus and Jasmeen had just been enjoying each other and reconnecting from Marcus's stint in jail, but now it was go time.

"Fifty thousand a kilo," Uncle Oliver said, his eyes on Wesley's footwork.

Marcus could tell from Uncle Oliver's clipped tone that he wasn't talking about fifty Gs on consignment as Marcus had hoped. Oliver wanted it all upfront.

Uncle Oliver was willing to deal with Marcus on the strength of Jasmeen, plus he took a liking to Marcus, yet it was still business, not to be confused for anything else. He wanted to know that Marcus was bringing something to the table, as Blue had when he plugged him in.

Uncle Oliver always believed that if a person has their own money tied up into something, then they'd be less likely to fuck over it. When he gave out consignment, there would always be a story followed by another story. Uncle Oliver ran a hand-over-fist operation—quick, easy, and always the best dope the region had ever seen.

Marcus didn't have anything close to $50,000, but he wasn't about to tell Uncle Oliver that.

"When can I see you?" he asked in complete confidence as if he had a bag of money right then.

"Thursday. Meet me at the club. I'll have it for you then. How many do you want?"

"Just one for now."

"One it is. And yeah, big bills only. Makes it easier to move."

"I got you."

Marcus said goodbye to Uncle Oliver, leaving him standing outside the ring. Marcus left the gym lost in thought because he had no clue where or how he'd come up with the money by Thursday, which was only two days away. He wasn't salty that Uncle Oliver hadn't fronted him the work instead. He understood why, although it would've been nice and would've made things a lot easier. But then again, nothing in Marcus's life had ever come easy. Always the hard way. Marcus was used to getting his off the floor.

Born to Die

He sat up and gripped the steering wheel with both hands as he pushed India's Jaguar down Woodward Avenue. He had the sunroof pushed back with the sun shining down on his oiled dreads. His favorite CD, *All Eyez on Me,* was in. Pac always got him ready to either kill something or get his shine on.

Marcus was ready to get his shine on as he dipped through lunch-hour traffic. He had a good feeling about the come-up money he needed to get on. He didn't know where it was going to come from, but when Thursday came around, he'd have that money in Uncle Oliver's hand.

CHAPTER THIRTY-ONE

The inside of the little greasy spoon, Connie & Barbara's, was packed to the hilt with the early morning crowd trying to get their fill of some of the famous breakfast being served up.

Lil' Keith stood wedged between Sin and her girlfriend, Nadine, at the counter as they ordered their food. It was six o'clock in the morning. Keith, Sin, and Nadine had been clubbing all night and drinking too much liquor, so they needed some grease to put on their stomachs.

Lil' Keith took them clubbing because he figured that since they were already some grimy bitches, he might as well use them for what they were worth, which was setting up niggas for the kill.

Lil' Keith played the V.I.P. upstairs, overlooking the floor of the club, watching all night as Sin and Nadine baked niggas' cakes, swapping numbers and setting up dates. The night had gone well; both Sin and Nadine had come up with good prospects. Sin was all in now that she had a full-blown heroin habit. She was doing half of a bundle daily, and she'd easily turned Nadine out as well.

As they waited for their orders to come up, two men cloaked in all black with hoodies on bust through the door, AKs in hand. They were pushing through the distracted crowd, almost going unnoticed.

Lil' Keith was on point, though. He kept his eyes on the door with his back to the counter. He didn't know who they had come for, but they were making their way toward them. As the first gunman raised his chopper, taking aim at Sin's back as she chatted with Nadine. Keith ducked down from the line of fire. The gunmen opened fire on Sin, riddling her body with burning-hot 223s. She was dead before her body hit the floor. As screaming patrons fled from the diner, the two gunmen stood over Sin and riddled her some more, ensuring her a closed casket ceremony.

When the smoke cleared, Keith lay beneath a stool at the counter, clutching his leaking shoulder. He'd been grazed by one of the bullets as the gunmen relentlessly slaughtered Sin. Her girlfriend Nadine was lying beside Keith in a thick, purplish pool of blood. She was staring up at the spinning ceiling fan, slowly losing her fight with the angel of death. She tried to speak as Lil' Keith stood from the floor. *Don't leave me here to die,* she thought as she watched Lil' Keith hastily making his way out of there.

What she didn't know was that Lil' Keith was a cold-hearted nigga. He'd leave his own momma stankin' if it came down to it. Self-preservation was the only rule in Keith's ill world, besides loyalty. And at that moment, his only concern was getting to the hospital.

As he drove along Outer Drive, smoking a Newport to calm his nerves, he lost consciousness at the wheel. He ended up swerving two lanes over, side-swiping a woman in a Grand Prix before climbing the sidewalk at the intersection of Outer Drive and Van Dyke. He burled into the parking lot of McTyrone's, crashing into the drive-thru window as cars sat waiting.

When Lil' Keith woke up, he was lying in a hospital bed at St. John's. His mind flashed back to the gunmen rushing into the diner and then Sin lying dead on the floor. There was no doubt in his mind who had put the hit down on Sin. It was the nigga T. Roy and the ten thousand he had promised to the streets.

Lil' Keith wasn't salty about Sin getting her issue because she knew the consequences of the game she was playing. Not only that, but she had been running a game since the night Lil' Keith first met her at the club. Come to find out, the nigga she kept claiming was her brother was really her man. Nadine had confessed this to Keith, trying to get close to him behind Sin's back. So, to Keith, Sin had got what she had coming. It was all G with him, though, because at least before she died, he'd gotten the full rundown on T. Roy and knew just how to catch him down bad.

A sharp pain shot through Keith's left shoulder as he tried to sit up in bed. He grimaced as he gave himself the will to fight through the pain. *How long I been in here? I gotta get the fuck up outta here*, Keith thought as he tore the I.V. out of his arm and swung his legs around the side of the bed. He had on a gown. *Where the fuck is my clothes?* As he sat on the bed, searching the cold room for any signs of his clothes, the shift nurse stepped in to check on him.

"My, what are you doing out of bed? You need to relax and get some rest, 'cause we nearly lost you. You lost a lot of blood."

"Have you seen my clothes?" Keith asked, disregarding the woman's concern. He was ready to be up out of there.

"They had to cut your clothes off when you came in because you were soaked in blood." The young white nurse tried to get Lil' Keith back in bed, but he stood and fought through the pain.

"I gotta get outta here."

192   Dorian Sykes

"But sir, the doctors haven't released you. You need your rest."

The nurse followed Keith out into the halls. He was searching for the elevators.

"Sir, would you please—"

Lil' Keith spun around with death in his eyes when he told the nurse to leave him the fuck alone and to stop following him. For all he knew, she was trying to stall him out until the police got there so they could try to get him to snitch on who had shot him.

Lil' Keith found the elevators and took one down to the lobby. *Where the fuck is my car at?* he thought, stepping off the elevator. He was barefoot in nothing but a gown. He caught stares as he used the payphone to call India at home, collect.

"We'll be right there to get you. Oh my God!" India said in a rush to get off the phone.

Lil' Keith was about to go stand inside the gift shop when the shift nurse rounded the corner with two detectives on her heels.

"There he is," she said, pointing to Lil' Keith.

The two pot-bellied black detectives quickly closed the space between them and Lil' Keith. They flashed their gold shields and introduced themselves as Detectives Cooper and Allen. "Young man, we need to get you back upstairs and into the bed so you can rest up. My partner and I here, we're going to find who did this to you, but we need you to answer some questions," said Detective Cooper.

"I'm checking myself out. My people are on they way to get me," said Keith.

"But the doctors haven't released you," spat the nurse.

"I'm releasing me. Or should I have my lawyer come down here? Am I under arrest?"

Born to Die   193

"No, we just want to find who did this to you," said Cooper.

"Well, I can't help you with that."

"And why is that?" asked Cooper.

"Because I don't speak Pig Latin. Now, unless y'all arresting me, I'm finna leave, ya heard me?" said Lil' Keith.

The Detectives took a step apart, allowing Lil' Keith to pass by. He waited outside the emergency room, wishing that India would hurry up because he didn't want the dicks pulling back up on him with more questions. He had no I.D. on him. The yellow band on his wrist had said "John Doe," and he wanted to keep his identity unknown to them.

Lil' Keith was relieved when he saw India's Jaguar whip into the parking lot. She sped around the turn and hopped from the car, double-parking beside an awaiting ambulance. She rushed around the car for Lil' Keith.

"Oh my God, are you okay?" she asked, examining him from head to toe. "Where's your clothes, baby?"

Lil' Keith turned her around by her shoulders. "I'll tell you about it in the car. Come on, let's get outta here, ya heard me?" He kept looking back over his shoulder into the lobby.

India rushed them out of there. She kept looking over at the blood-stained gauze on Keith's shoulder.

"Are you hurt anywhere else?" she asked.

"Nah, I'm straight. Just a scrape. Ain't nothing, ya heard me?"

"You call being shot nothing? You could have been killed, Keith. What happened?"

Lil' Keith really didn't feel like talking because the only thing he could think about was finding T. Roy so he could rob him, then stank his ass. But just to appease India, he told her that some niggas tried to carjack him at the gas station, and they shot him when he wouldn't get out. She had no reason not to believe him, and so naturally, she felt bad for Keith. Not to mention she was kind of turned on by the whole situation. She had been with her share of bad boys, but none who had ever been shot. Keith took being a bad boy to another level, satisfying her thirst for a troublesome, unpredictable man.

She was all too willing when Lil' Keith told her that he wanted her to buy some guns from the gun store in her name. She would provide him with the type of arsenal a street nigga could only get from Chet's back in New Orleans. He had her grab two AR-15s with 30-round clips and two Chinese AK-47s with 100-round titanium drums. He had her grab two .40 cal Berrettas with extra 30-round dicks and boxes of shells for each gun.

Lil' Keith faulted himself for the gunmen making it that close to him and Sin in the first place because he had seen them from the jump. If he had been armed, then he could have slumped both of them niggas. *Never again will I ever get caught naked without my yeah,* Lil' Keith thought.

He had to click back into mode and remind himself that it was still murder. He wasn't in the N.O. He still had to play the game in the raw.

CHAPTER THIRTY-TWO

When Lil' Keith got back to the house and ran the lick down to Marcus about T. Roy, there wasn't a question to be asked whether they'd be suiting up or not. The lick was just what Marcus needed anyway to come up with the money for him to plug in with Uncle Oliver.

He hadn't told Jasmeen that he needed $50,000 because he knew she'd only persist in being the one to come up with the money, and this was something he wanted to do as a man. Besides that, he didn't want Uncle Oliver to feel as though he wasn't man enough to front the money himself.

Marcus and Lil' Keith got suited in all black while both Jasmeen and India were sound asleep. It was going on two o'clock in the morning when Marcus and Lil' Keith crept out of the house, each toting brand new AKs.

T. Roy had spent the night balling out at his favorite strip club, 007, on the Eastside of Detroit. Every Friday night until the early morning, T. Roy and his Mack Avenue crew shut the club down, buying the bar out and commanding the attention of every bad bitch in attendance.

The club let out around 1:45 in the A.M. Usually, T. Roy and his crew would head over to Hoe Joe's, a raunchy after-hours joint where head, pussy, and anything else one was in search of could be found.

Nina, one of the strippers from 007, had been seducing T. Roy all night as she privately danced for him inside the V.I.P. section. She wanted to go home with T. Roy because he was known to drop five racks or better whenever he tricked. She was under his arm, working her ho skills as the club let out. T. Roy was liquored up, and Nina had him fiending to get between her chocolate thighs. T. Roy nodded to his crew, saying that he'd get up with them in the morning and that they should go ahead without him.

"You sure, Unc?" his nephew asked, looking from T. Roy to Nina. He didn't trust leaving anyone around his uncle.

"Yeah, it's straight. I'ma see you tomorrow," T. Roy assured his nephew as his white-on-white Lexus truck pulled into the valet.

Lil' Keith had gotten Sin to show him where T. Roy laid his head when he wasn't in the city. T. Roy lived in a nice colonial out in Southfield, Michigan, only minutes outside of Detroit.

Lil' Keith and Marcus were waiting inside the house in the dark. Sin was so vicious in her plotting that she made spare keys for all of T. Roy's key rings one morning when he had sent her out to buy some blunts. She had kept the keys, knowing that the day would come when she'd have him dead to the wrong, with goons waiting to relieve him of the safe he so openly flaunted around.

Lil' Keith and Marcus had found the safe embedded inside the closet of the master bedroom. Now all they needed was for T. Roy to come open it.

"Round," Marcus whispered through the darkness of the living room. "I think somebody's coming," he told Lil' Keith. He heard the garage door opening, and then a car pulled in.

Born to Die 197

Showtime, thought Lil' Keith. He and Marcus stood in the kitchen with their AKs dead aimed at the door leading into the kitchen and basement. Two car doors shut, then the doorknob turned and opened. Nina was still working her game on T. Roy, saying all the right shit as they entered the kitchen. She flinched and then screamed after walking face first into the cold steel barrel of Lil' Keith's rifle.

"Bitch, don't move," growled Lil' Keith as Marcus clicked the lights on. T. Roy stared, motionless, at the unmasked men in his house. "Do y'all know who y'all fuckin' with?" he asked, looking from Marcus to Lil' Keith.

"Yeah, nigga, a dead man, if you don't shut the fuck up and come open dis here safe," spat Lil' Keith.

T. Roy squinted his eyes down to a slit. He had never seen these two young niggas before a day in his life, but here they stood with balls bigger than King Kong's for having tried him.

T. Roy looked to Nina and asked heatedly, "Bitch, is this yo' work? 'Cause if it is, you finna die right beside these two niggas."

They had done too much talking for Marcus. He cocked back and split T. Roy's shit with the butt of his AK. He grabbed T. Roy up by his arm and steered him for the safe. "Tie that ho up, round," he said over his shoulder to Lil' Keith.

T. Roy was leaking from a deep gash over the bridge of his nose. His hands were covered with blood as he stood defiantly in front of the safe.

Marcus wasn't about to play no games with this nigga. Either he was going to open the safe up, or he was going to spank the nigga. He upped the rifle to T. Roy's face and ordered him to open it.

"Nigga, fuck you," T. Roy said, accepting his fate. He wasn't a nigga who was going to beg for his life under no circumstances.

Marcus respected the nigga's G, but that didn't stop him from blasting him twice in the face, killing him instantly.

"Say, round, help me back here with this here." Marcus came out, stepping over T. Roy's lifeless body on the floor.

"We gone have to snatch the bitch out the wall and take it with us."

"Step back," said Lil' Keith. "I just got an idea."

He aimed his AK at the safe's combination dial and squeezed five 223s straight through it.

"There! Problem solved," he said as the safe's door swung open, smoking from the gunfire.

Staring them in the face were neat stacks of hundreds and fifties. Marcus quickly snatched a pillow off the bed and used the case to empty out the safe. He knew they'd been in the house for too long, especially with shots fired, so he told Lil' Keith to go down T. Roy's bitch while he got the car.

Lil' Keith had Nina tied up inside the washroom, sitting on the floor with a gag in her mouth. Her pretty eyes watered as Lil' Keith stepped inside the washroom with his AK dead-aimed at her chest. He relentlessly rocked her to sleep—all chest shots—instantly killing her.

He slipped out of the house undetected and found Marcus waiting up the block in their getaway car. They slipped away from the scene, leaving not a trace of evidence, something that they'd never done before in their careers as head bussas.

CHAPTER THIRTY-THREE

Marcus and Lil' Keith got a cheap room at the Suez Motel on 8 Mile and Ryan Road.

Lil' Keith couldn't count to ten, so he posted up by the room's window, watching the early morning traffic, while Marcus put a count on their lick money. Marcus was on his knees in the middle of the twin-sized bed, counting in G-stacks.

"What we lookin' like, round?" Keith let go of the curtain and faced the small mountains of dead presidents neatly stacked on the bed.

Marcus was just finishing his count with the last thousand. "Exactly $196,000 to the good, ya heard me?"

Lil' Keith pulled back a cheap grin and thought, *I guess the nigga wasn't lying*. He pushed off the wall and joined Marcus on the bed.

"Look, round, I know you really wanna get ya thang going and off the ground, and I'm with you, ya heard me? Why don't you take $150,000 to get straight with and leave me the rest."

"Say no more, ya heard me? You already know you half with me down the middle," said Marcus, giving his partna some dap.

Lil' Keith squinched his face and shook his head, dismissing the partnership. That's yo' thing, ya heard me? I'ma die high, round."

"And I'ma still have ya back, ya understand me?"

"And same here, round."

Marcus pushed $46,000 at Lil' Keith, then pillow-cased the rest back up. Instead of copping just one brick, he was going to double up with two.

"So, when you going to get straight? 'Cause you know it's 'bout time we shake the spot and hit back to the crib, ya heard me?"

"I'm finna dip soon as the sun comes up good. And I say we should be back in the N.O. in two days tops."

"Good, 'cause I swear I miss the crib, round."

"Keep it a hunnid, round. What you missin' is that good 911, ya understand me?"

All Lil' Keith could do was flash his Aarons. His partna knew him all too well.

CHAPTER THIRTY-FOUR

Uncle Oliver did all his business from his office at the gym. He made Marcus wait until he finished his morning sparring session before they got down to business.

Marcus watched ringside as Uncle Oliver practiced his ground-and-pound technique. He moved pretty well for a man his age. Marcus doubted if he'd last two rounds in the ring with the old man.

Uncle Oliver and his partner slapped gloves, ending their session.

"Good work, Raul. Same time tomorrow," Oliver said as he made his way out of the ring. He patted at the sweat pouring down his face with a white towel he had swung around his neck. He gulped down an Aquafina bottled water, then smiled at the sight of the pillowcase clutched tight at Marcus's side.

"You always carry your money around in a pillowcase?"

"It all counts and spends the same," shot Marcus.

"I was just busting your balls. Come on and follow me," Uncle Oliver yanked his head, urging Marcus to step with him up to his office overlooking the gym floor.

"Can I get you anything to drink? All we got is water and Gatorade," Oliver said, entering the crisp, AC-cooled air inside his office.

"Nah, I'm straight."

"All business this morning. It's nothing wrong with that." Oliver settled behind his desk with his arms draped kingly over the armrest of his high-winged-back chair. "How much you bring me?"

"A hundred thousand."

"All big bills, I expect?"

Marcus answered his question by pouring the neat G-stacks of hundreds and fifties across the desktop.

"When can I get started?"

Uncle Oliver nodded solemnly at the money before him. "You know, I doubted that you'd be able to come up with the money without leaning on my niece, but as a man, I admit that I was wrong about you."

"No need for an apology. Let's just get to the business."

Uncle Oliver nodded, then slid back in his chair and stood for the wall locker behind his desk. He pushed it aside, revealing a safe built into the wall. He spun the combination, opened the safe, and then began tossing the money inside, locking it back after he finished.

"Follow me," he said, leading Marcus out of the office and through the gym into the locker room, where there were stairs leading down into the basement. Marcus followed him through the damp basement into a secret room, the walls of which were made of brown bricks. Uncle Oliver pulled three of the bricks from the middle of the wall and dug his hand around, pulling out a black duct-taped kilo, then another, and handed them both to Marcus.

Staring down at the two kilos in his hands, Marcus felt like he had a million dollars in his grasp. He'd handled many kilos before, but they'd never belonged to him. They were always from capers Tank had sent him and Lil' Keith on.

"I remember my first kilo," Uncle Oliver said, seeing the look on Marcus's face. He replaced the bricks in the wall, then led Marcus back upstairs to the gym, where they parted ways.

"So, when will you be ready for your next score?"

"It shouldn't be long, but I'll let you know."

Uncle Oliver put his hands on Marcus's shoulders and then gave him some Godfather advice about the game.

"Get in and get out, you hear me? This is not a game one should think he can play for the rest of his life. Hell, I wish every day that I could retire and spend the rest of my days on my yacht. Don't let this life take you under. Get what you came for, and that's it."

Marcus nodded solemnly at his advice. He had no plans of getting caught up by all the hype that comes with the game. He and Jasmeen had their game plan: five million, then game over.

CHAPTER THIRTY-FIVE

India was disappointed that Lil' Keith was leaving for New Orleans. She would have done anything to get him to stay there in Detroit. "I thought you loved me," she said with tears on the brink of falling from her pretty hazel eyes. She was following Keith around her master bedroom as he got dressed to leave. Marcus and Jasmeen were already ready and waiting for him downstairs.

"Shorty, look. I don't know what love is, ya heard me? You's a good girl. I'm sure some nigga gone swoop you up, ya dig?" Keith said, stopping for a brief moment to face India.

"But I don't want nobody else. I want you."

"Shorty, you's the type of girl a nigga marries. I'm the type of nigga a woman doesn't, ya understand me?"

"No, I don't understand. I love you, Keith."

Lil' Keith was no good at being sensitive. He didn't know what else he could tell her besides "bye." He turned and finished dressing, then made his way downstairs, where he found Jasmeen and Marcus waiting with their things in the living room.

India was crying with no shame, pleading for Keith not to leave or to allow her to come with him back to New Orleans. Keith was ignoring her pleas, though. He had only one thing on his mind: returning to the N.O.

Jasmeen was salty with her cousin because she knew things would end badly between Keith and India. That's why she hadn't wanted India messing with Keith to begin with. He was only good for having a good time, not for falling in love, and Jasmeen had tried telling her this from the start.

"Y'all go 'head and wait in the car while I say bye to India," Jasmeen told them.

Outside, Marcus and Lil' Keith waited in their rental truck. Their flight didn't leave for another two hours.

"Round, why you scared to bring her with you? You see she loves you, ya heard me?" wondered Marcus.

"That bitch don't love a nigga, ya dig? She love dis dope dick, ya understand me? Plus, I ain't got time fo' no bitch all up on a nigga when we get back to the crib, ya understand me?"

Really, Lil' Keith had been afraid to let anyone get close enough to hurt him. He felt that no one could ever hurt him if he were always the one walking out on people. And Marcus understood this about his partna.

The front door of the house swung open, and Jasmeen hugged India goodbye out on the porch. Her eyes were still pleading for Keith to let her come as she stared at him through the back window of the truck. Keith lit a Newport and refused to look her way, though. He wished Jasmeen would hurry the fuck up. He couldn't wait to be back in the sky and on their way back to the N.O.

Jasmeen climbed behind the wheel and slammed the door, letting her attitude ring out through the truck. She gave Marcus and Lil' Keith the silent treatment as they drove to the airport, refusing to cut on the radio.

But Lil' Keith didn't give a fuck. "Just get me back to the crib, ya heard me?"

There was plenty of pussy waiting on him back in the Boot, and plenty of beef he couldn't wait to dive into. He missed his hood—down in the dirty—and all the beefs they had going down between wards and sets. Detroit had been a nice getaway, but no place was like New Orleans.

Born to Die   207

The nervousness Lil' Keith first felt when they flew out to Detroit was now excitement. He couldn't wait for the plane to take off as they sat on the tarmac. The only thing he could think of was Tank and how he had left them for dead.

Looking out at the horizon from his window seat, Lil' Keith made Tank a solemn promise. . . . *I'ma down ya fat ass, ya heard me?*

CHAPTER THIRTY-SIX

Back in New Orleans

Detective Lewis got a call from his office that Marcus and Lil' Keith were on their way from the airport.

"Yesss!" he said, cradling an aged phone against the receiver.

He stood up and snatched his badge and gun from the stack of files decorating his battered steel desk. He rushed for the door, bypassing questions from his sergeant and lieutenants regarding the files he was supposed to be working on. He had bigger fish to fry. His two arch nemeses were back, and this time, he'd personally nail them to the cross if it was the last thing he did on God's earth.

Lewis peeled away from the Fifth District in his unmarked Chevy Impala. He shut off his police scanner, not wanting any distractions from his set destination. He pulled in front of Club 360 and parked at the entrance, leaving his hazards on and blocking the valet.

Tank leaned forward toward the video monitors upstairs inside his office at the sight of Lewis making his way into the club.

"Fuck this bitch want now?" he said just above a whisper. He stood from the blow job his new shot-girl was performing and fixed himself quickly, then ushered her out. Tank had come out of his rathole since there were no signs of Marcus and Lil' Keith around the city. Deeco and Courtney had been to every ward and every set looking for them so they could down them, but no one had seen or heard from Marcus or Lil' Keith since they had gotten out. Tank went back to his ballin' boss ways of running the dope game and tricking off on bad bitches. His life had returned to normal, except for this unwanted visit by Detective Lewis.

Tank was behind his minibar getting himself a cold bottle of Cristal from the fridge when Lewis knocked once, then came in bearing a wide grin across his scruffy face.

He got straight down to business. With his smile stretching to his eyes, he said, "Guess who's back in town?"

Tank wasn't for the guessing game. "Who, ya mammy?"

Lewis came over to the bar and grabbed a bottle of Scotch, removing its cork. "Even better," he said, turning up a good swallow, then said, "Your two henchmen. And I'd imagine that they're coming to kill your ass for leaving 'em out there. I know I would."

Tank took a swallow from his champagne. "Why you care? Either way, you win, right?"

"I win when I see those two shitheads with the needle shoved in their arms."

"And you think I'm finna help you with that?"

Lewis closed the space between them. "Yesss," he hissed his funky breath all over Tank's face.

Lewis was determined not to let the feds snatch Lil' Keith and Marcus from under him. He'd been on their tail for too long to let some stiff backs just move in and take all the credit. He was so close to bringing them down. All he needed was for Tank to play ball, and he'd have his convictions.

Lewis was so desperate that he did something he'd never before done in his career. He told Tank that in exchange for him helping bring down Marcus and Lil' Keith, he'd look the other way on Tank's drug operation.

"You gone have to come better than that," Tank said. He already had cops on his payroll.

"Fine." Lewis gritted his teeth. He wanted this bad. "You give me something that'll stick, and I'll open up the evidence room to you. Drugs, guns, and evidence to be used in court against you and your people will all be at your disposal. Everything!" stressed Lewis.

"Let me think about it."

"You do that, damn it. And you call me when you're ready to deal."

Lewis left Tank in his office to think things over. No doubt, Tank was an opportunist. He saw a gold mine with Lewis's proposition, but he still wanted to send Deeco and Courtney at Lil' Keith and Marcus before he jumped the gun and got in bed with the devil. That would be a last-resort option for fixing his problem.

CHAPTER THIRTY-SEVEN

Club Rockefeller was off the chain on any given weekend. It was a hood spot uptown that all the project chicks and street niggas flocked to. The Rock is what they called it for short. There was no telling which one of your enemies you might run into in there because the whole city was in the spot.

Deeco and Courtney were regulars at The Rock. They'd shut the club down every Friday and Saturday night, buying out the bar all night with their foreign whips parked in valet. Tonight was no different as they posted up in V.I.P., drinking Dom P and smoking kush.

Following his drop-in visit with Lewis, Tank had given them the news about Lil' Keith and Marcus supposedly being back in N.O.

"I want this done A.S.A.P, ya understand me?" Tank had told them.

Deeco and Courtney would start combing the streets first thing in the morning, but tonight, they were going to ball out how they'd been doing on the daily since they joined Tank's crime family. They had gotten spoiled and lazy by all the steady money coming their way from Tank's heroin ring. They'd put in some work here and there, but the streets were pretty much in check, leaving them to ball out whenever. They were slipping on their game as head bussas because while they were in the clubs all night, the next head bussas in line were in the shadows, lurking to take their spot in the game. It wasn't

214   Dorian Sykes

a secret they were eating with Tank. Everybody in the streets knew.

Lil' Keith got right fresh off the plane. He hit the set on V.L. and had a fiend take them up to Chet's gun store and bought all brand new choppers and .40 cals with extendos, 30 rounds dripping from everything, and two 63-shot clips for the AK-47s. He had got word that Deeco was home back when they were in The Parish, and he was ready to go see about the nigga for having sold him and Marcus all that death. Plus, Marcus and Lil' Keith came to the understanding that Marcus would focus on putting things together on the dope side, while Lil' Keith laid his murder game down on any nigga standing in their way. For Lil' Keith, it was the perfect arrangement because killing always came naturally to him. And besides that, he would've killed Tank and his flunkies just on the strength. They were going to get their issue regardless.

Lil' Keith was back on his bullshit. He suited up in his favorite black fatigues, ACG boots, and ski mask, then hit the streets with his brand-new Russian AK, riding in the stolen Camaro. He rode through his hood up Valance and Magnolia Streets. He spotted Samuel standing outside the store, nursing a pint of bumpy face and smoking a square. Lil' Keith hit the horn, then waved Samuel to come over.

Samuel squinted in the darkness, then pulled back a grin, exposing his blackened gums, seeing that it was his partna Lil' Keith. He grabbed the door handle of the passenger side and slid his bag of bones into the car.

"'Sup, round? Where you been at?" he asked, giving Lil' Keith some love.

Born to Die

215

"Shit, chillin', ya heard me? Where's ya stickman, Black Boy?"

"Ah, the Impalas rolled thru this mornin', ya heard me, and he had couple grams on him, so he down at The Parish."

Lil' Keith shook his head, not ever wanting to see the inside of that place again. He had made himself a promise on their last trip that he'd hold court in the streets next time before they ever took him in again.

"But dig, round, I came to holla at you 'cause I know you keep ya ear to the streets, ya heard me?"

"Shoot," said Samuel.

"Where can I find the nigga Deeco at?"

"Aw, that's easy. What's today, Saturday?" Samuel said, answering his own question. He and his partna Courtney be at The Rock out in the Seventeenth, ya heard me?"

Lil' Keith gave Samuel a couple of twenties for the information so he could get himself a fresh bottle and some cigarettes. If anybody knew where to find Deeco, Lil' Keith knew it would be Samuel and Black Boy. They hardly ever left the set, but somehow, they knew every move going down in the city from uptown to downtown.

Lil' Keith drove over to the 17th Ward, all the while massaging the AK-47 in his lap because he knew it was beef on sight with all them niggas. Eventually, he'd get around to spanking all of them, but tonight he only had reservations for Deeco.

Samuel had put Lil' Keith up on what Deeco was pushing around the city. And sure enough, as Lil' Keith pulled up to The Rock, a triple black S500 Benz sat on chrome blades at the curb. *Tank*, thought Lil' Keith.

Lil' Keith looked at the clock on the dashboard. The club would be letting out any minute as it was almost two

216

Dorian Sykes

in the morning. He parked at the alley, giving him a full vantage point of the club's entrance door.

As the club began spilling out, Lil' Keith sat up in his seat, waiting for Deeco to emerge. *There go my bitch*, Lil' Keith thought with a devious smirk as he spotted Deeco and Courtney step outside, seemingly checking their surrounding for any beef.

The valet first brought around Courtney's Range Rover. Courtney dapped up with Deeco for the night, then got in his truck and drove off.

Lil' Keith watched Deeco slip into his Benz and pull away from the club. He eased out into the buzzing traffic and kept his distance a good four cars back from Deeco until they made it a few blocks away from the club. He seemed to be heading into Hollygrove, but Lil' Keith wasn't looking to get into a shoot-out because he knew them niggas went dick hard, just like him.

Deeco got caught at the light right on the edge of Gert Town, a four-way intersection. That was all the time Lil' Keith needed. He put the Camaro in park, then crept from the side of stilled traffic with the AK under a sheet and the ski mask pulled down over his face.

Before anyone knew what was about to go down, Lil' Keith was at the back door of Deeco's 500, letting the K rip. Deeco tried to smash the gas, but he spun out and crashed into a crossing Jeep Cherokee.

As the Benz spun to a stop, all banged up, Lil' Keith ran up on the driver-side door and finished the 63-round clip.

Cars were blaring their horns and speeding out of there, but Lil' Keith was in a zone. He wanted to make sure he'd downed Deeco. He snatched the driver-side door open, confirming his kill.

Deeco slumped out onto the pavement, his flesh and clothes torn to shreds by the tumbling 223s.

Satisfied with his work, Lil' Keith slipped back into the Camaro and peeled away from the scene. He had gotten a rush from the body. It felt good to have blood on his hands again, especially from a nigga he'd been warring with since high school.

Lil' Keith's thoughts instantly flashed to Tank. He couldn't wait to have him on the other side of his gun, begging for his life like the bitch he knew he really was.

CHAPTER THIRTY-EIGHT

Meanwhile, Marcus had set up shop down the street from the methadone clinic on Congress Street in the Florida Projects in the 9th Ward. He rented a cheap hotel room at the Lucky Night's as a temporary setup until he got a steady clientele. Lucky Night's was a prime location because of the clinic, making it dope central, with junkie whores who kept a steady flow of incoming traffic.

Jasmeen was right there by Marcus's side, from helping him make his first bundles of testers that he planned on passing out at the clinic to watching his back with the .40 cal he'd given her. "Five million," she reminded him before he set out on the strip to advertise their new dope on the set. It was her way of letting him know that their plans hadn't changed now that they were in motion. "In and out" was still their motto and game plan.

Marcus had twenty-five bundles down in his briefs as he walked up to the clinic. He eyed every passing car and face out on the sidewalk. Everybody had something going down, it seemed.

As he approached the stained double doors to the clinic, an old familiar face stepped out, nearly bumping into Marcus.

"Nate?" Marcus said, taking in the old-timer. He looked good for a change, wearing clean clothes, and had even put on some weight.

"Ah, what's up, youngsta? Glad to see you out," Nate said, flashing a genuine smile upon Marcus. Nate had come up with Marcus's father in the trenches.

"And I'm glad to see you doing good ya self."

"Yeah, I just finished up two months of rehab. I was tired, you know?"

"So, now what you gone do out here?"

"Lil' bruh, the sky's the limit. I've been down for so long that ain't no place else to go but up."

"I feel that." Marcus remembered briefly the days of ole' Nate killing the heroin game and being a boss playa. "Say, I got something I want you to check out for me to let me know if I got something on my hands or not," said Marcus.

"What you got?"

Marcus looked up and down the sidewalk, then stepped under the awning of the clinic, where a gathering of heroin addicts stood. He peeled two testers out from his sack and handed them to Nate.

"You tryna get me to relapse already?" said Nate as he unfolded the foil packs.

"Damn, my bad." Marcus just knew that if anybody could stamp his new dope, it would be Nate.

Nate said a few words to two of the women amongst them, then handed each one a tester, where they sampled it up right there on the scene. After a few moments, the two women agreed that it was what the city had been missing.

"Who's got that here?" one of the women asked Nate, but instead, he turned and put his arm around Marcus, steering him out of there.

This was the big comeback Nate had been dreaming of. With all his knowledge of the game, with the dope Marcus had in play, he was sure they'd be riding high and millionaires in six months or less.

Nate gave Marcus his pitch as to why they should hook up and how much money they stood to make together.

Born to Die

"What you need, youngin, is two things: a partner and a stamp for your dope."

Marcus was kind of skeptical of bringing Nate in because he was fresh out of rehab, but at the same time, the old nigga could prove to be invaluable, and he had this serious hunger in his eyes that told Marcus he was ready to touch the sky again.

"Let me ask you something," said Marcus.

"Anything."

"How'd you fall off in the first place? I mean, I remember you was one of the flyest niggas when I was coming up. Next thing I knew, you was out there down bad."

Nate explained his plight with one word. "Tank," he said, now staring out against the mid-day traffic along Congress Street.

He gave Marcus the rundown of how Tank played him out of grace into a full-blown dope fiend. Hearing Nate's story only enraged Marcus because he, too, had been played to the left by the same nigga he once considered his Pa.

"Let's get this money, O.G.," Marcus said, hitting rocks with a smiling Nate.

Nate was in bliss about being back in the game.

CHAPTER THIRTY-NINE

Dinyell was on his way from the Bricks, having just checked on their dope spots. He was driving through uptown, recalling his last meeting with his new connect from Texas. They had plugged in, and by next month, their pipeline for heroin would be open to as many kilos as Dinyell could stand.

He was one step closer to knocking Tank out of the picture and taking over the family himself. For months, he'd been stealing money from the top in preparation for funding his first shipment with his new connect.

Dinyell was lost in his thoughts, oblivious to the black Firebird that had pulled up alongside him as he sat at the light on Covington Avenue.

The passenger door swung open, and Lil' Keith pressed his .40 cal to Dinyell's right temple.

"Drive," Lil' Keith ordered as he pulled his hoody over his dreads.

Dinyell growled for having been caught slipping. Lil' Keith pressed further into his wig for him to get going, to which Dinyell made a left turn, leaving the Firebird in the middle of traffic.

"Where is he?" demanded Lil' Keith.

"Where's who?"

"Yo' daddy, nigga. Tank. Who the fuck else?"

Dinyell saw a chance to save himself and a means to eliminating Tank even earlier than he'd planned. "You know, I thought it was fucked up how the nigga played y'all."

224   Dorian Sykes

"Nigga, save that weak-ass shit and take me to this nigga."

"You gon' let me live?"

"Bitch, we'll see."

Tank had gone back into hiding ever since Deeco got spanked leaving the club. Tank knew Marcus and Lil' Keith's work too well for him to mistake it for being someone else's. Thirty to one hundred shots every time, that's how they were coming. Tank had bodyguards around the clock surrounding his downtown estate. The only people who knew where he was were Dinyell and Detective Lewis, who was on his way to see Tank after receiving a call saying that they needed to meet.

Lewis walked into the chateau-styled estate wearing a victorious grin because Tank was about to sell him his soul. Tank received Lewis in his home library, where he stood at the window with his back to the door.

"So, you're ready to deal?" Tank said over his shoulder, never looking at Lewis because he couldn't believe that he was taking the ho route. "I don't want anything from you, or ya evidence room in return for what I'm 'bout to give you. All I want is for them two niggas to never see these streets again and for me to never see you again, ever."

"Done," said Lewis.

Tank half turned and nodded at the AK-47s and two .40 cals laid across his oak wood table. The guns were wrapped in plastic coverings, each with fresh fingerprints.

"Those are from the Lake Chateau Estates, when Marcus and Lil' Keith downed Brett. They should be enough, ya heard me?"

Lewis was like a kid in the candy store as he seized the murder weapons. He'd stash them at Lil' Keith's house and then get a warrant signed to raid the house. *Brilliant,* he thought.

"And you didn't get those from me," Tank said.

"No, I got 'em from that little fucker's house," said Lewis.

As Dinyell pulled up to Tank's downtown estate, Lil' Keith scanned the assortment of cars parked outside, and he stopped when he viewed the unmarked Impala, which he was sure was Five-O. He slapped Dinyell with the barrel of his .40 cal and told him to keep going.

"You tryna set me up, huh, nigga?"

"No!" Dinyell cried out like a bitch.

"Then whose Impala was that back there?"

"I swear, I don't know. I swear."

Lil' Keith was tired of playing with this nigga. He'd get down to the bottom of it himself. As soon as they hit back uptown, Lil' Keith made Dinyell pull over at a BP gas station, and he downed the nigga with four to the side of his head. He pushed his body over next to the pump and kept it moving. He had the drop on Tank now, and he'd most definitely be back to pay him a visit.

CHAPTER FORTY

Ol' Nate was dead on business, helping Marcus bust open spots all around the city, from uptown to downtown, in every project. The spots Tank once had were on their last leg because he was in hiding and Dinyell was dead, leaving all their runners dry.

The city was buzzing about this new dope Nate had stamped "Mix Jive." It had been a long while since the N.O. had anything better than the 911 everyone had grown to love, but what Marcus and Nate had was hands down the best thing going.

Jasmeen was pulling in money twice a day during the morning and evening rush. For the past three days, all she had done was money. Uncle Oliver had long ago taught her to always do her count by hand, for two reasons. He said that money counters made mistakes, plus the feds could plug them in and see how much money you'd been handling.

Jasmeen adhered to the rules set forth by her uncle. She already had the re-up money set aside for another four kilos. She figured they'd need about five flips and be right there at their five-million-dollar quota.

Meanwhile, her father had grown tired of watching his daughter destroy her life, especially knowing that his own brother had provided her with the means to do so.

228 Dorian Sykes

Daddy still had Agent Anderson's F.B.I. card from the last visit that Wallace and Anderson had paid him at his family's restaurant five years prior. Daddy phoned Agent Anderson and arranged a meeting down at the Federal Building. Agent Anderson gladly accepted, as he was eager to see what Mr. James had on his mind.

When Daddy made it down to the federal building, he elected to stand, saying that the meeting would be brief and to the point. He knew Jasmeen was in too deep with her new boyfriend and her Uncle Oliver. This was his last result of saving his daughter from shame and a lengthy prison sentence.

"I am aware of the government wanting my brother, Oliver. Well, in exchange for my daughter Jasmeen's total clearance on all charges that may be filed now or in the future, I will give up my brother and the history of the family business."

Agent Anderson and Wallace couldn't believe their ears. They'd known Jasmeen's father was innocent in the family's illicit drug business, but they'd always assumed he knew the score—more than he was ever willing to admit.

Anderson shot out of the office to inform Benjamin because any and all deals still had to be approved through him alone.

"Get it done," Benjamin told Anderson.

Agent Anderson re-entered the office, trying to seem as if he'd now gathered himself from earlier.

"So, do we have a deal?" asked Daddy, looking at Agent Anderson.

"Yes, we have a deal. Please have a seat." Anderson waved at one of the two chairs before his desk. His partner, Wallace, sat off to the side, pen in hand, ready to jot down everything.

"You can start by telling us your family history, and we'll go from there," said Anderson.

Daddy took a seat and folded his hands in his lap as he recalled over 50 years of his family being in the heroin business. For Daddy, this was the only way to save his daughter. He loved his brother, Oliver, but he loved Jasmeen more, and he'd do anything to protect her. Anything!

CHAPTER FORTY-ONE

Two days later, Detective Lewis got the call he'd been waiting on since taking the suspected murder weapons down to the crime lab.

"It's a match for them both," Brittney, the crime scene technician, told Lewis.

"Bag 'em and tag 'em." Lewis slammed down the phone in his office, where he'd been camped out the past forty-eight hours, awaiting Brittney's findings.

He snatched his Glock 27 and radio from the desk and rushed out of the office on his way to see Judge Victoria Curtis. She had an equal hatred for Marcus and Lil' Keith, having watched them make a mockery of her courtroom so many times. She and Lewis were allies in the fight against Marcus and Lil' Keith.

Her signing a warrant had to be done quickly and quietly before the feds stepped in and shut things down. Lewis secretly met with Judge Victoria inside her chambers, where he relayed his latest findings. She gladly furnished him with a warrant for both Lil' Keith and Marcus for the murders of Brett and Monay.

Meanwhile, the feds approached the grand jury with Daddy as their star witness. A sealed indictment was filed in New Orleans District Court, pending the roundup of all co-conspirators. The feds had upheld their promise

232   Dorian Sykes

not to indict Jasmeen thus far, as long as Daddy continued to cooperate and testify against Oliver at trial.

As soon as Daddy finished testifying in front of the grand jury, he rushed home and had his wife call Jasmeen to come over, stating that it was an emergency. When Jasmeen walked through the door of her parents' house, Daddy was standing in the living room alone, wearing a serious, distraught expression of concern on his face.

Jasmeen approached him cautiously, uncertain of what was happening. "Daddy, is everything all right?"

"Sit down," Daddy told her in a short, clipped tone.

Jasmeen sat at the edge of the pillow on the sofa, looking up at Daddy as he paced the Persian throw rug beneath his feet.

"The feds have indicted your uncle today."

"What? Why?" Jasmeen gasped.

Daddy took a moment. "They're charging him with running a criminal enterprise, among other things. They're also charging your boyfriend and his friend in a string of murders, unless you agree to—"

Jasmeen rose to her feet and closed the space between her and Daddy. "Daddy, what have you done?" she said, just above a whisper.

Daddy turned to put his hands on Jasmeen's shoulders, but she pulled away.

"Tell me you didn't do what I'm thinking you did."

"I had to save you."

"Save me from what?" Jasmeen yelled with tears filling her eyes.

"From a life of shame and prison. You are my daughter, and I will do everything within my power to protect you."

Jasmeen broke into tears. She couldn't believe what her father was telling her.

"The feds are going to arrest your uncle today, along with your boyfriend, so I want you to stay here with your mom and me. I don't want you anywhere around when they start rounding people up."

"I can't believe you," Jasmeen hissed, then proceeded to leave.

Daddy called after her, but she stormed into the foyer to grab her purse and keys. Her mother stood there with tears in her eyes. She was torn between loyalty to her husband and love for her daughter.

Jasmeen said nothing as she brushed past her mother, feeling betrayed and lost. Her only priority was finding Marcus before the feds did.

She called her Uncle Oliver first, giving the news to his voice mail. She was crying hysterically into the phone as she drove over to the spot where Marcus and Nate set up shop as their dope mill to cut and mix their famous Mix Jive.

Marcus wasn't answering his phone. Jasmeen could only hope that she wasn't too late and that the feds hadn't already picked him up.

CHAPTER FORTY-TWO

Lil' Keith was behind the wheel driving as Marcus answered his cell phone. Lil' Keith was zoned out in murder mode because they were on their way to go spank Tank. *This bitch has been skating by for too long*, Lil' Keith thought. He wanted to kill Tank so badly that it consumed him. It had been the only thing on his mind since coming back to New Orleans, and the only reason Tank had gotten a pass the other day was because of the unmarked Impala parked out front. But today, Lil' Keith didn't care if Jesus Christ was in the house. They were running up in there, choppers ready.

Marcus ended the call and turned in his seat to face Lil' Keith. He was filled with alarm after what Jasmeen had just revealed to him about the feds and her father's actions. Marcus explained everything to Lil' Keith, urging him that they needed to turn around and leave the city before the feds caught up with them. He was supposed to to meet Jasmeen at the Greyhound station in twenty minutes, and they would leave together. She was packing up all their money as they spoke.

"Fuck dat. Dis nigga gone die today, ya heard me? If we don't get him today, I got a feelin' we ain't never gonna get him."

Marcus sighed as he looked at the clock mounted into the dashboard of the stolen Mercury Cougar. They were almost at Tank's downtown estate, and Marcus didn't want to leave his partna hanging. Plus, he wanted to

236 Dorian Sykes

down Tank just as bad as Lil' Keith for having left them for dead.

"Fuck it. Let's do it," Marcus heard himself say. His mind flashed to Jasmeen waiting for him at the bus station. *I'm coming, baby. . . .*

Tank heard from his lawyer soon after the grand jury returned the sealed indictment charging Marcus and Lil' Keith. His attorney informed him that the feds were in the midst of rounding up everyone named in the indictment. Tank was happier than a punk with a bag full of dicks. This was the best news he could have ever gotten at a time like this. The murder weapons he'd given Lewis now seemed minute compared to the fed's indictment. Marcus and Lil' Keith would never see the streets again, Tank was sure.

Tank sent all his bodyguards home, feeling safe. He kept two Dominican bombshells with him to help relieve some of the built-up tension he'd been experiencing since Marcus and Lil' Keith came back to town.

Tank lay back in the center of his double king-size bed as the two imports serviced his manhood, taking turns pleasing him. He hadn't heard the patio glass door shatter. Lil' Keith and Marcus were downstairs in the kitchen, AKs in hand and on their way up.

Lil' Keith put his finger to his mouth as he heard Tank's bitchy moans of pleasure coming from the master bedroom. *You always been a sucka for a bitch*, Keith thought as he peered in at the orgy going down. He quietly pushed the door open and stepped in with Marcus by his side.

"You ready to die, bitch?" Lil' Keith said with menace in his voice and eyes.

Born to Die

Tank sat up, not believing his eyes. The two women scrambled from the bed into the corner, leaving Tank to face his fate.

Tank tried putting on a fake smile like he didn't know what this was about. "When y'all get out?" he said, flashing all golds.

"Round, you played us," Marcus said as if to say, "*Why?*"

Tank tried to sit up, but Lil' Keith raised his AK to his face. "Nigga, stay like that," he growled.

"I swear I paid y'all lawyers. Don't I always pay for y'all lawyers?" Tank said, his eyes pleading.

Marcus wanted so badly to believe him, but he knew Tank was lying. The nigga was no good, and he was full of shit. "So, you gone lie in my face, ya heard me?" Marcus was getting himself to the brink of slumping Tank. Lil' Keith was already there. He was just waiting on his partna.

Accepting the fact that he was about to die, Tank went into boss mode. There was no way he was going to go out like a bitch by begging these little niggas.

"I made both of you little niggas. Without me, both y'all asses would be in Angola doing life. This how y'all gone repay me? I should've killed you two bitches a long time ago, just like I killed yo' daddy back in the day," Tank said to Marcus. "That's right. I downed yo' dope-fiend-ass daddy. He wasn't nothin' but a fiend, just like you."

The young face that crackhead Danny had seen kill Marcus's daddy as he sat in his Cadillac was a young Tank, back when he was on a mission, by all means, to rise in the dope game.

Lil' Keith and Marcus raised their AKs to Tank's naked frame and riddled him from face down. When they stopped firing, Tank lay mangled in a pool of splattered blood. Feathers from the pillow drifted up in the air, and the mattress was torn to shreds by the 223s.

238 Dorian Sykes

Lil' Keith showed the two women no mercy as they cowered on the floor, hugging each other. Two dome shots apiece quickly put them to rest.

"Fuck, nigga!" Marcus growled with tears in his eyes as he stood in a trance, staring at Tank. He felt like a fool for ever having trusted Tank.

Lil' Keith put his arm around his partna, knowing that Marcus was going through it.

"Come on, round. We gotta go. It's over."

CHAPTER FORTY-THREE

Lil' Keith pulled the Cougar up to the curb outside of the Greyhound bus station in downtown New Orleans. He left the gear in neutral as his murderous eyes danced through both side mirrors, checking for any heat lurking.

"You comin' right, round?" Marcus said in a rush. He had the door ajar, looking back at his lil' partna.

"Nah, you go 'head and live ya life, round. I'm here, ya heard me?"

Marcus slouched in his seat, looking off into the distance inside the terminal. Somewhere inside, Jasmeen was waiting for him. It was a bitter moment. Marcus doubted if he'd ever see Lil' Keith alive again if he didn't come with him and Jasmeen. It felt like the end.

"You know I got nothin' but love for you, my nigga."

"And that's why I want you to get out this car, round, and go live ya life, ya heard me?"

A car horn blared behind them for Lil' Keith to move. Marcus pulled Lil' Keith in for an embrace.

"G'on get out of here," Lil' Keith said, not really wanting to see his partna go.

Marcus got out and tapped the roof. He stood outside and watched Lil' Keith fade into traffic, leaving the station.

"There you are," Jasmeen said, joining Marcus out on the sidewalk. She put her arm around Marcus's waist, and he kissed the crown of her head.

240   Dorian Sykes

"You ready, baby?" she asked as they faced the road still.

"Yeah, where we headed?" Marcus asked, just above a whisper, as they turned inside the terminal.

"Ever been to Miami?" she asked, smiling and looking up into his eyes.

"Can't say that I have."

"Well, I hear that it's beautiful this time of year. Guess we get to take our vacation after all."

Marcus was just happy to be with Jasmeen, no matter the circumstances. She made life worth living.

Jasmeen sat in the window seat as they boarded the awaiting Greyhound bus. Marcus sat, taking in his surroundings. Every face had their own story to tell.

CHAPTER FORTY-FOUR

Lil' Keith got caught by a red light as he sat on Freret Street in front of his old high school, Fortier, where it all started. It was a weekend, so the school was empty, but Lil' Keith could still envision him and his partnas walking down the cement steps after school, fighting with the 17th Ward niggas. It seemed as if it were only yesterday.

A brand-new pearl white Cadillac pulled alongside Lil' Keith as he sat at the light, breaking his daydream.

Lil' Keith turned and looked at the woman riding in the passenger seat. *Etta?* he thought, shocked. It had been over six years since he saw his sister, but he would know her anywhere. The light changed, and the Caddie scooted off, but not before Lil' Keith could catch who was behind the wheel.

Sherman! A'ight, bitch, I'm finna down you!

Lil' Keith shot after the Caddie, catching up to them as they got caught by the next light. Lil' Keith slapped the Cougar in park and jumped out, leaving the door open. In broad daylight, he walked around the driver's side, his .40 cal and 30-round clip in full view.

Sherman hadn't seen Lil' Keith coming, but Etta caught a glimpse of the gun and screamed.

Sherman locked eyes with a deep barrel of the .40, then with Lil' Keith. His mouth fell open in terror as his worst fears of dying were confirmed. Lil' Keith yanked the trigger back seven times, hitting Sherman center mask.

242   Dorian Sykes

Etta screamed to the top of her lungs as blood splattered all over her face and arms. She tried carefully touching Sherman's lifeless body in between sobs.

"Baby, please don't die on me. Wake up, please."

Sherman was slumped back against the door with his eyes staring out the sunroof.

Lil' Keith walked around to the passenger-side door and yanked Etta out to the street.

"Get the hell off me!" she kicked and screamed, fighting Lil' Keith.

Lil' Keith couldn't believe his sister was going crazy over the nigga who had killed their father.

"How you gone be with this nigga after he killed Daddy, huh?" Lil' Keith had a mind to kill her, too.

"What? What are you talkin' about? You're lying. Stop lying. Sherman wouldn't have done that. He loved me."

Lil' Keith felt his blood boiling with every second that passed. If he could have, he would have killed Sherman twice for ruining his family.

A shot rang out, warning Lil' Keith to get down on the ground. It was Lewis and his partner, Tate.

"Put the gun down and lay down on the ground, now!" yelled Lewis.

He and Tate were slowly approaching from across the street with their guns dead aimed at Lil' Keith.

Lil' Keith wasn't going back to jail. He had long ago told himself that he'd hold court in the streets before he ever felt another pair of handcuffs against his wrist. He snatched Etta and spun her around, using her as a bulletproof vest as he made his way to the Cougar. He let off the first lick of shots, to which Lewis and Tate returned fire, hitting Etta all over her body.

Lil' Keith clutched her tightly as she jerked from the bullets filling up her body. In his mind, she was a traitor

Born to Die 243

and no longer his flesh and blood. She could die on the streets with her man.

Lil' Keith shoved Etta into the hail of gunfire and peeled away, ducking low in the Cougar. As he blew past the stoplight, a host of Chevy Luminas with white men wearing blue-and-yellow F.B.I. jackets jumped behind him, signaling for him to pull it over.

"Fuck y'all. Y'all wanna do it, then we finna do it."

Court for Lil' Keith was in the hood. The set. On the corner of Valence and Magnolia Streets—the V.L. for short—where it all started and where it would all end. He took the feds and Lewis on a high-speed chase through uptown. He only wanted to make it to the 13th.

As he turned down Magnolia Street, he could see his whole hood buzzing in activity. He punched the gas while changing clips in his AK-47. He pulled up to the Chinese store and came out of the car, busting the chopper on the feds as they pulled behind him.

"You bitches wanna do it, huh?" Lil' Keith yelled between gunfire. He was tearing through their engine block, the 223s rapidly spitting from the assault rifle he so expertly was handling.

"Let's do it!" Lil' Keith zoned out.

He had the F.B.I. cowering low inside their Luminas. He was oblivious to Lewis, who came from the opposite end of Magnolia Street, creeping slowly in his Impala.

Lewis eased out to the street and took aim at Lil' Keith, who fired relentlessly upon the agents.

Lewis shot Lil' Keith twice in the shoulder and once in the back, briefly sending him to his knees. Pain shot through Lil' Keith's body as Lewis ordered for him to stay down.

"Cracker, fuck you, ya heard me?" Lil' Keith spun around to his feet, shooting wildly. He stumbled back from the shots Lewis and Tate had pumped into his chest.

A hot, burning sensation filled Lil' Keith's chest as he stood up into the sun, unable to move.

The AK slipped from his hand, and he stumbled over behind the Cougar and fell to the curb. He managed to roll over on his side, where he lay with a smile on his face. He'd always imagined that this was the way he would go out: on the set, as hard as a mothafucka.

Lil' Keith dug into his blood-soaked Girbaud jeans for the Mix Jive pack. He lifted the coin-sized envelope to his nose and snorted hard. He closed his eyes and enjoyed the mellow feelings of the dope. *I'ma die high*, he thought, accepting his fate. What better way to go?

CHAPTER FORTY-FIVE

At the end of the day...

In New Orleans, if you're anybody from the streets attached to the official culture, your funeral ain't complete without a second line.

Angel, from Angel's Bar, and Eugene got together and paid for Lil' Keith's final arrangements because to them and all of Valence and Magnolia, he was family. They wanted to send him out in style and in proper fashion.

A second line is something like a parade. Bands walk through the streets, playing second line music, something like a funky, soulful jazz, while being followed by anywhere from five hundred to three thousand people, depending on how big the second line band is. It usually starts at a bar, travels a pre-planned route, and ends at the same bar. Along that route, it stops at about six or seven bars in different hoods, traveling through different wards and projects, and then back to where it started. All the while, people are dancing, hooting and hollering, and buck jumping.

Rebirth Brass Band led the hearse with Lil' Keith's body away from the church where his funeral was held. The band brought Lil' Keith through a final ride through the streets before making it to his final resting place.

With over two thousand people following the band, Angel's Bar was where Rebirth really cranked up. The

246 Dorian Sykes

whole set of V.L. was out there wearing white Ts bearing Lil' Keith's picture underneath the phrase "R.I.P." The hood loved him because he had always been one way: *real.*

The band led the hearse down Valence and turned on Magnolia Street, where it all began. Down in the Dirty.

Meanwhile, Marcus and Jasmeen had settled into a nice mini mansion down in Miami Beach. Marcus had gotten word about his partna Lil' Keith. He wished that he could've convinced him to leave with them that day at the bus station, but that was life. Lil' Keith would always be close in Marcus's heart as the only brother he ever had. It was just crazy how life could tear you in two different directions.

Jasmeen found Marcus standing out on the beach behind their home. He was facing the water with his toes sunk into the fresh, plush sand.

"What you thinkin' about?" she asked, wrapping herself up in Marcus's arms.

Marcus took in her sensual scent and sighed, appreciating her essence. He said, "Just thinkin' how sometimes people have to die so that others can live."

"Lil' Keith loved you. You know that, babe."

"Yeah, I know. . . . I know. . . ."

18 Years Later

CHAPTER FORTY-SIX

Aaron and Leo had been following the new Infiniti truck since it pulled out of the Show n' Glow Car Wash in the 10th Ward. Big Prince was behind the wheel of the black Infiniti truck. He was a major player in the New Orleans heroin trade. Big Prince controlled most of the lucrative heroin spots downtown, but he'd made the deadly mistake of moving his stamped product into uptown, which was mostly controlled by the twins Ronald and Deshawn.

Aaron and Leo were the twins' guns. They were on the twins' payroll to do one thing and one thing only: kill on command. Aaron was a year younger than Leo at just seventeen, but both held equal status on the grimy streets of New Orleans. The murderous duo repped the 13th Ward.

Aaron was a pint-sized killer, standing a mere five feet and five inches and weighing 110 pounds soaking wet. Aaron had no disagreement with his being ugly. He had gapped yellow teeth and nappy hair. His beady eyes stayed red from the weed and heroin he stayed high off. Leo was tall and thin as a rail. His shoulder-length dreads masked his young age, giving him at least ten extra years. The duo only cared about two things: getting and killing their vics so they could stay high. The twins fed Aaron and Leo with heroin and pocket money, but nothing more than just enough to get by.

Aaron was behind the wheel of a tinted black Yukon XL. His beady eyes danced through the side mirrors out of precaution. His partner, Leo, leaned back beside him, his skully pulled low over his eyes. Atop both their laps were fully automatic AK-15s equipped with drums. A murderous verse from Souljah Slim faintly played throughout the SUV, but neither Aaron nor Leo needed any encouragement to down somebody. They were the real deal. They did what rappers rapped about in their songs.

"We got that bitch, round. Pull up," said Leo as he sat up with his AR-15 on the ready.

Big Prince had gotten caught at a red light on Congress Avenue. His truck was boxed in by cars blocking all lanes in front of him. Aaron pulled up beside Big Prince. As soon as Prince looked away from the fine yellowbone riding shotgun in his truck, the last thing he saw was the barrel of Leo's AR-15 coming out the passenger window.

Big Prince tried stomping the gas, but it was far too late. Leo had already riddled the driver's door with a barrage of bullets. Big Prince tried shielding himself from the onslaught, but he lost control of the wheel and crashed into the car in front of him.

Leo wasn't known to leave his vics alive. Once he had them in his sights, it was lights out. Leo jumped out of the SUV bare-faced as cars sped to get away from the murder scene. Leo walked up to the Infiniti and snatched the driver-side door open. Big Prince's heavy yellow frame lay face down against the steering wheel, and the woman beside him squirmed in her seat with blood seeping through her fingers from the bullet wounds in her stomach.

Leo raised the rifle to Big Prince's head and fired a series of shots, then silenced the woman's screams by turning the barrel on her. Leo jogged back to the SUV, and Aaron casually pulled away, making a U-turn against traffic. Not a single word was exchanged between the murderous duo. They each had a mini graveyard of their own, and they lived by the murder game rules, which was never to speak on it once it was done.

Aaron reached in the center console for an ounce of weed he and Leo had been blowing on. He tossed the Zip-loc, along with a pack of blunt wraps, onto Leos's lap.

Leo took to the duty of rolling up. Both of their stomachs, however, longed for a good hit of blow. Aaron grunted and thumbed his nose at the thought of it. He pushed down on the gas and headed back uptown.

The twins were from V.L. as well, but their good dope gave them a ghetto pass in much of uptown. Ronald ran things out of the Calliope Projects, while Deshawn ran things out of the Magnolia Projects. The twins had respect in the streets for having put in their share of work, but they were hustlers at heart and gangsters only when forced to be. Their pops, Junie, had long money from the 80s, having run dope spots in the same projects as his sons. But Junie had been indicted by the feds and went on the run, leaving the reins to the twins.

Aaron pulled into the Magnolia Projects, his eyes scanning the many faces for potential enemies. He and Leo had done so much dirt that they were always on high alert. Enemies to them were everywhere, and wherever they so happened to run into their enemies was where they'd leave them. It was called on-sight beef.

Aaron eased the SUV through a huddle of shirtless men shooting dice in the court. Leo pointed to one of Deshawn's cars parked further back into the projects. "Call his ass, round," said Leo.

Aaron was already on it as he speed-dialed Deshawn's cell number. Aaron listened to the phone ring in his ear. "Yeah, I'm out here in the parking lot," said Aaron, then he ended the call.

252   Dorian Sykes

Deshawn came out of the apartment he'd been stashed in. He had a blunt dangling from the corner of his burnt purple lips. He was shirtless and sagging his jeans. Both twins were tatted up to their chests, backs, sleeves, and hands. They embodied the thug life culture to the very core.

Aaron hit the horn, then rolled down his window. "What's up, wodie?" asked Aaron. His grin was a sign that their latest business had been handled.

Deshawn pulled back a knowing grin, revealing a mouth full of golds. He gave Aaron some dap.

"What's good, round?" he said to Leo.

"Ah, you know," said Leo, holding up his AR-15 for emphasis. He was ready to get high, and the only way they could do that was if Deshawn went ahead and paid them for their work.

Deshawn's eyes scanned the projects for no one in particular. His mask of deception had slipped back on. He tapped the hood of the truck as he stepped away. "I'ma put you boys together. Just give me a minute."

Aaron and Leo watched Deshawn slip back into the apartment and shut the door. They needed a fix, and bad. Between the both of them, they had a four-grams-a-day habit. Aaron had graduated to banging his dope, while Leo still stuck to snorting. The only reason Leo hadn't joined the big leagues of banging was because he hated needles. And besides that, snorting made him feel like he was less of a dope fiend. He'd tease Aaron from time to time for banging, calling him names like "Dope Fiend Negro in a Cadillac."

"I wish round would hurry the fuck up," said Aaron as he raked his dirty fingernails over his track marks.

The door of the apartment swung open, and Deshawn emerged with noticeable lumps in his pockets. Deshawn approached the passenger window so that his back would

Born to Die 253

be to the onlookers. He dug out the two bundles from his pockets. "There's one for each of you."

"Where's the yeah?" asked Leo, almost in a panic. "It's in there," said Deshawn. He tapped the hood and made his way back toward the apartment he'd been holed up in.

Aaron and Leo tore into their brown paper bag packages like Christmas gifts. They bypassed the three thousand dollars, stacked in twenties, and found what they'd been waiting for.

Deshawn had blessed them both with half an ounce of raw dope. He gave it to them uncut, how it came to him before he put his mix down on it. It was his appreciation for the work they'd put in because with Big Prince out of the way, the twins were about to double their profits in the streets.

By the time Aaron got his spike hooked up and was ready to bang his first hit of the day, Leo was already in his lean on cloud nine.

CHAPTER FORTY-SEVEN

Aaron still lived at home with his mom, Kenya. They lived next door to Eugene's homemade barber shop. Kenya had grown up on V.L., having been raised by her late grandmother, who had passed away some years ago and left Kenya the house. Back in the day, Kenya used to vie for the attention of her childhood crush, Lil' Keith. She would go to school a few days out of the week whenever Lil' Keith wasn't running the streets with Marcus. They kept their relationship a secret from most because Kenya's strict, churchgoing grandmother would never have approved.

Kenya hadn't known she was pregnant with Aaron until after Lil' Keith's death. It was a hard blow to Kenya's grandmother and had practically put her on her deathbed. Kenya had never grown out of her hood and ratchet ways. She was still sack-chasing and living like a teenager. She and Aaron had a more like brother-sister relationship. Kenya only played her momma role when she had to go to court on a new case for Aaron, or when she was begging for some money, which she always figured Aaron had since he kept himself out in the streets. She knew what her only child was up to out there.

"You're your father's son," she would often tell Aaron. She couldn't help but picture the day when she would bury her son as she did his father.

Aaron was barricaded in his room upstairs, high out of his mind from the night before. He was passed out across

256   Dorian Sykes

his bed with his clothes and shoes still on. The pounding on his bedroom door jerked him out of his sleep. His hand raced for the .40 cal he kept beside him, but his fears subsided at the sound of his mother's nagging voice.

"Goddamn it, Aaron. What I tell you 'bout locking my doors in my house?"

"What?" yelled out Aaron. He knew Kenya, as he called her. All she wanted was some cigarette money and a shot of blow.

"Boy, open up this damn door!"

Aaron reluctantly rolled out of bed and stuffed all valuables in his jeans pockets before heading downstairs. He unlocked the door and pushed by Kenya, who stood in her house clothes, barefoot and ashy. She was thin as a rail, with her hair pulled back into a meager ponytail.

"Where you been all night?" she quizzed, following Aaron into the kitchen.

"Why?" Aaron slammed the refrigerator back shut, disgusted that it was empty aside from a box of Arm & Hammer and a jar of grape jelly. He opted to have a Newport for breakfast instead.

"Give me some money so I can get some cigarettes and milk."

Aaron shook his head as he eased two loose bills out of his pocket. It was pointless not to give it to her because Kenya was something else with her shit. Deny her loan if you wanted to, and the next time you took inventory of your belongings, you'd be sure to be missing some items.

Besides that, Aaron knew how it was waking up with that gorilla on his back, and he did not have the slightest idea how he would get his morning fix. He hated seeing his mom like that. So, in that regard, he had a soft spot for her. Aaron sat down at the kitchen table and fished out his spike and a small stash he kept separate to limit Kenya's begging.

Born to Die 257

"You got your hook-up ready?" asked Aaron as he unfolded the lotto ticket containing the raw dope Deshawn had given him.

A wide grin creased Kenya's thin face at the sight of the dope before her eyes. She fished her own spike from out of her bra and joined Aaron at the table. They both prepared their spikes in silence. Peace had been restored in the Clarksdale residence.

It had been Kenya who had graduated Aaron from snorting to banging dope. She even bought him a spike to get him out the gate. Kenya did all this for her own selfish reasons of wanting another dope fiend buddy she could always pinch off. And what better candidate than her very own son?

It was still early morning, so the rest of her dope-fiend associates wouldn't be pulling up for at least another forty-five minutes once they scored their morning fix. Kenya used her downstairs as a shooting gallery, selling $2 spikes at the door and a piece of whatever action her patrons were banging. Kenya had become a bonafide dope fiend over the years. When she first starting getting high, she would at least hold a job down and even used to cook and look after Aaron from time to time. But those days were far behind her. Kenya lived for a good hit of dope, period.

Aaron knew just how larceny-hearted his mom could be when it came to dope, which was why he knew to decline her offer to prepare his spike. Kenya was infamous for switching spikes or watering down a spike while cuffing the dope. Aaron had learned the hard way after coming up empty a few times, messing with Kenya's crafty ass.

Aaron had his morning blast and fought off the urge to nod because of Kenya's presence. He'd surely wake up with his pockets molested. Aaron pushed to his feet and left Kenya to her spike.

258   Dorian Sykes

"Grab my cigarettes before you get lost in the streets."

Aaron was at the front door, checking his appearance in the mirrored table beside the loveseat.

"Damnit, Aaron, did you hear me?"

"I got you shit. Ya ass needs to get a job," said Aaron on his way out of the house.

Aaron fired up another Newport and stood on the porch for a beat, taking in the movement on the block. Eugene's crib was buzzing with early morning customers trying to get a fresh cut. Aaron ran a hand over his head as he started down the steps. His shit was nappy and unedged. He was thuggin', though. He was content with being ugly, but a bitch better not speak on it.

"What's up, round?" called out Samuel as Aaron crossed the street.

"Ain't shit, ya heard me?" said Aaron, climbing the curb. He gave Samuel and Black Boy each some dap. He had mad respect for the duo because they had been holding down the set of V.L. since back in the day. They could always be found standing outside the Chinese store, which was what the hood called it. "What's the word?" asked Aaron, putting his back to the storefront.

"The dicks done slid through couple times, ya heard me?" advised Black Boy.

"Don't know who they lookin' for," added Samuel.

Aaron always got an eerie feeling when talking about the law. As far as he was concerned, they were always looking for him.

"Y'all want something outta here, round?" offered Aaron.

"Get us a half-pint of bumpy face, ya heard me?" said Black Boy.

Samuel and Black Boy would stand outside the store and drink from sunup to sundown, and the crazy part about it was they wouldn't have paid for a single drink.

Born to Die 259

People who knew the duo were accustomed to treating the two legends to a taste of their favorite gin, which was the cheapest liquor in the store. They were the eyes and ears of V.L., so to speak, so in turn, people paid homage.

Aaron came out of the store and handed Black Boy the small brown paper bag containing the gin.

"Good looking out, round," said Samuel.

As Aaron shook a few loose Newports from his pack to give to Black Boy, his attention was arrested by the gunning sound of a police engine. Aaron knew that sound from anywhere. He didn't have anything on him, so he wasn't worried about getting caught dirty, but still, it was V.L. law to take them bitches on a foot chase.

Aaron dropped the pack of cigarettes and turned around for the corner. The dicks knew about V.L.'s no-surrender street law, so they were prepared for a tour through the hood. The driver of the Crown Victoria gunned the engine as he turned the corner after Aaron.

Aaron was so small and crafty that they'd be lucky to have caught him on foot. Aaron looked back over his shoulder, flashing a victorious grin into the faces of the two white detectives. Aaron had made it into the alleyway behind the Chinese store, and by the time the detectives pulled into the alley behind Aaron, he had vanished. The two dicks were left slamming their fists against the wheel and dashboard.

CHAPTER FORTY-EIGHT

Leo wasn't so lucky that morning. He had dozed off in the living room after snorting his morning fix. The front door flew off the hinges, and a storm of police dressed in S.W.A.T. gear rushed inside with their rifles on the ready. Leo was snatched from his crease on the sofa and slammed to the floor. His mom could be heard in the back of the house, screaming at the officers to get out of her damn house.

Detectives Rayford and Edwards walked into the house as if they owned it. Both were middle-aged white boys from the country, dressed in cheap blazers and slacks. Rayford thought of himself as the lead homicide detective. The streets called him Redhead because of the red, mullet-style haircut he wore.

Edwards and Rayford stood over Leo, both smiling down at him. "You missed us?" cracked Edwards.

"Yeah, like ya wife missed this big black dick, ya heard me?" shot Leo.

Rayford turned beet red around the collar. He wanted so badly to kick Leo's teeth down his throat, and he would have, except there were too many other departments present. Rayford and Edwards were there to I.D. Leo, then have him transported into custody.

"It's him," Edwards advised the two masked officers restraining Leo.

They stood Leo up and searched through his pants pockets.

"Oh," said Rayford, rubbing his hands together at the dope found in Leo's pocket. "Look at what we have here."

Just then, a plainclothes detective came out of the back carrying a .40 cal with a 30-round clip hanging from it.

"You're on a roll, shithead," joked Edwards.

"You know dope plus gun equals feds," said ol' Rayford. He finally had something solid on Leo. "Get him outta here," ordered Edwards.

"Daddy!" Lil' Stevie came weaving through the sea of officers. He was only five and loved Leo to death because, all in all, Leo was a good father to his son.

One of the detectives detained Lil' Stevie before he could make it to Leo. The last thing Leo saw was the tears streaming down his son's face.

"You might wanna take a good look around, 'cause this will be your last time ever seeing it again," said Edwards as he escorted Leo to an awaiting patrol lock-up van.

Leo was a solider. He'd been down this long, dark road before. He and Aaron had fought and beat countless murder charges, shootings, and gun cases. It had gotten to the point where every time a shooting took place and the police didn't have any clear suspects, they'd pick up Aaron and Leo and hope to pin the case on them.

However, since they worked for the twins, paid lawyers were always on standby when Aaron and Leo took a fall. They were too valuable to the twins' organization to leave them for dead, and besides that, they knew too much dirt on the twins for them not to play it fair.

Leo rode with his eyes closed. He could tell from the bumps in the road and from the turns how far they were from The Parish, which was every man's nightmare, but also their reality at some point in time if they were in the streets. The Parish was almost like a second home to Leo, with all the time he'd spent there fighting his cases. He and Aaron were living legends. From the streets to

Born to Die

263

the pen, their names rang bells. The only difference between the streets and The Parish was how enemies solved their beefs. In the streets, AKs and Glock 40s were the weapons of choice, but behind the wall, the guns got checked in at the door, separating the real killers from the wannabes.

Leo was definitely the real McCoy. He was down to butt his gun, push a knife, or throw hands, whatever the beef called for. The Parish was dangerous on a lot of levels, but what made it the most dangerous was the fact that it was a meeting ground for enemies at war on the streets. It was on sight, and whoever was the unlucky one to be outnumbered just had to roll with the punches.

The police often knew what beefs were going down in the streets, so they did their best to keep both sides separated. But that was a double-edged sword because if they wanted to fuck you over, they'd just put you in with your enemies and let them kill your ass.

Leo was a vet, though. If the police were to try him like that, he would just swing on whatever officers were escorting him. Sure, he'd get an ass-whooping, but at least he'd live to talk about it. One thing for sure was that he wasn't about to let them decide when and how he would die.

Leo arrived at The Parrish and was led to an interview room. The detectives knew from experience Leo wasn't going to make a statement, but it was protocol to take a crack at him.

The legend himself, ol' Detective Lewis, was waiting for Leo inside the small, steel room. He snatched the lone chair out for Leo to have a seat, and then Lewis waved the guards away.

"Well, you really did it this time, shithead," said Lewis as he shoved his hands into his worn jeans. He had aged badly, maybe from the booze and chain-smoking, but his

264   Dorian Sykes

detective skills were still keen. "The feds are gonna want to take a look at you after we're done with you for Big Prince's murder."

Leo showed no emotion as he sat in silence. They had him on Big Prince's murder . . . so what? He'd fight it and beat it, just like all the other bodies Homicide had tried to pin on him and Aaron. Jail was just part of the game—the part no one wanted to experience. But Leo knew what came with his lifestyle: closed caskets and tight prison cells. It was what it was.

Lewis circled the room a bit. He had a hard-on for Aaron and Leo, simply because Aaron was Lil' Keith's son, and Homicide had never been able to make anything stick on Lil' Keith, not to mention the fact that Marcus had never been found.

"So, what are gonna do this time? Are you going to keep playing badass here and fuck the rest of your life up, or are you going to give me something to help yourself?" asked Lewis.

"Take me to my cell," said Leo.

Lewis hated the fact he couldn't break Leo or Aaron whenever he brought them in. It was like looking at Marcus and Lil' Keith in the flesh. The arrogance and fearlessness they all embodied irked Lewis.

CHAPTER FORTY-NINE

Aaron had been lying low at his cousin Denise's house. She lived down the street on V.L. Denise was an attractive, thick, and chocolate little thot. There was always traffic in and out of Denise's crib because she sold weed as much as she smoked it. She also did hair out of her living room.

Aaron didn't feel safe being at her house because he learned from watching the news that the police and federal task force had ten thousand dollars in reward money on his head. He knew that niggas would turn in their own momma for that type of money. He was beginning to feel like a prisoner, stuck hiding in Denise's bedroom all day because of the steady traffic in the house. Besides the paranoia, Aaron's stash was nearly gone, and he needed to go score some more dope from the twins.

Aaron always went with his gut instinct, and his gut told him to get out of the house. He didn't bother telling Denise he was leaving because she was too busy entertaining her company and serving her weed. Aaron climbed out of the bedroom window and hopped the fence into the alleyway. He had his hoody pulled over his beady little head as he blended into the night. He kept a tinted-out DTS Cadillac stashed around the corner.

Aaron slipped inside the blue Caddie and pulled out of the garage of an abandoned house. He sparked a Newport to ease his nerves. Out of all the murder cases he and Leo had fought, never once was there a reward being offered, nor were the feds ever interested in them. It was unnerving just knowing that the entire city was looking for him. The easiest thing to do would've been to find another place to lay low or get out of town. But Aaron didn't have any places he could've gone to lay low out of town, and then there was Leo. Aaron couldn't just leave him for dead. He had to figure out what the police knew and then take care of it. Leo would've done the same for him if the shoe was on the other foot.

The Calliope Projects were buzzing with midnight traffic and drug deals as Aaron pulled inside the maze of crime. He clutched the butt of his Glock 40 as he made out the faces of the people in the courts. He needed a good hit of dope to settle his nerves and clear his mind.

Ronald was posted outside amongst a group of shirtless men. They all wore gold chains, boasting their ghetto wealth. Glock 40s with extended clips hung from several of the men's waists. All eyes were on the Caddie as Aaron brought it to a slow creep. He had enough sense to call Ronald's phone to let him know it was him behind the tint.

Ronald said a few words to his men, then got in with Aaron. "Boy, you hot as fish grease, ya heard me?" said Ronald.

Aaron kept the Caddie moving, driving in circles around the projects. "What the lawyer say they got on Leo?"

"Shit, they got a couple witnesses. They say round got out bare-faced and downed wodie," advised Ronald.

Aaron didn't confirm or deny. He and Leo had taken to going bare-faced, more so out of arrogance than anything else. They were so confident that they'd kill their vics that it didn't matter if they saw their faces or not. But then there were always witnesses too nosy to get the fuck down when they heard gunshots.

"I should have their names by the morning, ya heard me?" said Ronald.

"Yeah, I'ma need those A.S.A.P., round."

"You know I'm on top of it."

Aaron nodded. The twins had always lived up to their end of the bargain when it came to paying for lawyers and getting crucial information, such as the names of potential witnesses.

"I need some blow, Ronald. Enough to hold me over a couple days," said Aaron. He needed a good hit if he was going to press on.

"Gimmie a minute, ya heard me?" Ronald slipped out of the car and had an exchange of words with one of his runners.

The young boy jogged away and came rushing back with a folded package. Ronald accepted the package and made his way to the driver-side window of the Caddie. Aaron let his seat back to keep out of view of anyone passing by. Ronald leaned inside the car and dropped the package of heroin onto Aaron's lap. He then peeled off a thousand dollars in fifties and handed them to Aaron.

"Call me if you need me, round," said Ronald with all sincereness. Aaron and Leo were more than just the twins' hitmen. They were family and would be treated as such.

Aaron nodded as his fingers flirted with the package of dope on his lap. Ronald faded back into the shadows of the projects, and Aaron pulled the car over toward the entrance of the front court. He had to take a hit now. Within mere seconds, his arm was tied up, and he prepared his spike in a fury. All the while, his murderous eyes danced in the side mirrors for any signs of danger.

Aaron nodded for a minute before regaining his bearings. He backed out of the parking space and clutched his Glock 40 out of habit. He knew that he needed to get off

268   Dorian Sykes

the streets until Ronald got him the information in the morning. He was high, riding with a gun, and a wanted man. Aaron's hiding options were slim to none at that point. He really doubled if he could trust anyone with ten grand being offered for his capture. But he had to get off the streets.

His heart sank in his chest at the sight of the police in his rearview. Aaron checked the dash to make sure he was doing the speed limit. The dicks got right behind him, and he could see the passenger's head going up and down. They were running his plates, undoubtedly.

Aaron put on his blinker and changed lanes over to his left. The dicks changed lanes behind him. The car was legit, and the plates were up to date, so there was no way the dicks would've known it was Aaron behind the tinted windows. But then again, Aaron wasn't about to let them pull him over, either. His face was all over the news, and besides that, every cop in New Orleans knew him by name and face. So, it definitely wasn't a good look that the dicks had followed Aaron onto the service drive. They feared letting the Caddie onto the expressway because, in Louisiana, only the State Police were authorized to stop a vehicle on the highway. The driver flicked his lights, signaling for Aaron to pull over.

"Yeah, right," said Aaron, and he punched the gas to the floor. His eyes stayed in the rearview. He was hoping the dicks would abide by the law and back off because he had slipped onto the expressway.

But the flashing blue-and-red lights followed the Caddie in hot pursuit, as if they knew it was Aaron behind the wheel. This unnerved Aaron because he knew from experience it would only be a matter of minutes before they had the ghetto bird on top of him. As crafty as Aaron was, even the best had problems shaking the helicopter.

Aaron began driving recklessly in hopes the dicks would call off the chase, but they were right there with him, making every dangerous lane switch, even sideswiping two vehicles. Aaron let down his sunroof and stood up a bit with his Glock aimed at the hood of the cruiser in pursuit of him. *Boom! Boom! Boom!*

The police cruiser swerved to the left and scraped the divider, but the driver managed to catch the wheel and kept after the Caddy.

Aaron stomped down on the gas and came up on the next exit. Two cars were also exiting in front of him, and they were taking their sweet time making the turn. Aaron panicked and abandoned the Caddie, leaving the car in neutral and causing it to roll backward into the speeding police cruiser.

He raced around to the passenger side of the Navigator that had been blocking his escape and snatched the door open. A woman screamed and tried to stomp on the gas, but Aaron was already inside the truck. He slapped the woman a few times with the barrel of his Glock. "Bitch, shut the fuck up and drive!"

He had the woman by the collar of her blouse, with the gun shoved under her throat. They made it away from the scene, with the older woman crying for her life. "Please don't kill me. I have a family I just want to go home to," pleaded the woman.

"You don't think I wanna go home, huh? Ya nosy ass sittin' there tryna block me in so the police could catch me. I oughta blow ya fucking brains out."

"I swear that's not it. Please!" begged the woman. Her eyes were already swelling from being pistol-whipped.

Aaron scanned the darkened streets ahead and pointed for the woman to make a turn. They were in Hollygrove. Aaron had a few spots in the area where he could lay low for the night. "Pull over," he instructed the woman.

They were on a blackened side street with no street-lights. "Turn off ya lights," ordered Aaron as he began riffling through the woman's purse. He pulled out her cell phone and snatched the back off, leaving her with just the battery.

"Bitch, what else you got in here?" Something told Aaron to look inside the glove box. When he opened it, there was a stack of white envelopes with addresses scribbled on the front sides.

"That's my rent money," cried the woman. She looked the part of a landlord with money. Aaron tore into the first envelope, finding an array of big bills. His little fingers raped the glove box for the remainder of the en-velopes; then, he turned the gun suddenly on the woman.

"Bitch, when I get out, make a U-turn and get the fuck on. If you even think 'bout callin' the police, I'ma find you and I'ma kill you."

"I'm not. I swear."

Aaron left the woman with her life as he slipped from the truck and disappeared into the night.

CHAPTER FIFTY

Aaron ended up spending the night at Karen's house in Hollygrove. She was still in high school and lived with her aunt, so she had to sneak Aaron into the house through the side door. Overall, Karen was a good girl compared to the other fast-tail girls her age. She had a thing for Aaron, not because of his looks or his money. Karen was drawn to his I-don't-give-a-fuck lifestyle.

She stayed up with him, helping him count the $9,600 in rent money he'd taken off the lady he carjacked. Aaron gave Karen a thousand dollars, not because he was trying to impress her, but because he never knew when he would need to stash away at her crib again. No one would ever suspect him to be hiding out in Hollygrove.

Karen was a pretty little something, about five-foot-six, 125 pounds, with a phat ass and a flat stomach, a pretty face, and shoulder-length hair. She was just a couple of shades lighter than Aaron, who was dark as night.

Aaron loved watching Karen bounce around the house in her boy shorts and tank tops. Her camel toe got his dick hard instantly every time he laid eyes on it. Her aunt worked mornings, so she had already left the house. As much as Aaron loved having sex with Karen, he couldn't that morning because his mind was consumed with the police being on his trail and his partner in crime being on lock.

Aaron had talked Karen into lending him the keys to her car so he could get around. She had a used Dodge

272   Dorian Sykes

Intrepid that her aunt bought her for her sixteenth
birthday. It was clean and ran well, but it wasn't tinted
out, which was a problem for Aaron. He rode behind tint
not only because of the police but also due to citywide
enemies. The quickest way to get caught slipping in New
Orleans was riding in a clear fishbowl, as they called it.
So many had gotten their issue from riding without tint.

Aaron clutched his Glock 40 extra tight as he rode
through the city. He mostly took the back streets to avoid
the police. That way, at least if they made out his face and
he had to run, he stood a better chance of getting away,
being in the confines of the hood.

The projects were coming to life with its early morning
traffic as Aaron whipped the cranberry Intrepid into the
first court. Dope fiends stalked the pavement in pursuit
of their morning blasts being sold in the fourth court.
Aaron followed the walking dead until they all reached
the action where money was exchanging hands for sure-
fire dope. In the midst of it all stood Ronald. He wasn't
handling any dope or money, but he was sure dictating to
his runners and granting shorts on behalf of a select few
customers.

Aaron eased the car into an empty space, and Ronald
saw that it was him, so he excused himself away from
the action. He approached the car with a blunt he'd been
unwrapping.

"What it do, Ronald?" asked Aaron.

"I got that info for you," said Ronald, cutting to the
chase. He dumped the tobacco from the cigar down onto
the pavement, then fished a small yellow folded piece of
paper from his pocket.

Aaron accepted the paper as if it were gold, cuffing it
for safekeeping.

"You need anything?" asked Ronald as he licked both
sides of the blunt leaf.

Aaron put the car in reverse. "Nah, I'm good, round. Good lookin', ya heard me?"

Ronald gave a solemn nod and stood back. Aaron was his little man, outside of the dealing he had in the streets. If Aaron was ever to come to Ronald for anything, and he had it to give him, the twin wouldn't have hesitated to help Aaron out because they had a real love for him and Leo. They all took on different roles in the game, but what made them all equal was loyalty. The twins knew Aaron and Leo were loyal not only to them but to the game as it should be played.

Aaron unfolded the piece of paper as he drove. Two names were scribbled in the blue ink, along with a lone address in downtown, not far from where Leo had killed Big Prince.

There wasn't a second thought in Aaron's murderous mind as to what needed to be done. He sparked a Newport and eased along with the mid-morning traffic heading downtown. Aaron found the residential street scribbled on the paper. He was a couple of blocks from Congress Avenue in the 9th Ward—definitely enemy territory. Aaron hadn't a single ally he could turn to in the area if the need were to suddenly arise. He clutched his only lifeline, his Glock 40, as he inched down the residential street, squinting at the addresses on the houses.

Aaron spotted the house he'd been looking for. He did a ride-by to scope out the scene. The front door of the brick home was open, with the white screen door shut. He couldn't make out any movement within the house, but there was an Explorer parked in the driveway. A man's truck, he guessed, from the rims and dark tint.

Aaron drove around the block and parked a couple of houses down. The street was deserted, with the exception of a loose pitbull circling a tree in pursuit of a cat. Aaron got out of the car and started for the house with no real

274   Dorian Sykes

plan other than to kill Leo's two witnesses. The problem was, he hadn't the slightest clue as to what either of them looked like.

As Aaron climbed the steps up to the porch, he could hear the Isley Brothers playing softly throughout the house. A woman's voice yelled for Germaine from somewhere in the house. *Bingo*, thought Aaron. To his surprise, the screen door wasn't locked. He eased into the house unnoticed and withdrew his Glock from his jeans.

"Germaine, I know you hear me calling you!" The woman's voice was coming from the back bedroom to the left. A stampede of feet came rushing down from the upstairs bedroom. "I heard you, Ma."

The door swung open, and a young man around Aaron's age walked toward the back bedroom. Aaron came from around the corner in a flash. He dome-checked Germaine execution-style as he entered the room. His body slumped to the floor, revealing the tiny figure of Aaron. Ms. Carter yelped from the sight of her dead son and the knowledge that her life would likely be next.

Aaron grimaced as he closed the space between them. He had a thing about missing. He hated missing. And he gave himself extra points for killing his vics with the first shot.

Ms. Carter couldn't bring herself to scream. Aaron looked her dead in her eyes, then squeezed the trigger, knocking a bloody patch from the crown of her head. Aaron grimaced because he knew from experience that it wasn't a kill shot, so he stood over her and fired two more shots into her temple. On his way out, he fired two shots into her son for good measure.

As he was leaving the house, the next-door neighbor was standing in her driveway in her housecoat, talking into her cordless phone. Aaron assumed she was on the

Born to Die 275

phone with the police because of the way she was talking with her hands and looking over at the house. Her mouth dropped wide open when Aaron withdrew his Glock from his waist. She let the phone fall to the ground while trying to make a dash for her side door, but Aaron grabbed her by the arm before she could make it inside the house. He swung her around and planted two bullets between her eyes.

He didn't even stay to see the body drop. He could hear sirens nearing in the distance, so he jumped into Karen's Intrepid and made his getaway.

CHAPTER FIFTY-ONE

"Just promise me that you'll be careful, baby," said Jasmeen, watching Marcus pack his things. Part of her understood why Marcus felt the responsibility to try to save his godson, but another part wanted to be selfish and forbid him from leaving her side. They had a three-year-old daughter and a beautiful life they split between Miami and traveling. Jasmeen sat crisscrossed at the center of her bed, watching helplessly as the man she lived for prepared to re-enter the life they had escaped over eighteen years ago.

Marcus had always known of Aaron, Lil' Keith's son back in New Orleans. And he had always considered himself Aaron's godfather, even if it was from afar. Over the years, Marcus had made sure he sent money to Aaron's mother. But then again, Marcus also knew what lifestyle Kenya was leading and where the money was likely to be going.

Marcus had caught the news about Aaron and his crime partner being wanted by the feds. They were making national news, being called the nation's youngest-known hitmen. Their pictures were all over the papers, which were blasting that Aaron was wanted for questioning in a string of recent murders. Marcus felt responsible for not being there. Lil' Keith was like his brother, and yet he had allowed the streets to take hold of his brother's only begotten son.

278   Dorian Sykes

Jasmeen got up from the bed and stalked into her massive walk-in closet. She stopped Marcus from his packing and steered his eyes to hers.

"Look at me," she demanded in an even tone.

"I have to save him. I can't let Keith down, bae."

Jasmeen could see the hurt in Marcus's eyes. For years, he'd blamed himself for Keith's death.

"Okay. You do what you gotta do. But just know your daughter and I are here waiting on you, Marcus. We're not about to lose you to this."

"I'm coming back to you, bae. On my word," said Marcus. He kissed the crown of Jasmeen's head, and she closed her eyes with a prayer that he would return home as he left, safe and in one piece.

Marcus was a legend throughout New Orleans, not just for all the work he'd put in alongside Lil' Keith, but also because Marcus was the only one to escape the feds and the wrath of Detective Lewis. Many believed the only reason ol' Lewis hadn't retired yet was because in his heart, he believed he'd one day catch Marcus and see him sentenced to death. No one was supposed to escape the game and all the ills that it embodied, but Marcus proved it could be done, making him more than just a living legend. He was a mythical figure, especially throughout uptown. The younger generation had taken to swearing by his name whenever their credibility was in question. They would say things like, "On Marcus, ya heard me?" The word "Marcus" took on a whole new meaning and spread throughout the southern states, meaning "real."

Marcus slipped back into the heart of New Orleans by renting a car from the private airport. He had the jitters as he drove the Expedition through his hometown. Everything he remembered had changed or was abandoned and on the verge of being knocked down. But even with everything changed, Marcus still could feel the beat of his city. New Orleans had its very own heartbeat, unlike any other city he'd ever been to.

It was midday, and the sun was blinging off the skyline of the high rises in the downtown district. Marcus cracked his window and smiled as he caught a good whiff of what he was sure to be crawfish gumbo. It felt good to be home. Marcus had to remind himself why he had returned and that he was very much a wanted man.

Marcus checked his reflection in the rearview. His appearance had definitely changed from eighteen years ago, especially since he'd cut his dreads and put on some grown-man weight. He felt assured that he had become the alias printed on his fake Florida state driver's license.

Marcus knew that some things in New Orleans would never change, and Eugene's crib was one of them. Marcus figured he'd kill two birds with one stone. He'd pay his old homie a visit, and through Eugene's knowledge of the streets, Marcus would find out where Aaron was at.

Marcus felt nostalgic as he turned onto Magnolia on his way to Valance. Where the old phone booth once stood, an empty liquor bottle marked the place where Lil' Keith had taken his last breath. It was almost as if Marcus could see Keith lying there with his life escaping his young body. At that moment, Marcus had the urge to find Lewis and kill him. Whether Lewis realized it or not, he had victory in killing Lil' Keith, but his personal trip had always been sending them off to Angola with life sentences.

That was exactly what Marcus wanted to avoid happening to Aaron. He pulled across the street from Eugene's and parked. A few cars were in the driveway, and the front door swung open a few times as customers entered Eugene's barber shop. Marcus watched the comings and goings for a while, just happy to be back on the set. Then

Eugene emerged from the house with a customer he had just finished cutting, a younger guy sporting a new-style Mohawk faded at the sides. Marcus couldn't identify the young man, but he'd recognize ol' Eugene anywhere, even with the extra pounds he had picked up.

Marcus tapped his horn lightly and rolled down his window. Eugene and the young one glanced at the truck, but neither approached it. Marcus didn't want to startle them, so he checked his side mirror for traffic before getting out. The youngin and Eugene exchanged dap, with the youngin starting down the block. Meanwhile, Eugene kept his eyes on the man crossing the street.

"What, you put on a few pounds and don't recognize ya partna no more?" asked Marcus as he came into full view.

Eugene couldn't believe his eyes. It was like seeing a ghost after all those years. He pulled back a wide grin and embraced Marcus with open arms.

"My mothafuckin nigga. God, I missed you," Eugene confessed as they hugged.

"I missed you too, my nigga," Marcus said, releasing the embrace. He scanned the block with a wary eye, prompting Eugene to suggest they take a ride. As they crossed the street, the front door to his house swung open.

"All right, bunch," called out a youngin, throwing his hand up.

"I'll be right back."

"You sho' you wanna leave ya crib?"

"They ass can wait till I get back. Besides, who else they gone go to but me?"

Marcus smiled as he slid into the truck. It was true, Eugene was the coldest nigga uptown with a pair of clippers. Niggas would rather wait an extra day if that's what it meant to sit in Eugene's chair.

Born to Die

Marcus had another moment of nostalgia as they pulled off. He realized that he and Eugene were about the only two still living out of their homies.

"So, what's up, round? What are you doing coming out of hiding? I know it wasn't just to see me," asked Eugene.

Marcus gripped the wheel tight with both hands. "I need to find Keith's son."

"Aaron?"

Marcus turned to Eugene. "Yeah."

"That young nigga worse than his ol' man. Feds and shit all lookin' for him. He got the hood hot as shit."

"That's why I need to find him, ya heard me? I can't let them crackas get a hold of him. He'll never walk again."

"You right about that," agreed Eugene. He was scrolling through his contacts on his phone.

"So, can you help me find him?"

"Hold on, this him right here," said Eugene as the phone rang. He put it on speakerphone.

"Yeah," answered Aaron.

"Round, this Eugene."

"What's good, my nigga?"

"I got somebody here who needs to meet you."

"Who?" Aaron's tone was laced with paranoia. He didn't know who he could trust at that moment.

"Round, you already know I wouldn't ever bring no poison to you."

"Yeah, but shit. Who is it, ya heard me?"

Eugene looked to Marcus.

"It's ya godfather, Marcus. He's in the car with me, and he wants to see you."

There was a beat of silence.

"Aaron, it's me, Marcus. Son, where are you?"

"Shit, I'm straight, ya heard me?" said Aaron, then the line went dead.

Marcus was crushed. How could he have let Keith's son slip into a life of destruction when he was alive and well? Marcus hated himself at that moment for not having a bond with Aaron. If they had been close, Aaron would've listened to him. But Marcus felt like just another nigga in the streets.

"I'm sorry, round," offered Eugene.

Marcus shook his head in disbelief. "I gotta find him, ya heard me? I gotta find him. . . ."